JAKE'S PROGRESS

David Simmonds

First published in 2018 by
Bethannie Books
105 Cornerswell Road
Penarth CF64 2UY

To Mary,
the girl in the suede coat.

Diolch am bopeth. Gyda llawer o gariad.

Foreword

He was, he had to admit, a lucky bugger. Sitting in his favourite armchair, his feet on the low sill of one of the penthouse apartment's huge windows, he gazed out at the panorama of the London skyline stretched before him, occasionally sipping from a glass of very good single malt whisky.

It was his favourite time – early evening, with the lights of the city coming on and behind him, the room darkening. It was very much a man's room, leather armchairs and sofa, expensive and comfortable but by no means new. A Turkish rug lay in front of the sofa which faced a large plasma television screen on one wall; bookshelves lined much of the remaining wall space. Many of them held mementoes he'd gathered from around the world, souvenirs of what even those of his contemporaries who didn't care too much for him would agree had been a distinguished career. There were awards in myriad shapes and sizes, framed certificates and many photographs of him formally dressed, smiling with the great and the good, and others in which he wore much rougher clothes and stood in jungle or desert alongside men carrying cameras or guns.

He eased his shoes off, dropping the battered brogues to the floor and wriggling his toes. The pink tip of his left big toe peeked at him though a hole in the sock. He regarded it thoughtfully and wriggled it again. Well, he'd need a shower and to change anyway before the taxi came to pick him up for tonight's speaking engagement. These days he insisted on a car to and from whatever function he'd agreed to attend; no more late-night Tube journeys or searching for parking spaces. Not that the sock and its hole really mattered, he didn't expect to be taking his shoes off in front of anyone else later tonight.

He had aged well. The hair, now grey, was still thick and although he wasn't tall he stood straight and slim. His face belied his age and the lines there were lightly etched; he exuded an air of calm, of imperturbality, that many women found attractive. Among those who lingered after these occasions were over, there were often one or two who made it obvious that they'd be happy to extend the evening on a more intimate basis. Sometimes he took up the offer, but increasingly he preferred the empty space in his bed at night and solitude in the morning.

His eyes closed and he savoured the tranquillity of the room. Over the years he'd come to appreciate silence more and more, perhaps because most of his working life had been so dominated by noise. Especially the noise of weapons being fired, of shells detonating and bombs exploding. He'd seen and heard so many explosions that he had trouble differentiating one memory from another now, they all seemed to meld into one overwhelming impression of noise and confusion.

Except the first, of course. Without looking, he dropped his hand onto the small table beside him. It fell on an irregularly shaped piece of brass and his fingers traced its contours: the arc of a rim, and from it a jagged wing of twisted metal. If he wanted to, he could still recall the dull flat boom of the explosion, the sound of windows shattering, the tremor underfoot, the shock on the faces of those who'd gathered round this little piece of excitement...

Of course, technically, that was his second bomb. But he didn't feel the first really counted.

Chapter 1

'Don't stop. Please don't stop.'

A bead of sweat trickled down Jake's spine; his shoulders, his whole upper body, were rigid. His eyes strained straight ahead as he muttered his little prayer.

'Nearly there. Oh please, just keep going...'

The little blue Ford Popular - three forward gears, top speed with a following wind about 65 miles an hour - crawled forward at considerably less than that. In fact it was barely keeping pace with a middle-aged couple on the path beside the road, out for a walk on this fine late summer Welsh afternoon. On the dashboard the engine temperature gauge was edging steadily towards the red zone; if Jake glanced in the car's rear view mirror he could see the long ribbon of traffic that had gathered behind him, following him as he wound his way, ever slower, up the mountain road from Cardiff towards Caerphilly and then into the South Wales valleys.

Not that he looked into his rear view mirror; he was focussing all his mental energies into willing the car into making it the next fifty yards to what looked like the crest of the hill. He'd been in first gear for five minutes now, although it seemed much longer, and the sound from the engine had become increasingly strained as the road grew steeper and the speed had dropped – now the car seemed on the brink of grinding to a complete halt. Jake had read somewhere that its strongest gear was reverse, but how was he supposed to do a three-point turn with what looked like most of the cars and vans in Glamorgan on his tail? And then the ignominy of reversing up the hill, travelling backwards to his future. The shame of it all sent a little shudder through him when he, very briefly, considered it.

Jake had bought the car for £30. Casual work on building sites around his parents' home in St Albans, just north of London, was well paid and easy to come by in the summer of '68. He'd saved enough not only to buy the car, passed on by one of his parents' neighbours who had reached the age where he'd decided to give up motoring for good, but to pay for two weeks in Spain with Amanda, his university girlfriend of the last two years.

And he'd started doing something about his future. He'd read English in Aberystwyth's university college and found that he quite liked writing essays. That, and a naturally inquisitive nature, had made him decide in his final term that he might try journalism.

After not too many letters to newspaper publishers, he'd got himself a job as a trainee reporter, conditional on his degree, on the Edwardstown Enquirer, covering part of the South Wales valleys. His parents had simply been relieved he'd found a job. Amanda, though, was not impressed.

'But surely there are weekly papers in London? Or Surrey?? Or Kent??? I mean, they're so much <u>nicer</u>.'

'Yes of course there are weekly papers there. But I can't get a job on them because loads of other people want to work there too, and to be honest, I don't fancy living in Tunbridge Wells or Epsom. Anyway, the Tomkins Group owns the Enquirer and they've got Fleet Street papers too so there'd be a career path.

'Look, it's just till I qualify; two years indentures, I get my Proficiency Certificate and then the world is our lobster.'

'You get your what?'

'Proficiency Certificate. It's like your licence to be a journalist.'

'And it takes how long?'

'Um, two years.'

'Oh good God almighty...'

In fact, Jake had noticed Amanda becoming increasingly distant of late, and Jake had wondered more than once if the flame of their love affair was beginning to cool in the harsher post-uni world.

Certainly his poor little car wasn't. The needle on the temperature gauge was now lodged firmly in the red and the walking couple, leaning into the slope but striding along easily, were moving steadily away from him. Slowly, agonisingly slowly, Jake's knuckles white on the faux-leather covered steering wheel, the little Ford heaved itself over the brow of the hill. Ahead of him the vista of the valleys opened and in the distance a shower of rain had produced a rainbow that curved spectacularly over the downhill road. With a sigh of relief he began the descent towards Edwardstown.

An hour later, Jake raised the gleaming brass knocker on the front door of 17 Llanberis Terrace, a smartly painted double fronted terraced house set back from the road by a small forecourt and a low wall topped with black painted railings. With some trepidation, he brought it down smartly and rather harder than he had intended. Seconds passed, then footsteps approached down the hallway and the door swung open to reveal a sturdily built middle-aged woman wrapped in a worn but clean floral apron, her hair tied back in a rather severe bun.

She looked him up and down and saw a young man with a pleasant, open face and unfashionably short fair hair that spiked on top of his head but was saved from being a crew-cut by slightly longer back and sides. He was around five feet ten inches, solidly built, wearing a blue zip jacket, a Fred Perry tennis shirt, jeans and brown shoes. He looked rather scared.

She sniffed.

'Mr Nash, is it? I am Mrs Rosemary Probert but you know that already since your new employer fixed you up here. Right then, you'd better come in. Straight through and into the kitchen, if you please.'

Jake carried his case down a dark hallway, hung with ancient photographs of serious looking men and women, and stood awkwardly in the spotless kitchen.

'Sit down then. I expect you'll be wanting a cup of tea after that journey.'

As she busied herself with teapot and kettle, Mrs Probert carried on talking to Jake.

'So to be clear: I charge £7 for the room, which is shared with one of your colleagues, payable in advance on Friday. That includes breakfast, of course, and Sunday dinner. I can do you an evening meal on weekday nights too, I charge seven and sixpence for that but I have to know before you go out in the morning. Is that all right?'

'Um – yes, that sounds fine.'

'You can use the front parlour, there's a desk there if you need to work and a radio, to be used up to but not beyond ten o'clock. Home Service only, please. There's a telephone in the hall, incoming calls until 8 o'clock, no more than two a week, please keep the conversations brief, outgoing calls in cases of emergency only. For other calls, there's a public telephone just down the street.'

She turned and looked at him over her shoulder.

'Do you play any kind of musical instrument – trumpet, guitar, anything like that?'

'Er, no.'

'Well if you're thinking of starting, don't do it here, please. And there's to be no drinking in the house, and no… <u>funny business</u> of any other kind.' There was a significant pause before 'funny business' and a heavy underscoring of both words.

'I trust we understand each other, Mr Nash.'

Jake was pretty sure he did. Amanda was not going to be impressed.

Mrs Probert turned and put a china cup full of very strong tea and a plate with two digestive biscuits on it in front of him.

'There you are, sugar's on the table. Then I'll take you up to meet Mr Harris.' She sniffed again, and this time conveyed a disapproval too deep for mere words. 'He's probably asleep'

Gareth Harris was not asleep when Mrs Probert knocked once on the door and, not waiting for a reply, swept into the large and rather dark back bedroom. He was though lying on one of the two beds, staring at the ceiling.

'Mr Harris, this is your new roommate. Mr Nash, I'll leave you to introduce yourself.' And with a lighthouse-beam look around that checked every item in the room she exited, closing the door firmly behind her.

Gareth got up and walked over to Jake, extending his hand. He was a slim, pleasant faced man, a couple of years older than Jake, fashionably dressed in dark velvet flares and a blue flowered shirt, with black hair just curling over his ears and collar

'Gareth Harris, pleased to meet you. You must be a bit knackered after that trip, she told me you were going to drive down. Londoner, is it?'

'Just about. On the northern fringes.'

Gareth grinned. 'Don't worry about it, butt, someone's got to be. That's your bed by the far wall; I have the one by the window since I was here first. You get the bottom two drawers in the chest of drawers and the left hand side of the wardrobe. And of the cupboard in the bathroom – down the landing on the left, lav is next door to it. Next door from here is the spare room, and The Dragon's lair is in the front.'

Jake sat and bounced experimentally on the bed. It creaked a bit but was reasonably soft and the sheets looked crisp and clean.

'Seems all right.'

'Aye it is, really, and she's all right too. Food's good, the place is always spotless and she's softer than she looks. It's just that the sixties haven't quite been ushered in with open arms through the doors of Number 17. And what with you coming here from England, and from London, she probably reckons you've got a Rolling Stone in the boot of that car and your case is stuffed with marijuana.' He paused. 'It's not, is it?'

'No, 'fraid not. I'm more of a beer man, me.'

'Well there you go, me too. Tell you what, drop your things and we'll go and have a wander round town. I'll show you the hot spots – that'll take about two minutes but they do a tidy pint in my local and we can pick up some fish and chips on the way back.

Chapter 2

Edwardstown was a substantial community at the foot of one of the industrial valleys that extended northwards from the southern coastal belt. Branching off from the main road that took drivers from Cardiff into mid-Wales, the valley road ran alongside one of the railway lines spared when the chairman of British Railways, Dr Beeching, had axed thousands of miles of track. It went through the town and into the valley beyond, where row upon row of terraced houses lined the sloping sides. Above them on the hillsides were the piled slag heaps, and below on the valley floor the pits that both produced the spoil that dominated the landscape and the income of many of the men who lived in the town.

At the town's heart was a thriving market, the local council offices and magistrates' courts, a small and rather soulless new shopping plaza and the host of shops, cafes and pubs along its streets that drew families in to spend their money. Jobs were plentiful on the recently opened industrial estate nearby where new businesses were expanding, and the miners were still the well-paid aristocracy of the working class.

The hot spots, it turned out, were congregated around the crossroads in the centre of Edwardstown. Gareth pointed them out as they passed them by.

'That's Tolaini's, our local caff – their boy works with us, trainee photographer, nice lad. That pub on the left is Y Llew Coch, tell you a bit more about that one in a minute, and the paper's offices are just down that lane beside it so it's only a five-minute walk from Mrs P's. And on the opposite side of the road, The Colliers' Arms.

'Looks a bit rough.'

'I would say that's a fairly accurate assessment, and it's also the favourite pub of our chief reporter, which might be another reason for avoiding it. And this is mine, The Greyhound.'

They went though the single front door, down a corridor lined to dado level with tiles and into the wooden floored bar. Most of the clients were men but there were a few women there too. Jake paid for two pints of bitter and they found a table near the back.

'So then, Jake, this little corner of paradise is new to you, is it?' said Gareth.

'Well, yes and no....'

Gareth raised a quizzical eyebrow.

'Actually my mum is from one of these valleys', Jake went on. 'She left when she was fourteen, went up to London to join her older sister Eve – she'd left a bit earlier and was working up there. My mum had a bad chest, and the doctor reckoned even London was better than down here.'

'And she never came back?'

'No, met my dad, he was a gas fitter who came to check a boiler at the house where she was working, a companion to an old lady; eventually they got married and she stayed up there. We used to come back to Wales when I was small to visit my grandparents at Christmas but to be honest, all I can remember of that is big roaring fires in very cold rooms, steep streets and a wooden bridge over a black river – I suppose that must have been the coal dust. There were big gaps between the planks, or that's what it seemed like to me, and I was always terrified that I'd slip through somehow and drown.'

'Still, you've got a bit of Welsh blood in there somewhere. I could tell there was something fundamentally decent about you beneath that urban sophistication.'

Jake grinned. 'How long have you been here?'

'Five years or so. I'm from the Swansea Valley, a small village called Cwmtwrch, Upper Cwmtwrch actually, because there is a Lower and it's important to get it right. I came straight from school. My uncle's a journalist in London and I always wanted to follow him.'

'You must have finished your indentures then, so you could leave at any time.'

'Yeah, I've got my Proficiency Certificate so I suppose the next move would be to the South Wales Echo in Cardiff or the Evening Post in Swansea, or maybe the Western Mail, but I thought I'd hang on for a while and see if anything else a bit more exciting turns up. I quite like it here, to be honest – digs are OK, money's not bad, I've got a little bug-eyed Sprite convertible to whip around in; real tart trap in the summer, I can tell you. Not so good in the winter, mind, bit draughty and the rain gets in but it's swings and roundabouts, isn't it?'

He stood, draining his glass.

'But you're right, it's too easy to opt for the quiet life and what you know. Wouldn't do to get trapped here.'

He gestured towards Jake's still half-full glass.

'Same again?'

'Oh yes, right. Thanks.'

When Gareth had made his way back through the rapidly filling bar, swaying deftly through the clumps of drinkers with the two pints perfectly balanced in front of him, Jake asked him about Y Llew Coch.

'There's nothing wrong with it but being a Londoner you might feel a bit uncomfortable in there at times. It's where the Cydmeithas yr Iaith boys gather, that's the Welsh Language Society – oh sorry, the boss mentioned you'd been to Aber, you'd know all about them.'

He took a sip of his pint.

'It's also – and I may have to kill you when I've told you this – the unofficial headquarters of our local Free Wales Army detachment.'

Jake's glass, en route from table to lips, stopped just short of its destination. Jake stared over its rim at Gareth.

'Really?'

'Well, it's a bit grand to call it a detachment, there's only one of them: Goronwy ap Siencyn, but most people call him The Captain. I suppose you might count the lad who lives with him as another half but I'm not sure about that.'

'Lad who lives with him?'

'Oh, nothing funny about that', said Gareth. 'He's a relative of some kind, The Captain took him in when he lost his parents. You see them out and about together sometimes but I don't know what his political views are.

'Anyway, the Llew Coch is The Captain's local. He keeps pretty quiet in there, the landlord's told him that if there's any trouble at all, they're both banned for life. And since The Captain is already barred from just about every other pub in the town he's not keen on losing the only place he can get a pint.'

'Does he get much support?'

'No. Some of the Cymdeithas boys are a bit sympathetic but mostly they keep him at arms length and everyone else just treats it all as a bit of a joke, really.'

Jake had known a good many members of the Welsh Language Society at Aber. They were dedicated to non-violent direct action and their destruction of English language road signs, demonstrations and their readiness to accept arrest had raised the profile of the language and won the tacit support of many in the Welsh establishment.

But the Free Wales Army was another matter. Founded by the charismatic Cayo Evans a few years previously, its members had marched in Dublin as part of the fiftieth anniversary celebrations of the Easter Rising, and a year later a television interview by David Frost with Cayo and the movement's Commandant, Dennis Coslett, had raised its profile. With their homemade uniforms and talk of explosives-carrying dogs and arms trades with the IRA, they attracted little organised support and generated humorously sceptical articles in national newspapers. But there were dark rumblings of unrest in Northern Ireland, and although the uneasy suspicion that something might really be starting in Wales was a minor worry to most people, it didn't seem to go away.

Might be a bit of investigative reporting to be done there, thought Jake, but immediately followed it with another, that it might just be wiser to keep his head down until he was more familiar with the lie of the land.

'Right then. Well I think I'll be staying clear of Y Llew Goch for the foreseeable future.'

'I wouldn't worry about it too much. I don't think a searing expose of Edwardstown's militant underbelly is high on the list of our editor's expectations. You'll meet him on Monday, anyway, him and his lovely wife. A treat in store indeed.'

Gareth raised his empty glass to his eyes and stared pointedly at Jake through the bottom of it.

'Have you noticed how you can see right through these glasses when they're empty...??'

At that precise moment, The Captain and Siôn were sitting in a corner table in Y Llew Coch. A heavy silence hung between them. The Captain stared at the flaky remains of a pork pie on a plate in front of him; Siôn thoughtfully swilled the dregs of a pint of bitter around his glass.

'Well, that's disappointing', said Siôn eventually.

The Captain said nothing but heaved a deep sigh.

'Nothing at all then?' said Siôn, after a pause.

'No, nothing.'

When Gareth had described them as the Edwardstown contingent of the Free Wales Army, he was rather jumping the gun. The Captain had never made any secret of his support for the FWA; in recent weeks he'd been telling anyone who'd listen that the time for simply vocal support was past and more practical action was required.

He'd written a long and passionate letter expressing his determination to help rid Wales of the English yoke and offering the services of a ready-made unit (he described it 'compact but highly motivated and ready to sacrifice all'). Addressed to 'Free Wales Army HQ, Carmarthen', it had found its way, via the police Special Branch offices in Cardiff, back to the Edwardstown CID. Brief telephone discussions had taken place between the two offices, then the letter had been placed in a file marked 'For attention' and left in a drawer.

Siôn swilled a bit more.

'So what do we do now?'

'Well we're not bloody giving up, that's for sure!'

They'd known each other for all of Siôn's twenty years; in fact, they were related – Siôn was The Captain's nephew. Siôn's father, a collier, had been killed in a pit accident when the boy was just eight, a blow that had plunged his mother into a deep and inconsolable grief. From a mid-Wales farming family, she'd been determined that her only child would not follow his father down the mines. She'd pushed the quiet and thoughtful boy into excelling at school, and she'd passed on her love of the language and culture of Wales.

She died when he was fifteen, of sadness, Siôn always believed, although the death certificate said ovarian cancer. He'd moved in with The Captain, his father's brother, on his small farm on the hills outside the town. The Captain, already a father figure to him in those long years since his real father had vanished from his life, began to play an ever-more significant role in his developing view of his world.

But The Captain and his brother were very different people. Siôn's father had been gregarious, outgoing and optimistic; The Captain, two years younger, had been much more awkward, growing up in the shadow

14

of his popular brother and finding himself always pushed into the background.

Conscripted into the army at 18 to do his National Service, he'd had an unhappy two years. With that randomness that seems to dictate much of military life he'd been posted to a Home Counties regiment where his thick valleys accent had been the source of much amusement to the sergeants and corporals who ruled his world.

He'd left the army with a patchy disciplinary record and a permanent grudge against authority, particularly English authority. Back in Edwardstown he'd drifted from job to job without being able to settle. His grandmother's side of the family had been farming people; he found casual work on farms with those relatives and eventually, with a loan from his grandmother, he'd bought the small run-down farm he now worked and lived in, alone until Siôn moved in.

In many ways, they'd been the salvation of each other. The Captain, nursing his grievances in solitude, had become increasingly withdrawn and bitter. Compensating for his loneliness with aggression, he'd eventually been thrown out of most of the pubs in the town and had taken to drinking at home. But he could give Siôn, still grieving for his mother and with no close friends, a continuity of family life the boy craved.

In return, Siôn's lively intelligence and inquiring mind had opened new horizons for The Captain. Spending much of their days together, they'd talk about what they'd heard on the radio news that morning or seen on television the night before. Events such as the flooding of the Tryweryn Valley in 1965 to create a reservoir for Liverpool had outraged them both; Siôn had seen it as another example of establishment indifference to his country, The Captain, more prosaically, as more bullying by those who held authority.

A powerful fusing of youthful idealism and smouldering resentment had led them both to the conclusion that democracy had failed; although Siôn was much quieter about it than his uncle – he was much quieter about almost everything – he too had come to the regrettable conclusion that direct action was the only way to bring about swift and radical change. Now that option too seemed to be fading.

'So, what are we going to do?' asked Siôn.

The Captain pensively poked a bit of pork pie crust with his fork.

'We've got to show the FWA we're a force to be reckoned with, a force that could make a real contribution to the struggle. Let's have a little think now...'

Gareth and Jake bought chips on the way home then while Gareth went ahead to warm up two plates, Jake stopped at the public call box just down the road from Number 17. He'd promised to call Amanda as soon as he could. He dialled her parents' number and munched on a chip while he waited for an answer.

'Hampstead 3721, hello?'

Jake's heart gave a familiar little flip at the sound of her voice. He jabbed a chip-greased coin into the slot to complete the connection.

'Hi, it's me.'

He began to tell her about his awful journey, the embarrassment of the hill climb, his dragon landlady, his new roommate and the pub. Every now and then she'd ask a question or make a comment – 'I warned you about that car', 'She sounds awful', 'He sounds nice' – but to Jake, she sounded polite rather than engaged.

Amanda had never really liked Aberystwyth. Despite the beauty of the countryside, she'd never managed come to terms with the difference between west Wales and north London and she'd been happy to spend her summers

16

working in her mum's boutique. Jake's decision to go back to Wales was, to her, plain contrary.

So it was without a great deal of hope that Jake tentatively suggested she might want to come down some time to see where he'd be spending at least the next two years of his life. The invitation was met with silence.

'I think you'd like it down here', he added quickly and rather desperately. 'We could find something to do, perhaps go down to Cardiff for the evening. And it would be lovely to see you.' Which, even to his ears, sounded rather pathetic.

'We'll see', she said. 'We've been absolutely frantic in the shop, and Mummy wants me to go stock buying with her sometime... Listen, we'll stay in touch and sort something out. Good luck when you actually start work, and don't upset the Dragon. Bye.'

Jake gathered up his cooling chips and wandered disconsolately along Llanberis Terrace towards his new home. The flame of love, it seemed, was fading faster than he'd thought.

'A press release, that's what we need!' said The Captain.

He'd been pondering the next step forward all the way home from the pub; now, halfway through the preparation of two mugs of bedtime cocoa, inspiration struck.

'Announcing what?' said Siôn from his seat at the kitchen table.

'Well, that we're here for a start.'

'And who are we? We can't call ourselves the local branch of the FWA since they apparently don't want us.'

'They will. How about... the Glamorgan Popular Front for the Liberation of Wales?'

''It's catchy, I'll give you that.'

'OK smartarse, if you're going to be sarcastic, what do you suggest?'

'Um... Wales Liberation Front?'

'Trouble with that is it makes us sound like a rival to the Free Wales Army and they might not take too kindly to that. We want to give the impression that we're an active local unit, ready to do our bit but not against being part of the bigger organisation.'

'How about compromising then? Glamorgan Liberation Front.'

The Captain considered. 'Aye, go on then, that sounds all right.'

'And should we have a slogan too, something to put underneath the GLF heading? How about 'Rhyddid!'? With an exclamation mark. It would be good to have something in Welsh that's not too complicated.'

'What does it mean?'

'Freedom!'

'That sums it up.'

'And what are we going to say in this press release?'

The Captain thought for a couple of seconds as he stirred sugar into his cocoa. 'We'll announce our formation and what are aims are: getting rid of the British government, our establishment as an independent nation, 'cetera, 'cetera and then... basically we'll say that the press should hold themselves in readiness for further announcements.'

'And what will they be?'

'Look, you're supposed to be a thinker, why don't you come up with some answers for a change instead of constant bloody questions? For now, let's just get the ball rolling. I've got a stencil somewhere; that'll do for the letterhead and you've got that typewriter of your mum's I can use for the rest'.

The Captain put the mugs down on the table so violently that the cocoa slopped over the sides.

'I'll get cracking now. We can drop it off at the paper tomorrow evening when they've all left.'

Energy and optimism renewed, he hurried off in search of the typewriter.

Chapter 3

At half past eight on Monday morning, Jake strode out of the front door of Number 17, off to the first day of the rest of his life. In a small briefcase he carried 'The Simple Subs Guide' and 'Essential Law for Journalists', both textbooks suggested by the National Council for the Training of Journalists, along with a reporter's notebook and two pencils. He had no real idea what awaited him and he was more than a little nervous.

It had occurred to him on Sunday that writing essays on Romantic Poets and The Role of The Knight in Chaucer's 'Canterbury Tales' might not be ideal training for news reporting but Gareth had been unconcerned.

'Golden rule: who, what, when, where, how, why in the first paragraph. And make it punchy; that's the bit where your reader is going to decide whether it's worth reading on or skip to something else. Don't start with a name unless it's instantly recognisable to everyone, and that would rule out almost everybody, except possibly the Queen, Gareth Edwards and any of The Beatles. Even then, maybe not George Harrison. Then expand, but get all the important stuff in near the top, then in descending order of importance; if they cut your story when it goes to press it'll be from the bottom up because it's just easier that way.

'And always check you've got the names spelled properly. You'll find that people are tolerant of you making up quotes, as long as you get the general sense of what they mean in language they would have used, but they really get annoyed if you get their name wrong.'

Gareth had driven off to his base in a small shop front office in Croesybont, a small town about five miles north of Edwardstown. From there he filed enough stories every week to fill two change pages of The Edwardstown Enquirer and thereby justify its rebranding as The Croesybont Courier, covering the north end of the valley.

Jake had asked him if it wouldn't just be simpler to find digs up there; Gareth had looked at him for a moment, then said 'Look, I know Edwardstown isn't exactly London's West End but compared to Croesybont, it's bloody Las Vegas.'

Both papers were part of Gwalia Press, a group of of a dozen valleys papers, which was in turn part of the national Tompkins Group. The Enquirer and the Courier came under the editorship of Roland Griffiths, whose empire was based in an old hotel in town, The Castle. It was a big, rambling, shabby building, converted without a great deal of imagination or expenditure into newspaper offices. Mavis the receptionist sat behind a desk by the front door, dealing with callers and booking in small personal ads; the rest of the floor acted as a distribution point for the Tompkins Group's Cardiff evening newspaper and an office for their district reporter.

At the top of a broad flight of stairs was the Enquirer's reporters' room, a large space in the centre of which four tables had been pushed together to make one large desk, with four typewriters and a small mountain of old newspapers, press releases and general bits of waste paper covering most of the surface. Off the corridor to one side were the photographers' room with its en suite darkroom and the advertising salesmen's, the ad reps, office to the right; to the left, Roland's office with a small adjoining room for his wife.

Roland and his Dorothy had been running the papers for more years than anyone could remember. He was responsible for overseeing the editorial content, she for laying it out around the display advertisements sold by the reps and for writing the headlines. Roland would determine the front page and first two inside pages lead stories every week; thereafter Dorothy determined priority of stories mainly by their length, compiling pages like an elaborate jigsaw puzzle. For her, size of stories was everything, although neither she nor Roland understood why her habit of shouting 'I need six inches!' down the corridor to the reporters' room was the cause of much stifled mirth from the younger members of staff.

It was 8.45 when Jake arrived at The Castle. Directed upstairs by Mavis, he glanced into the empty reporters' room as he passed it and suddenly felt a little shiver of excitement at the prospect of joining its currently absent quota of real journalists. Hard-bitten, hard-drinking, cynical, world-weary... he could be all those things. Did anyone actually wear a trench coat and a trilby these days? Probably not, he thought, with a slight pang of regret.

The excitement died and the nervousness returned, in spades, as he arrived at Roland's firmly shut door. He paused, gathered himself and knocked.

'Come', called a muffled voice.

Roland sat behind a large and untidy desk – Jake was already beginning to appreciate that tidiness was not a virtue held in high regard among journalists - with his back to the window. He was scanning a piece of copy; after a few seconds, he uttered a sigh of disgust and impaled it on a large spike that stood on a metal base on his desk.

He stood up and extended a rather limp handshake.

'Mr Nash, I assume. Have a seat.' He waved a hand in the vague direction of two battered dining room chairs that stood in front of his desk.

Roland was middle-aged, with thin grey hair and heavy jowls that gave him the look of a particularly disappointed bloodhound. Large and rather poorly maintained teeth did not add lustre to the appearance. He was wearing a thinly striped off-white nylon shirt, a nylon tie and over a well-developed paunch, baggy black trousers that came up to just below chest level, supported by grey braces. Jake had never seen trousers like that on sale anywhere; he assumed that they were only sold to old men, and at a future and hopefully far distant point in his life he imagined he would receive a discrete letter from a government ministry telling him where they could be bought. Or perhaps someone would sidle up to him in a pub or a bus queue and slip a piece of paper into his hand with a roughly scrawled address.

For the next twenty minutes, Roland laid out Jake's immediate future. He suggested Jake should spend some of the morning reading through some old copies of the paper, all filed in the reporters' room, to get a feel for the kind of stories they ran. To Jake's relief, he told him he wouldn't be expected to cover the really small stuff, the garden fetes and flower shows; Jake's friends at home had enjoyed themselves coming up with headlines for the kind of stories they anticipated he would be covering in his first few months: 'Dahlia Delight for Delilah!', 'Clean Sweep for Blod's Bara Brith!'

These events, church and chapel reports and anything else that struggled to be rated as news to more than a small group of people were covered by unpaid correspondents who did it out of a sense of community spirit and to get their name in the paper.

Sports reports too were usually written by correspondents in the clubs, but Roland made it clear that Jake was a general news reporter and would be expected to tackle anything that came up. The magistrates' courts were generally the domain of the chief reporter but Jake would cover for him if necessary; he'd get his share of council meetings too. There were features to be written, sometimes advertising features to go with the display ads that the reps sold. He should get himself an A to Z address book and start accumulating a list of contacts, people whom he could trust to give him expert guidance, valuable steers and pithy quotes on a variety of topics. And above all, he was expected to develop a nose for news, a sense of a good story.

'Remember, my boy, news is what someone, somewhere, doesn't want revealed. Everything else is just propaganda.'

A diminutive woman with a tight perm and dressed in a blouse and skirt that reminded Jake of his mum, entered the room from the adjoining office. She put a cup of instant coffee of Roland's desk, smiled briefly at Jake, and exited.

'My wife, Dorothy.'

They would, he continued, be arranging for Jake to go on a training course as soon as possible but in the meantime, a couple of things to bear in mind: 'I know you've got a degree in English but you're not here to enrich our literary heritage and to show us all the extent of your vocabulary. Keep it simple and keep it plain; if you have to look up the meaning of a word, don't use it. If you do I'll take it out anyway and put something in its place all our readers can understand.

'Make sure you get your facts straight. An axiom you'll hear over and again in the next couple of years: 'if in doubt, leave it out.' And as C P Scott - you can look him up later - said, 'comment is free but facts are sacred.' In fact, free or not, we don't want comment at all; you can leave that to the editorial, and our local vicar writes a fairly feisty column which usually gets a few people going.'

He stood and hauled the trousers a little higher. Jake winced.

'Right, come and meet your fellow seekers after truth and justice. If they've managed to drag themselves in yet.'

The Reverend Iorweth Stanley of Holy Trinity (Church in Wales) and the querulous vicar in question, sat at his desk in the back room of the vicarage and gazed bleakly out of the window at his rather unkempt garden. He was an angry man. Not at anything in particular. Just angry.

He hadn't always been. He'd had a happy childhood, secure in a warm and loving family. When he began to think more about life he'd believed that mankind was essentially good, that unkindness and unfairness were lapses from the norm; he felt only sorrow when it displayed its capacity for wickedness. He'd gone into the ministry believing that he could reinforce the goodness that lay within all men and women.

But as time went by, optimism became frustration, and then frustration became anger and occasionally rage. And that rage was sometimes fuelled by the feeling that he was banging his head against a wall that was never going to crumble.

From his pulpit he'd berated his congregation, haranguing them on everything from the wars and famines that engulfed parts of the globe to the small acts of individual selfishness he witnessed around him every day.

Perhaps not surprisingly, this hadn't gone down too well. Most of those who sat silently in front of him on Sunday mornings felt they couldn't do much about war and famine in foreign parts apart from putting an extra shilling or two in the collection plate, which they would willingly have done except that they were a bit short of change this week. While comments about the individual lack of Christian charity and kindness might well apply to others in the congregation, and certainly they could name a few, they themselves lived, if not entirely blameless lives, then at least they were doing their best.

Tired of standing condemned every week, they voted with their feet. The dwindling size of his congregation - and of each collection – hadn't gone unremarked.

Quiet words of advice had come down the Church hierarchy, but the Reverend wasn't inclined to blunt his message to curry favour with the Bishop. Each week he gazed, seething, over the emptying pews, but if his congregants were disinclined to be taken to task for their failings every week, Roland had seen an opportunity and invited the vicar to write his weekly column.

Although not a churchgoer himself, Roland had heard that the vicar wasn't at all adverse to expressing controversial views and he'd always believed that a little bit of controversy never hurt sales.

Plus it relieved him of the necessity from ever having to say anything that anyone could disagree with in his weekly editorial. Being a champion of free speech while not having to argue with anyone worked just fine for him.

So every week, 'Views Across The Pews' (Roland's choice of title; the Reverend, mindful of the open spaces on those pews, was less than impressed but put up with it) took up a cause or challenged an authority in some shape or form. With passion, conviction and eloquence, the Reverend chided the local council on its failure to provide enough leisure facilities for its poorer citizens and young people, he wrote incredulously of the occasionally bizarre decisions of the courts, he vilified the health service for its shameful neglect of the elderly and the mentally ill, and he championed anyone battling with a faceless bureaucracy that made illogical decisions.

His current concern was homelessness. Two years earlier he'd been moved and shocked, as had many others, by the television drama 'Cathy Come Home', a devastating story of a young family torn apart by their inability to find affordable, decent housing. The Reverend had been almost equally shocked at how quickly people seemed to forget.

After some tutting and head shaking, Edwardstown had seemed to sink back into a conviction that this was only a problem over there in England and had very little to do with them.

He'd been trying to convince them otherwise ever since, and now he'd come up with a plan. He'd been thinking about announcing the campaign in his column but on second thoughts, perhaps it deserved a bigger platform. Maybe he could persuade the editor to give him a bit more space for a separate splash. He would outline his ideas in a letter and drop them off at The Castle when he went out for his evening stroll. He pulled a fresh sheet of paper towards him, uncapped his fountain pen and began to write.

As he followed Roland down the landing, Jake became aware of a furious staccato rattle of typewriter keys; walking into the reporters' room he found two of the chairs at the central island of desks now occupied, one by an extraordinarily pretty girl in her early twenties who was filing her nails and the other by a short, dark middle-aged man. Both looked up as the editor walked in; the girl smiled brightly, the man nodded briefly and returned to punishing the typewriter keys, using only his two index fingers with impressive speed and venom.

'Terry, Lotte, this is the new trainee reporter, come down from London to raise the whole tone of the newspaper. Look after him for a bit, Lotte', said Roland. He turned and trudged back to his office.

Lotte stood up and walked round the edge of the desks to shake hands. Her blond hair hung in curls over her shoulders and her tight top emphasised fulsome curves; a short skirt revealed long, slender legs. The attraction of Edwardstown and its newspaper for Jake increased immediately.

'Hello. Lotte Protheroe', she said, smiling broadly.

'Hello. Lotte – that's an unusual name.'

'I was christened Regina, my mum was a bit of a Royalist but my dad got a crush on Lotte Haas, that German diver who was on TV with her husband Hans doing lots of underwater exploring and looking at glamorous fish. I liked swimming then so he started calling me Lotte and it just sort of stuck. I can't stand the water now, plays havoc with my hair, but I don't mind the name. Bloody sight better than Regina, anyway. It usually gets abbreviated to Lotts; some of the young wits about town – that's wits with a w - like to add what they think I've got lots of, but you get used to it.'

She half turned and glanced over her shoulder at the man seated behind her.

'This is Terry Jenkins, our chief reporter.'

Terry stopped his hammering of the typewriter for a second to consult a notebook open of the desk beside it, his finger poised over the keys. He read for a couple of seconds then fired off a final volley of key strokes, ripped the piece of paper from the machine and, adding it to a small pile on the other side of the typewriter, picked up the bundle and stood.

'Aye-aye kid', he said, nodding briefly to Jake and making only fleeting eye contact.

He picked up a coat from the back of the chair and started towards the door.

'Just going down the nick, Lotts.'

She smiled at his departing back, then turned and raised her eyebrows to Jake.

'He likes me a lot already, I can tell', he said.

'He's OK really. He's chief reporter because he's been here longest. He usually does the court stuff, which fills a big chunk of the paper, and the crime stories. He gives us to understand he has extensive contacts in the town's underworld; anyway, he certainly spends a lot of time outside the office cultivating them. Come on then, I'll show you where Lord Snowdon and his trusty sidekick hang out.'

Jake stood aside to let her through the door first, not entirely out of politeness; walking behind her let him enjoy the view as she led him down the landing and into the photographers' room.

'Morning boys, how are we both today?'

The two men who'd been sorting out camera equipment on a large table at the end of the room turned. One was in his mid-forties, with unruly hair and metal rimmed glasses; his clothes, a tweed jacket and mismatching fawn cord trousers, had a lived-in look and suggested that keeping up with fashion wasn't a major preoccupation of their wearer.

The other was much younger, slim and dark, probably a couple years junior to both Jake and Lotte, and by way of contrast to his colleague wearing a well tailored navy blue single-breasted suit, black shoes and a narrow tie.

'All the better for seeing you, Lotts, as always', said the older man, gazing at her with undisguised pleasure.

'Ah, you silver-tongued devil, Reg. And how was your weekend, Wayne, seduced many of Edwardstown's few remaining maidens?'

The younger man had been staring at Lotte with an expression that suggested he was in pain, or at least extremely anxious about something.

'No, no... spent most of it helping my Mam and Dad in the caff. They're too bloody mean to employ enough waitresses so I have to help out when we're busy. Which is all day Saturday, unless I'm working.'

'Never mind, I expect Rocco Forte started the same way.' She turned to Jake. 'Reg and Wayne, our ace snappers.'

'All right?' they said, almost in unison, by way of greeting Jake.

There was some polite small talk about where he was from and where he was staying, then they invited him to have a look at their darkroom, a windowless room immediately off their main office smelling strongly of chemicals. It was the heart of their workplace and a place of refuge; when the red light over the door was switched on from the inside, a sign on the locked door informed the world that photos were being developed and printed and not even Roland could get in.

Back in the reporters' room, Lotte made them both a cup of instant coffee from the kettle on a corner table then sat down to give him a bit of background.

'Wayne's not been here long. His parents aren't too happy because they want him to take over the business; he's got a sister but she was off to London as soon as she finished her secretarial training and I can't see her coming back. But he's really enthusiastic about his work, perhaps like we all are when we start. I expect it'll get knocked out of him though.'

Jake half smiled and grimaced at the same time.

'Bit cynical, isn't it?'

'No, just realistic. I expect Reg and even Terry were the same when they started, but at some point you have to make a choice. In the beginning we all want to break big stories, name the guilty, make it big even if it's only in a little pool, show what we can do, but in the end...

'I mean, take St David's Day, for example. What we run every year is pages and pages of pictures of school classes, all the girls in their black hats, shawls and flannel, all the boys in their waistcoats and Dai caps.

'Wayne will go out and want to shoot a daffodil reflected in a pool of water, with a boy and girl in soft focus in the background. It may be a nice picture but how many extra copies of the paper will it sell? Maybe three or four, if you can make out the kids' features. But a bog-standard class photo in the paper, with maybe thirty or forty kids in it? Count the kids, multiply by two – one for Mam and Dad, one to send to Auntie Gladys in Toronto... no contest really, is it? Head count journalism.

'Same with news really. Very occasionally, once in a lifetime, we get a really big story like the Aberfan tragedy. There's the odd serious crime, the occasional minor disaster, sometimes a planning row or an industrial dispute; by and large though, life is pretty quiet. But people like to read about what does go on, we've got a decent readership and it's not a bad way to earn a living. So eventually, you have to make a choice: do you want to settle for this, and a quiet but comfortable life, or do you want to test yourself out a bit, make a bit of a mark? Because at some point it's too late to make that choice, the options disappear, and that point can creep up on you and pass you by if you're not careful.'

Jake sipped his coffee, and thought, I seem to have heard that before.

'How about you, Lotte? You seem to be pretty much sorted out here.'

She smiled.

'Oh me, I am sorted. I'll be married in a couple of years'. He noticed for the first time that the hand around the coffee cup had an engagement ring. 'Richard. I've known him since we were at school. He's a trainee manager at the County Bank in town now; once he qualifies we'll make it official, and I'll give up work, have three kids and become a kept woman. Not very ambitious, I know, but it's what I want.'

'What if he finds someone else in the meantime, though?'

She smiled and ran one hand down a long and elegant thigh.

'Nah, he knows what he'd be missing. Not that he's had it all yet; just enough to keep him keen. I've seen too many girls round here end up with a kid and a resentful husband before they're out of their teens to go down that route.'

She pushed back her chair and stood.

'Right, I've got to go out for a bit. Got something to do?'

'Roland suggested I should read up on some back numbers.'

'Good idea. Wash the coffee cups up first? Toilet's down the landing on the right. I'll catch you later.'

Jake washed up the cups as ordered, then spent an hour ploughing through the old Enquirers and Couriers bound into year-long bundles on a table along a side wall. When that palled, and lacking any instructions to the contrary, he decided to practise his typing.

He was pecking away at the keys, trying to copy an article from the previous week's paper and wondering despairingly how he'd ever get work up to Terry's speed and élan, when Reg and Wayne stopped in the doorway.

'We're off to lunch, want to come?'

'Yes, right, thanks. I'll just finish this – can I catch you up?'

'Silver Slipper, tidy pub, does nice sandwiches. Out of the front door, turn left, it's down on the right. Can't miss it.'

Jake finished copying the article ten minutes later and went in search of the Silver Slipper but either the directions were wrong or he'd misheard them. The Prince Llewellyn, The Caradog Jones, The Red Hart... He walked up and down several times but there was no Silver Slipper. In the end he gave up and bought a pasty from a chip shop, which he was munching at the reporters' desk when Reg and Wayne returned.

'Where did you get to then?' Reg demanded.

'I couldn't find it. There were a few others: The Red Hart, The Prince Llewellyn – '

'Oh right. Yes, well it's The Prince Llewellyn. The brewery changed its name a few years ago, but it was the Slipper for years before that.'

He grinned at Jake's blank expression.

'We're a bit slow to pick up on change around here. Don't worry, butt, you'll get used to it.'

Jake spent a pleasant afternoon driving around the area with Lotte in her bright red Austin Mini as she showed him the sights of Edwardstown and gave him an idea of the geography of the place. She drove quickly and with confidence, but then she seemed confident about everything she did. Jake envied her.

She dropped him back at the crossroads in time to meet Gareth for an evening meal at Tolaini's. He watched from the kerb as she accelerated away before he went into the café. Gareth was already there and had ordered; Jake went to the counter, asked for chicken pie, chips, peas and a cup of tea, declined the offer of a slice bread and butter with the meal and took the tea back to join his fellow reporter in one of the booths that lined one wall.

'Good day then?' Gareth asked.

'Yeah, good. Lotte's been showing me the ropes. Nice looking girl.'

Gareth snorted. 'If you're going to join the I-Fancy-Lotte Club, you might find there's a bit of a waiting list. Here comes the Club President now.'

Wayne was crossing the floor, now suitless but still smart in pressed jeans and a dazzlingly white T-shirt, carrying a tray loaded with two dinner plates, cutlery and a bottle of coke. He put the tray down in front of them then slid into the seat beside Gareth and reached for the coke.

'Jake was just saying that he thought our Lotts is a nice looking girl', said Gareth, beginning to sort out the constituent parts of a large mixed grill.

The same look of anguish that Jake had seen that morning flitted over Wayne's face. 'Nice?? She's bloody gorgeous, man. What she's doing mucking around with him when she could have me...' He shook his head, totally mystified by the illogicality of it all. 'I just don't get it.'

"Him' is Richard the budding bank manager?' said Jake.

Wayne and Gareth glanced at each other. 'Him too', said Wayne.

'Aaahh', said Jake, his budding reporter's nose for a story already twitching. Or perhaps he just liked gossip.

'So who is the other competitor for young Lotts' hand? Or other parts of her delightful anatomy?'

'That would be salacious speculation and I'll have no part of it. You'll find out soon enough', said Gareth. 'Anyway, I thought you were already betrothed to another in London.'

'Not exactly betrothed. And just because you're on a diet, doesn't mean to say you can't appreciate the menu.'

Gareth smiled knowingly and turned to Wayne. 'Speaking of which, will there be enough of your mam's delicious apple pie left for two portions by the time we finish this or should we reserve them now?'

A few minutes later, had Gareth and Jake not been deeply involved in demolishing their dessert, they might have noticed the Reverend Stanley walking past the window of Tolaini's. When he arrived at the closed front door of the Enquirer he reached into an inside pocket of his coat, took out an envelope and posted it through the letterbox.

Much later, long after darkness had fallen and the pubs had shut for the night, a Land Rover pulled up outside The Castle. A short, wiry figure emerged from the driver's seat, walked to the same door and posted a similar envelope.

So it was that the Observer's receptionist found two delivered-by-hand letters on the front mat when she opened up the offices the following day.

Chapter 4

'Morning Mavis.'

'Morning luv.'

Mavis looked up from the envelopes she was opening and sorting as Jake walked past her desk and began to climb the stairs to the first floor. Terry was on his way down and they passed at the mid point.

'All right, kid? Just off down to the nick, if anyone's looking for me,' he muttered as they passed, not looking at Jake.

'Right-oh, Terry.'

There was no one about in the Enquirer's offices. Jake pulled up a chair at one of the typewriters in the reporters' room and practised typing his name as rapidly as he could. It was quite depressing how quickly the two fingers he was using got tangled up with each other and the keys.

Just after nine, Jake heard the sound of heels on the stairs and Lotte breezed in carrying a pint bottle of milk. She smiled at him, walking across to the table in the corner and talking to Jake over her shoulder.

'Morning. Back for more then? We didn't put you off?'

'No, but I don't think I've grown on Terry.'

'Ah don't worry about that', she said, shaking the kettle to see if it had any water left in it. There was a sloshing sound so she plugged it in and turned it on. 'He's fine. He's not Mr Affability with anyone.'

'What's his background then?'

She perched on the edge of the table, waiting for the kettle to boil.

'He used to play semi-pro football apparently. Quite good, bit of a hard man. He'd put in match reports which were decent enough and it sort of grew from there. Roland gave him a trial doing other stuff and he came up with some good stories. He provides Roland with a steady stream of copy that isn't going to win any awards, but it's accurate and doesn't cause any problems and that's more than enough to keep him in work. Coffee or tea?'

'Coffee, please. Strong, milk, no sugar. Does he live on his own? It's a bit difficult to imagine him with someone else.'

'His wife's name is Margaret. I've met her a few times when she's come to work's parties. She's really nice, just the opposite to him – very bubbly, talkative, used to work in the opticians, but she's had to pack that in a while ago. She's been quite ill. He spends a lot of time looking after her now; he's always been quiet, but maybe that's made him quieter.'

The kettle boiled. She put coffee into two mugs, added milk and carried them over to the reporters' desk. She pulled up a chair beside Jake.

'Right, good boy, let's get you earning your wages.'

She leant across to the middle of the desk, rummaged in a pile of paper and retrieved a small sheaf of documents, mostly bearing official headings.

'Press releases. Some will be notifying us of upcoming events; if they look interesting enough, make a note in the diary, the large desk diary on the corner there. Roland uses that to decide what we're going to be covering but if you're particularly interested in something, prompt him with it. If it goes in the diary, put the press release in the appropriate day file – top drawer of the brown filing cabinet over there, 31 files for every possible day in any month. Clever, eh?

'Some will be council meeting agendas and minutes, you can bung them straight over to me. I generally do those but you'll get your share too. Some will just be from local organisations and businesses keeping us in touch with what they do.

'They're all written by people who wouldn't recognise a good story if it bit them on the bum. Some can go straight in the bin and you'll probably get a good idea of which ones as soon as you start reading, but you need to be careful. Sometimes buried in the middle there'll be a short paragraph saying that the company's development of a death ray machine is coming along nicely and now has the capability of wiping out a large village, or that the local residents' association has decided to step up its campaign against a proposed travellers' camp site by investing in a second-hand tank.'

She paused, and they looked at each other.

'I exaggerate slightly. Anyway, try to get a couple of paragraphs out of most of them if you can, they're handy fillers for odd bits of the page where Dorothy needs to fill a corner or the bottom of a column; she'll be in a bit later with a few more from this morning's post. Any doubts, ask me. When you've done a few we'll go through them together.'

She turned away to her own typewriter, pulled a notebook out of her bag and after checking a page inside it, reached for the phone and began dialling a number.

Jake took the top sheet from the small bundle of press releases.

'A meeting of the Glanclwyd Residents Association was held at the Scout Hall in Glanclwyd on the 28th September 1968. The meeting was chaired by the chairman, Mr Ivor Griffiths, and commenced at 7.30 pm. Present were Mrs Rosalind Emanuel, Mr Ianto Rees...'

He scanned down the page. No mention of a tank or even a Bren gun carrier but they were concerned about street lighting in Daisy Avenue. He took two sheets of the A5-sized copy paper from the pile on the desk, slid a sheet of carbon paper between them and rolled them carefully into the typewriter. He stared at the blank sheet of paper in front of him. It was falling to him to alert the whole population of Edwardstown to the worries of the people of Glanclwyd.

'It won't write itself', said Lotte's voice to his right.

OK. Very carefully, he began pecking at the keys. 'Broken street lights in parts of Glanclwyd are a danger to motorists and are encouraging loitering, say concerned residents ...'

He worked steadily, occasionally turning to Lotte with a query in between her phone conversations. Half listening, he was impressed with her telephone manner; she obviously knew many of the people at the other end of the line, beginning her conversations with enquiries about partners, children, recent activities. Even when she had to introduce herself the to-and-fro always seemed friendly, more a casual chat than an interview. He noticed though that she often asked the same question in different ways, never hectoring, leaving a topic then returning later, gently but insistent, and all the time, she jotted down notes on the pad beside the phone.

Dorothy came in and put a small sheaf of papers underneath the ones he was working on. One jutted out from the pile and bold black lettering at the top caught his eye. He pulled it out and read it.

Jake read it through twice. He recognised 'I'r gad' - 'to arms' – as the title of a popular song by a well-known Welsh folk singer and political activist, Dafydd Iwan. He knew the next line too: 'come Welshmen, old and young...' It was certainly a rather stirring rallying cry.

'What does 'rhyddid' mean?' he asked Lotte when she put the phone down.

'Er, 'freedom', if I remember my O-level Welsh. Why?'

39

He passed over the sheet of paper. 'What do you reckon to this?'

She studied it for a minute or so.

'Not sure. It could well be The Captain, but on the other hand it might be something a bit more serious. Go and show it to Roland.'

He took the press release back, crossed the room and knocked on Roland's door.

'Lotte thought you might like to have a look at this. It was with this morning press releases.'

Roland scanned it quickly.

'It's either The Captain or some nutter who had his wallet nicked on a day trip to Blackpool and has a lasting grudge against the English. Either way I'm not giving them any publicity.'

He screwed the paper into a ball and lobbed it into the bin beside his desk. He reached across, pulled a handwritten letter from a pile and passed it over to Jake.

'Have a crack at this. It's from our local vicar, the one who writes a column for us. Currently he's worried about the homeless. He's always got a bee in his bonnet about something and personally I don't think this one's a major problem around here but it might make something. Give him a call, fix a time for an interview. If you think it's worth it, find out when he's free for a photo; get some background information on homelessness if you can and do me about five hundred words in total. All right?'

Delighted to be relieved of press release duties, Jake had a quick conversation with the Reverend on the phone then spent most of the rest of the day ringing press officers at the Welsh Office, the local authority, housing charities and anyone else he could think of. That evening he occupied the desk in Number 17's front room, writing detailed questions to put to the Rev. Stanley the following day.

He showed Gareth the closely written foolscap sheet over breakfast. Gareth read it as he slowly chewed a slice of toast and marmalade.

'What time are you doing the interview?'

'Ten, at the vicarage.'

'OK. Nothing wrong with these questions, although you need to reduce them to bullet points, but what's the most important thing about doing an interview?'

'Um... preparation?'

'No, though that is important, obviously. The most important thing is – listen. Sounds obvious doesn't it, but when you're preoccupied with the fear of drying up, just sitting there looking at the interviewee without a question in your head, there's a real tendency simply to plough through your list of questions. You've got to listen to what he says and then respond to it; it's not difficult if you're half way interested in what he's saying, and if you're not a curious sort of person then you're probably in the wrong job. And don't worry, it'll be fine.'

Jake wasn't so sure, particularly in the three or four seconds between ringing the vicarage doorbell and waiting for the door to open. In fact in those few seconds, he became more than ever convinced he was going to make a complete fool of himself. He was in the wrong job. What madness had persuaded him that because he could knock out fifteen hundred words on the plays of Bernard Shaw over a week he could question a clergyman on a subject that until yesterday he'd known nothing about and then write something that might actually interest someone else? They'd laugh at him. He'd have to go home, in disgrace, and look for something else. Maybe a postman, maybe a...

The door swung open. Jake smiled brightly.

'Reverend Stanley? Jake Nash from The Enquirer. We spoke on the phone yesterday.'

The Reverend regarded him gravely.

'Yes, we did. Come in, please.'

He was a tall and severely imposing man in his late forties, dressed in a clerical black suit with a shining white dog collar above his black shirt. He was quite thin, with an aquiline nose, bushy grey eyebrows over bright dark eyes and a mass of wiry grey hair. He stood aside to let Jake walk into the long dark hallway.

'Go through to the study, straight down and it's in front of you. I'll just get us some refreshments – tea? Coffee?'

'Coffee please; strong, milk, no sugar.'

The vicar disappeared through a side door, and Jake walked through to the study. It was a large, light room dominated by a solid wooden desk facing out to the garden. A rather old and overstuffed sofa faced an empty fireplace and was flanked by two matching armchairs. Two bookcases contained a cross section of volumes – history, theology, novels, autobiographies – in English and in Welsh. On the mantelpiece there was a row of framed photographs: an older couple on their wedding day, three young boys who looked remarkably similar, the middle one, about ten years old, almost certainly the Reverend, a group of soldiers grinning at the camera, the man in the middle quite definitely the Reverend, the dog collar looking incongruous against the battledress.

'Here we are then.'

The Reverend walked across to a small table in front of the sofa, carefully balancing a tray with two coffee cups and a plate of biscuits.

'You were in the army then, Reverend?'

'Yes, I was. I come from a military family; I was the first of us to go into the church but I did serve as a padre for a while. I expect it's in the genes. It was an interesting experience, not always comfortable but it did make me confront some issues. Would you like a chocolate digestive, Mr Nash?'

While they drank the coffee, Jake asked the Reverend about his background. The Reverend told him that he'd been born into a Welsh speaking family near Carmarthen, had known from an early age that he'd wanted to go into the ministry and had served in several parishes around Wales, mostly in Welsh-speaking areas.

'The language is important to you, Reverend?' Jake asked.

'Extremely. As is our culture and way of life, amusing though it may seem to those who think themselves more sophisticated.' He smiled, thinly.

'You must be pessimistic about its future though,' said Jake.

'We cannot give in to despair, although I admit that when I look at the world around me I sometimes struggle to maintain an optimistic outlook on life.'

He shifted forward onto the edge of his seat, looked intently at Jake and spoke with a quiet vehemence.

'I believe that the Welsh people, for all their apparent indifference, will realise in time what a treasure they are losing, that life is about more than the acquisition of a bigger television set or a shinier car, and the appropriate action will be taken to save it.'

He paused and looked at Jake intently. When he spoke again, his voice was even softer but had lost none of its intensity.

'And it's action we need, isn't it, Mr Nash? There comes a time when mere words do not suffice, although what form that action might take I have no firm idea. Or would you, as an Englishman, not agree?'

Jake had the distinct impression that he was being tested.

'Er, no, I can see where you're coming from, Reverend' said Jake and nodded slowly in what he hoped was a thoughtful way. He shifted uncomfortably in his seat. Time, he thought, to begin the interview.

It went well. The Reverend had what sounded to Jake like some good ideas. His plan was to borrow a load of bricks from a local builder then get people to 'buy' a brick for half a crown to build four pillars in a space by the market entrance on a Saturday in the near future. When the four pillars were high enough they'd make a rough roof and walls with timber and tarpaulins, then the vicar and anyone else he could persuade to join him would sleep out under the shelter overnight before walking to the morning service in church the following day.

'I think I can get a couple of the international players, soccer and rugby, to come along and maybe a television presenter, possibly even persuade them to stay overnight. I've found that celebrities' – his face, at that point, looking rather as though he'd just realised that Jake had carried with him into the room a very large portion of dog poo on his shoe – 'celebrities tend to be more enthusiastic in attending when what I believe is called a photo opportunity presents itself, so I'm sure they'll be happy to buy a brick or two and crouch under the makeshift roof for as long as it takes to get a picture.'

The long-term aim was to raise enough money to buy and convert a house somewhere in the area to provide temporary accommodation for homeless people, a refuge to give them some stability in their lives and a breathing space to organise a future.

'So who'll run this refuge and pay the running costs?' asked Jake, by now over his initial nervousness and feeling bold enough to depart from his prompt sheet.

'A good question and one I can't immediately answer. I think the important point is to get the project up and running; I hope that if we can get off to a good start and get a level of enthusiasm going, perhaps the project will develop an energy of its own. And perhaps, for once, we will forget our own problems and think of the bigger picture.'

Jake was happy he'd got all he needed. He thanked the Reverend, closed the notebook, then glanced across to the photographs on the mantelpiece. There was something else he was curious about.

'This may be a bit trite, Reverend, and I'm sure it's a question you've been asked before, but you served as an army padre; how do you square the commandment 'Thou shalt not kill' with providing spiritual solace and moral support for a group of men whose job it is to do just that? Are they sinners? Are you a sinner for serving with them and tacitly approving their sins?'

Again, that intense stare.

'Again, good questions, fair ones, and ones I had to ask myself before I signed up. I think in the end I decided that the taking of life is a bad thing and should be avoided whenever an alternative course of action allows, but that sometimes a bad thing can be justified if it is intended to prevent or mitigate a worse thing, and so serves a greater good. I don't believe any of the men I served with enjoyed killing.'

He pointed towards the photograph on the mantelpiece, the one of him standing with four very young men. 'Certainly those four did not; they found themselves where they were because the British government sent them there and told them they had a job to do. They realised that their work might, perhaps would, entail the taking of life and they seemed to accept it. I'm not sure any of them thought too deeply about it. But I know that young soldiers endured great trauma and subsequent doubt because of what they did, and if I could alleviate some of that... suffering, then I saw it as my duty to do so.'

'So you, and they, were perhaps doing something that might be thought to be wrong in the abstract but in the end was in fact good?'

The Reverend looked at him steadily for a few seconds before replying.

'Yes, something like that.'

The shadow of a humourless smile crossed his face. 'Some found the choice easier than others.'

Something like a cold chill ran momentarily down Jake's spine, and it occurred to him that there was steel in this man.

On his way back to the Castle, Jake made a short detour to a small office in a back street of the town. He was there for half an hour then carried on back to the paper. He called in to the photographers' room, confirmed an appointment for Wayne to get some shots of the Reverend Stanley tomorrow, and asked the photographer to do another job for him. Then he sat down at one of the typewriters in the reporters' room, flicked back through his notes for few minutes and began to write.

He worked steadily for three hours, through his lunch hour, only acknowledging briefly the comings and goings of Lotte and Terry. He stopped twice to make himself coffee and occasionally he leant back from the keyboard with a thoughtful expression on his face; two or three times he yanked the paper from the machine, screwed it into a ball and flung it into the waste paper basket. When he'd finished, he read through the typed sheets, then tapped them together into neat pile and took them into Roland's office.

'The Rev's homeless story, Roland' he said, putting the stack down on the corner of the desk.

Roland glanced at it. 'That looks more than five hundred words to me. All right, leave them there' and he turned back to the story he had been reading.

Jake went back into the reporters' room and for lack of anything else to do washed up the morning's coffee mugs, dried them and restacked them next to the kettle. Then he thought he'd try to restore some order to the desk;

he'd been at that for five minutes and was about to give up when his name was shouted from the editor's office.

'Jake! In here.'

His heart sinking, Jake walked into the office. Roland, still looking at Jake's story, waved in the direction of one of the two chairs in front of the desk. Jake lowered himself onto one, sitting upright on the edge of the seat, his hands clasped nervously in his lap.

Roland read on for a few more seconds, flicking through the sheets, then he looked at Jake over the top of his reading glasses.

'First of all, if I ask you for five hundred words, I expect five hundred words. Maybe a dozen either way. If you think it's worth more or less, then you come and talk to me about it. What you don't do is take it upon yourself to decide what you're going to give me. OK?'

'Yes. Sorry.'

'Having said that, this isn't too bad.'

Jake had written up the Reverend's proposals with a good dash of human interest. He'd brought out the personal impact on individuals and families of being without a home and the Reverend's conviction that this was a problem we could all help in solving, not least because it was a lot closer to all of us than we like to think. He'd included a separate section highlighting some of the most dramatic statistics of homelessness he'd gleaned from his research the day before – the number of people affected, the relatively low level of resources devoted to helping them, the increased risk to life and health that the homeless suffered.

And he'd added another element that his phone calls had yielded. Jake had contacted a small charity in the town; someone there had known of a man who'd been living rough for a year in a shed in a disused colliery yard. He'd been a surveyor but an accident at work had meant he'd lost his job. Unable to cope with the changes in his life, he'd started drinking, his wife and child had left him, he'd lost his home. Now he got by as best he could.

The charity had thought they could persuade him to be interviewed by Jake, and they'd succeeded. He'd met the man, Richard, in the charity's offices that morning on the way back from the interview with the Reverend because Richard was ashamed to show anyone where he now lived. But he'd been surprisingly honest, not blaming others for his plight and frank about his own weaknesses but eager to underline how quickly circumstances can convert the possibility of being without a home, apparently too remote for most people to worry about, to a frightening reality.

Jake had considered incorporating it into the main body of the story but had decided it ran more powerfully as a separate piece. He'd even written a headline; 'Richard's Story: The Cost.'

'Is Richard his real name?' asked Roland.

'Yes. He's embarrassed by his circumstances in one way but he really feels what happened to him could happen to an awful lot of people. I said we wouldn't use his surname but he knows a lot of people will identify him anyway.'

'Don't make promises on the paper's behalf. Pictures?'

'Wayne's going to do the vicar tomorrow morning. I suggested he get him at the site where they're going to build the temporary shelter, maybe get the vicar with a placard announcing the idea but with people hurrying by and apparently ignoring him. It might take a while to get right but it could stir a few consciences.

'Then he's going to do Richard in his shed. Richard was a bit reluctant at first but I pointed out that he'd already said a lot of people would know who he was from information in the story and it would be much harder-hitting if people could put a face to the facts and actually see the conditions he lives in. He agreed in the end. I told Wayne to be a bit dramatic.'

Roland looked at him silently for a few seconds, then shouted 'Dot!'

His wife put her head round the door to her adjoining room and looked quizzically at him.

"There's not much on page 7 we can't do without or hold over, is there?' he asked.

'Well there's the -

'Drop what you have to and get all of this in, will you? And two pics. Wayne can bring them up to Trefoes tomorrow.'

Trefoes was where all the Gwalia Press newspapers were printed; Roland and Dot went up there every Thursday to oversee last minute adjustments to the pages.

Roland looked back at Jake. 'You'd better come with us. You might as well see the dying days of an industrial process before it's gone forever.'

Jake hadn't skipped for a good many years, but it was only with a major effort of will that he stopped himself doing it on the way back to the reporters' room.

Chapter 5

At half past eight the next morning, Jake slid into the back seat of Roland's Austin Cambridge for the journey up the winding valley road to Trefoes. The print works was on a new industrial estate on the Heads of the Valleys road, a major route that ran from east to west linking the tops of the north-south running valleys. Sub-editors and editors from all over the area travelled there once a week to see their papers off the presses.

The building was unimpressive, a single story industrial unit, but inside Jake found a scene he would have found hard to imagine. This was printing on an industrial scale. When he walked through the door that separated the reception and small suites of offices from the printing area, the first thing that hit him was the noise. Seven-foot high Linotype machines filled the area. At each sat an operator, tapping away with what seemed to him incredible speed at a ninety-character keyboard, composing lines of type that were then cast in molten metal.

Jake and Dorothy went over to the steel frames where those lines were being set into a page. Standing beside her, Jake casually reached out to run a hand over the solid mass of metal, curious as to what it felt like. Dorothy snatched at his arm. 'Don't touch it!' she said, looking anxiously around her.

Jake was startled. 'I don't think I'd do it much harm.'

'That's not the point. It's strict demarcation. We're National Union of Journalists, they're National Graphical Association. We write it, they print it. If a shop steward sees someone who isn't an NGA member touching their stuff, they'll all stop work for a union meeting and the whole distribution schedule gets knocked back.'

Chastened, Jake thrust his hands into his pockets and kept them there for a good while.

Back in the side office where Roland was checking page proofs, Wayne arrived, dumped his coat and immediately disappeared into the building's dark room with his camera; he came back with the black and white prints he'd taken earlier that morning. They were good. He'd used a long exposure on the shot of the vicar so that the people passing in front and behind him were slightly blurred, adding to the impression of their indifference. In the other, Richard's face was large in the frame but set to the right; lit dramatically from the left side, he was looking up into the camera, his face drawn and slightly grubby, his eyes dark-rimmed, the stubble on his chin clearly visible. In the background, a broken window was partially blocked with cardboard, and on the floor of the hut, a rough bed of blankets.

Roland studied them for a while, then sniffed. 'I suppose they'll do.'

Wayne smiled, and Jake nudged him in the ribs. 'Nice one', he whispered.

Later that day, Jake stood at the end of the production line, watching the papers coming off the press. He was deeply impressed with the process, watching the whirling drums of the presses and the paper being fed from what looked like a huge toilet roll into the machines. It seemed incredible that virgin paper could go in at one end and complete printed, assembled and folded newspapers could come out the other but the operation was excitingly noisy and dynamic.

Occasionally one of the print workers would take a copy off the line and check it through for print quality. Seeing Jake watching, he handed a copy over after he'd finished with it.

Jake turned as slowly and casually as he could to page seven, feigning an interest in the earlier pages, which in truth hardly registered.

Then there it was, his first published story. And under the headline 'Homelessness: "A Stain On Our Society"' (a quote from the Reverend Stanley lifted from the body of the text) were an extra three words – 'by Jake Nash.'

Dorothy appeared at his shoulder. 'What do you think?' she shouted over the noise of the press.

He grinned at her. 'Great', he shouted back.

He didn't think he'd ever been so happy.

The Edwardstown Enquirer was in newsagents the length and breadth of the valley the following morning, and just after nine, The Captain and Siôn sat side by side in Tolaini's, drinking frothy coffee and sharing a copy.

Starting at the front page ('Council Threat To Cut Bin Collections') they worked their way through steadily to the back page sport ('United Slump in 7-0 Shocker').

'Not a mention. Not a bloody word,' said The Captain in disgust. He folded the paper roughly in half and tossed it back onto the table.

The press release had taken him the best part of the afternoon to produce and he was hurt that his industry hadn't been rewarded. Siôn shrugged.

'Well there you go. Free press? Don't make me laugh. They do what they're told by their bosses, who in this case are all up in London going to garden parties with the Prime Minister and Her Maj and conspiring to keep the working classes down. Any hint of dissent, any little trace of stepping out of line and they ignore it if they can or demonise it if they can't.'

The Captain stirred another spoonful of sugar into his coffee and took a sip.

'That's the answer then. We have to do something that they simply can't ignore.'

'Like what?'

'Well, something that shows we mean business, that demonstrates we're not just going to march around town and wave a banner and shout a few slogans. A proper military exercise, that's what we want, a show of force, and get the paper along to report on that.'

'It's not going to be much of a show of force with just two of us.'

The Captain tapped his spoon thoughtfully on his saucer. 'What about the Jenkins brothers from Cwmphil? They were in The Llew a few weeks ago saying that nothing short of a rebellion was going to shift the bloody English out of Wales, and when it happened they'd be there.'

'They were drunk. And they find it difficult to be anywhere but home in bed before ten in the morning. And as for politically engaged, I doubt if they could name the current Prime Minister.'

'Look, it swells the numbers, doesn't it? Once we get some publicity we'll get the momentum going, and they'll flock to the banner.'

'We haven't got a ba-'

'WE'LL GET ONE LATER!! Right, let's have a think.'

The Captain took another mouthful of coffee and grimaced slightly. By now it was quite cold. He put the cup down and stared into space for a few moments.

'Have the shops started selling fireworks yet?'

'Don't think so. But there's a shop down in Cardiff you can get them, they sell them all year round for parties and stuff.'

The Captain pulled out his wallet, extracted a five pound note and gave it to Siôn.

'Go down to the model shop in Glanrafon Street...no, second thoughts, find a model shop in Cardiff and buy some Jctex fuse-' seeing Siôn's mouth open to ask a question, he carried on quickly 'just ask, they'll know what it is. Whatever size packet they sell it in, get two. Then go to the firework shop and spend the rest of that on as many bangers as you can get. That should be quite a few, so don't sit next to anyone who's smoking on the train back.'

'And what are we going to do with them?'

'You'll find out.'

The Reverend Stanley was reading his copy of the paper on the sofa in his study, his mid-morning coffee and chocolate digestive on the table in front of him. He read the homelessness article with a cold satisfaction. The reporter was obviously new to the job but he'd made a reasonable fist of it.

He turned to page nine to read the single column The Enquirer ran every week in Welsh; their correspondent was musing on the possibility of a Welsh language television channel. His face twisted in a parody of a smile.

Well, I won't he holding my breath for that, he thought. He was about to turn the page when a short story at the bottom caught his eye.

Memorial Plans On Track was the heading, and below that:

The rededication of the Edwardstown War Memorial is set to go ahead before this year's Remembrance Sunday ceremony, a senior councillor has confirmed.

After the controversial decision to move the memorial from its original site in Cyfartha Road to a new location in Griffiths Park to make way for what the council claimed was essential road widening, there were fears that the work would not be completed in time for this year's annual commemoration of the dead of two World Wars and other conflicts.

But Coun. Arthur Jones, Chairman of the Parks and Leisure Committee, has confirmed that the rededication will take place on Saturday 2nd November.

'I'm delighted to say that the Lord Lieutenant of the county, Brigadier Ormsby-Kirkwood MC, has agreed to

perform the ceremony, in good time for the Remembrance Day ceremonies that are so important to us as a community', he told *The Enquirer.*

The Reverend slowly lowered the paper to the table then, hunching forward to smooth the page out with a hand that shook very slightly, he reread the story.

When he'd finished, he sat back and gazed, unseeing, out of the window to the garden. The autumn had left the flower beds untidy and the grass unkempt, and the bare branches of the rose bushes bent before a gusty wind. It was a drab and chilly day, but the Reverend was back in a much colder place.

Chapter 6

March 1952. Yongdong, South Korea

Captain Stanley (not that he or anyone else ever thought of him as a captain, it was a nominal rank) dropped from the passenger seat of the truck into the semi-frozen mud then, pulling the collar of his greatcoat tighter around his neck, waved his thanks to the driver as he crunched his gears and drove away. The padre shivered in the cold of the late afternoon air and began trudging across the compound towards one of the sandbagged bunkers on its periphery.

He'd been coming here every couple of Sundays for three months now, ever since this unit's own padre, Captain Connolly, had approached him in the base NAAFI canteen one evening. Connolly was sorry to ask, he was sure Stanley had more than enough on his plate anyway, but there were four Welsh lads in his unit, all National Servicemen, all struggling in this alien environment so far removed from their own experiences. Would Stanley mind coming over now and then to conduct a small service in their own language? Connolly was sure it would help.

Stanley made the first trip with some reluctance; it was bitterly cold and anything that entailed travelling, especially when he had to scrounge lifts from wherever he could, wasn't to be welcomed. He hated the army and Korea. Most of the men he was supposed to serve seemed at best indifferent to him, another irrelevance foisted on them from the hierarchy that ruled their lives.

But after that first time he'd come to look forward to these evenings with his congregation of four.

Two of them, Davies 167 and Jones 42, were lifelong friends from the same village in North Wales who had somehow managed to stay together through training and posting. The other two, Morgan and Preece, came from mid and west Wales respectively but all four had their rural background and chapel upbringing in common. And all four, trying to behave like men but still really boys, seemed lost in this harsh landscape amidst the machinery of warfare.

They and Stanley would gather in one of the smaller bunkers that had been set aside as a recreation room, mostly used by soldiers who just wanted a little time away from the claustrophobia of their own living quarters. Stanley would read a passage from the Bible then, rather than preach, he'd ask them what they thought of it, hoping – usually successfully – to promote a discussion about whatever was most on their minds.

Together they would sing a couple of the old hymns, 'Gwahoddiad' or 'Blaenwern' perhaps, falling naturally into harmony. Davies and Jones would sing with a solemn intensity, their eyes unselfconsciously closed, and Stanley knew that for those few minutes they were home again, far away from the cold and the mud and the guns and the dead.

And he too found a certain peace in those moments. For a short while, his doubts about his role there faded, his growing anger at the inanities of military life subsided and he seemed to find a true purpose.

Stanley was heading now for a bunker that had a sign propped against the wall, 'B Company HQ'. He pushed aside the blanket across the doorway and ducked into the gloomy interior. It was empty except for the Company Sergeant Major, sitting behind a typewriter at a rickety table and laboriously filling in a form by the light of a weak electric bulb.

'Evening, Sarn't Major', said Stanley, unbuttoning the coat. 'Bit early, I know, but I thought I'd better take the lift I was offered.'

The CSM looked up, seeming slightly surprised. 'Evening, padre. You didn't get the message then?'

'Message?'

The CSM looked a little embarrassed. 'I left a message for you earlier. I'm afraid there won't be a service this evening, padre.'

Stanley frowned. 'No service? I don't understand. I thought this had all been agreed. And it's been a regular thing now, every two weeks.'

'Well, yes it had. Major Nash was happy enough with it but you won't have heard that he's gone down with pneumonia and been evacuated back to the base hospital. He'll be all right but he's going to be away for a while.

'Anyway, the new CO's arrived. Very keen, padre, very keen indeed. Wants to put a more aggressive spirit into the men, more patrols, more contact, all that sort of thing.'

Stanley shook his head in frustration. 'But why does that mean our service has to be cancelled?'

The CSM lifted his hands from the table, turning the palms upwards and apart in a hopeless 'who knows? - it's the Army' gesture.

'He's sending out a patrol tonight to stir things up, and he says he doesn't see why your lads should be exempt just to sing hymns.'

Stanley looked down and stared at the earth floor for a few seconds, then looked back up at the Sergeant Major. 'It's barely an hour and it's good for morale,' he said softly. He was suddenly more angry then he'd been for a very long time. 'Look, this is nonsensical and quite unfair. May I speak to him, this new CO?'

The CSM rubbed his hand across his brow. 'I don't think the Army's too concerned about being fair, do you padre? And if you ask me, he's not the kind of bloke who's open to discussion.' He shook his head. 'I don't think there's much of a chance to be honest, but I'll see if I can find him if you like.'

'I would like, Sergeant Major. Thank you.'

The CSM hauled himself wearily to his feet and, pulling his greatcoat around him, pushed his way through the curtain. It had barely fallen back behind him when Stanley heard his voice again.

'Oh, there you are sir. The padre's just arrived, the Welsh one who comes over every couple of weeks – I mentioned him this morning? Wondering if he could have a word about holding a short service for the Welsh lads, same as he usually does. To be fair, sir, it's quite a trek over here, and we could probably spare the boys for tonight, they've done their share of patrols these last couple of weeks.'

There was a pause, and when the response came it was in the clipped, carefully enunciated tone that Stanley had come to associate with the product of English public schools.

'I thought I'd made it perfectly clear this morning, Sergeant Major, that the men in question will not be excused tonight's patrol to attend an unofficial church parade. If the padre wasn't informed that's not my concern, nor do I have time to talk to him now. I'm about to brief the patrol.'

'Yes, sir.'

'And, Sergeant Major, I will decide who can or cannot be spared from any duty, not you. These men are here to fight, not sing hymns in some Godforsaken language that hardly anyone understands. Now carry on.'

'Very good, sir.'

The CSM shouldered his way through the curtain back into the bunker and shrugged at Stanley.

'You probably heard that, padre. Like I said, I didn't think there was much chance of him changing his mind. He seems to be pretty...' The CSM paused and seemed to be choosing his words with some care. '...certain about how he wants things done. I wouldn't say he's the flexible type, if you know what I mean.'

Stanley gazed at him, expressionless, his fists tightly clenched by his side.

'No, I see that'. His voice was calm, controlled. 'Thank you for trying, Sergeant Major.'

The CSM looked slightly embarrassed as he shrugged the greatcoat off and settled back on his chair.

'I'm sure things will be back to normal in a couple of weeks. Why don't you see if you can get yourself a cup of cha and I'll get someone to run you back as soon as I can.'

Stanley, his body rigid, nodded abruptly. He moved towards the curtain, then stopped and turned back.

'What's the name of this new CO, by the way?'

'Kirkwood, padre, Major Ormsby-Kirkwood.'

Things did not get back to normal, the services were never resumed. The patrol was ambushed by the Chinese; survivors reported that Davies 167 and Preece were killed outright, Jones 421 and Morgan were missing, believed captured. But after the war ground to an end and an armistice was signed they were not among the prisoners released to return home. Eventually they were numbered among the scores of soldiers who disappeared into Chinese prison camps, never to be heard of again.

No matter how angry Stanley felt, he had always tried to live by the maxim 'hate the sin, love the sinner' and he endeavoured conscientiously to keep any issue free of personal dislikes. But from then on, he struggled with that. Oppression now had a face and a name.

Lost in his thoughts, the Reverend stared out onto the garden for some minutes. Then he slowly stood and walked over to his desk. Opening a bottom drawer, he rummaged in it for a while and after some time searching, took from it a battered notebook. He turned the pages until he found what he was looking for; he sat down at the desk, pulled the phone towards him and consulting the notebook once or twice, dialled a number.

In a small house in County Cavan in Eire, not far from the border with Fermanagh in Northern Ireland, a phone rang.

Jake was allowed to bask in tl
while that morning, but not fo.

As he'd climbed the s
Terry had managed a half sm
way down.

'Nice story, kid. Just go.

Terry carried on dow
paused and seemed to make :
turned back and looked up at Jak

'If you ever need any clo   _., son, any gear – shirts,
jackets, anything like that - I know a few blokes who can get
stuff...well, a bit cheaper than you'd pay in the shops.
Know what I mean? Just say the word, kid.'

'Thanks Terry, I'll bear it in mind.'

'Fair enough. Catch you later.' The chunky frame
turned and clattered off down the stairs.

And Lotte had greeted him with a broad smile.

'Well well, byline on your first story, eh? Took me
about four weeks, if I remember correctly. Well done,
anyway; are we allowed to talk to you while seated or
should we kneel?'

'That's going a bit far, Lotts. Maybe just incline
forward slightly from the waist with the eyes respectfully
downcast?'

Then Roland, making no mention of yesterday's
story, had sent him off on his day's tasks. First to talk to a
group of residents in one of the outlying parts of the town
who were worried about flooding from a nearby stream;
then on to a charity who were setting up a scheme to divert
young offenders away from a career in stealing cars by
acquiring some old ones for them to repair and drive
around a farm track.

By the time he'd come back and written them both
up, it was time for his first council meeting.

He sat on the pres
council chambe
governed th
seemed a

bench next to Lotte and surveyed the
. By and large the men and women who
affairs of Edwardstown Urban District
retty normal group, with one or two exceptions.
Who's the bloke with the medals?'

'Arthur Lewinson, one of the two Independents on
e council. If you're going to ask me why he's wearing his
medals, I've no idea, except that he's never seen out
without them. He's a tad eccentric, but at least he asks
awkward questions sometimes.'

'Is that good?'

'Oh absolutely. This council has 24 members, 22 of
whom are Labour. It hasn't had a Conservative in living
memory and most decisions are actually taken the night
before the council meeting in the Labour group meeting.
To which the Press is not admitted. If it's a potentially
embarrassing issue for them they've been known at the
council meeting to move that the matter is put straight to
the vote as soon as it's reached on the agenda so there's no
debate, and with a 22 to 2 majority, they get away with an
awful lot.'

'Who's the other Independent?'

'The lady in the too-large hat. Maude Tinsley,
rumoured to be a closet Conservative with a bit of a pash
for Edward Heath. But of course she couldn't stand as a
Tory or she'd never get in.'

'So how did they manage it as Independents?'

'Every now and then the council will do something
that gets people in a ward really hacked off, appoint a
headmistress at the local school who isn't up to the job but
happens to be the niece of the chair of the education
committee, something like that, and there'll be a protest
vote. The turnout is always phenomenally low so you don't
need that many angry people to cause an upset. In Arthur's
case, though, it's more of a sympathy thing. He's

represented the Brynmill ward since the Second World War but his only son was killed in the Korean War; he'd lost his wife a couple of years earlier and it hit him really badly. He's not been quite right since.

'The Labour group asked him to resign because they thought he'd damage their chances; he did but then he stood as an Independent and the locals backed him. Bully for them. To be honest, it's a bit like that joke 'whoever you vote for, the government always gets in.' Most people think it doesn't really matter where they put their cross on the ballot paper, the council runs things the way it wants to anyway.'

'It all sounds a bit corrupt', said Jake.

'A bit, but not in a really nasty way. In the old days, a fiver to your local councillor would get you moved up the list for a council house but now the process is much more transparent. The council officers run things much more tightly and they're not about to risk their jobs for a few pints and a packet of chips.

'Sure, the councillors like to treat themselves to the odd inspection tour or familiarisation visit to somewhere vaguely attractive, they're not adverse to the odd dinner and maybe they exaggerate their expenses a bit. But then on the other hand they spend a lot of time on council work, they have to, and they don't get anything out of it other than a bit of status. Most of them seem happy enough to settle for that.

'And national politics aren't really reflected at this level. They call themselves Labour but most of them are pretty reactionary, and I doubt if more than three or four of them could give you any clear idea what Labour Party policy is on any given subject. It's a bit like the social clubs in the town; if half the people who drink in the Conservative Club actually voted Tory they might have a decent chance of getting some councillors.'

On their way in, Jake had noticed Lotte seemed to be on good terms with a good many of the members and officers; most had said hello, a few had waved across the room, one or two had stopped for a few words.

'I thought you'd have to guard against being too friendly with them?'

Lotte screwed her mouth up in an expression that said well, yes and no. 'The thing is, it's a mutually dependant relationship. They need us to get their plans out and to stay in the public eye; we need them to fill the paper. It's not like the nationals where you can charge in, flail about and then leave, knowing you're very unlikely to bump into the people involved again. We see these people all the time, we all live in the same community.

'They know that if we've got a story we'll chase it down, and as long as we're fair and don't take cheap shots, they'll go with that. Lots of these guys are working men without a lot of education, you know, they ain't Winston Churchill or Nye Bevan when it comes to a debate, so we can help them a bit.'

Lotte smiled. 'Last Christmas one of them actually moved a vote of thanks to me 'for writing what we meant to say rather than what we actually said.' I'm not sure if I should have felt happy about that, but I did.'

She turned back to the agenda. 'Right then, what delights await us tonight?'

She'd already put asterisks besides some of the items. For Jake, none of them seemed particularly promising but Lotte, in between making notes, quietly filled him in on the background to each item and its likely interest to their readers.

'How can you tell what's newsworthy and what isn't?' Jake asked.

'It gets easier when you know the area. But I suppose it comes down to figuring out whether what you've just heard weighs down the 'oh really?' side of the scales or the 'so what?' side. If it's the former, it's news, if it's the latter, it isn't. And if it's 'bugger me!!' it's definitely news.'

They'd reached one of the items that Lotte had highlighted.

'Rededication of the War Memorial. Councillor Jones?' said the chairman.

'Yes, Mr Chairman, delighted to say that things are moving ahead smoothly in accordance with the stipulated schedule.' Councillor Ronald Jones was about fifty, dressed in a well-worn three-piece blue pinstripe suit. An impressive paunch strained against the waistcoat and he seemed proud of it; he sported a pocket watch and chain that drew the eye to the size of his stomach. He had the contented air of a man who was, on the whole, rather pleased with himself.

'As already reported in the local press' – he glanced over to Lotte, smiled and inclined his head, she smiled slightly and gave a brief nod back – 'the Lord Lieutenant will be attending, as will representatives of all the armed forces and various youth organisations. The Reverend Stanley' (not, the slightly raised eyebrows and significant pause seemed to imply, the Councillor's favourite minister, too opinionated by half and a troublemaker if you asked him, but nonetheless acknowledged to be The Almighty's senior representative in Edwardstown) 'the Reverend Stanley will as you know conduct the religious side of the dedication with the assistance of Nonconformist ministers, their number to be confirmed but not more than two; I can also inform the council that plans are in hand for a reception afterwards for dignitaries in Pembroke Villa. This falls within the budget already agreed for the project. The usual caterers have been engaged.'

There was a murmur of approval from the room. Councillor Jones was obviously a man who knew a good caterer from a bad one.

'What's Pembroke Villa?' whispered Jake to Lotte.

'A Victorian mansion at one side of the park. It was gifted to the council by the descendants of a coal owner who probably felt a bit guilty about all the money he'd made from his pits here. Local organisations can use it for meetings but it's good for functions too, it's got big rooms and lovely gardens.'

'Seems a bit tame to be much of a story.'

'Ah you're wrong there, these things can loom large in a small community. There were ructions when the council decided to move the memorial to make way for a new road, a lot of older people felt it was almost sacrilege. We found some of the descendants of the men whose names are on the memorial from the British Legion and the old comrades' associations, spoke to them to see how they felt, got some of the stories of the men who'd died, and the whole thing brewed up into quite a nice little row.

'It's mostly died down now but it's a story that needs closing. Human interest, you see – it's always there if you look for it, even in a planning row.'

Chapter 8

A week later, Siôn came down for breakfast in the farmhouse to find The Captain already sitting at the kitchen table, smoke curling from a cigarette in his right hand as he stared thoughtfully at the old typewriter in front of him. As Siôn drew nearer, he saw that a piece of paper with the GLF logo was in the machine.

'Morning. Tea in the pot if you want some', said The Captain.

Siôn poured himself a cup, sat down and reached for a piece of toast from the two slices on a plate in the middle of the table. 'What's up?' he asked, spreading a thick layer of honey over the bread.

The Captain leant back in his chair, still looking at the sheet of paper.

'I think we're ready to go.'

'Really? You've spoken to the Jenkins brothers then?'

'I went over there yesterday.' He sighed. 'To be honest I'm not that impressed. They'll do it, in fact they're very keen to do it, but I'm not sure how far they're really committed to this in the long term. They seem to think it's all bit of a lark more than anything.'

Siôn chewed thoughtfully.

'I did warn you, but as you said, the main thing is to get some momentum going, generate some publicity, let people know we're here and that we mean business. There are people out there who feel the way that we do; we've got to give them a rallying point. Once we've gathered enough of them together we can be a bit stricter about who we take on, we can weed out the weak links and make sure we only stick with those who are absolutely prepared to go forward with us, whatever the cost.'

'Yes, you're right. It's just that I get a bit disheartened sometimes.'

'It'll be fine. What's the plan?'

'I'm going to write to the paper, tell them we'll be staging an exercise and say we're willing to be accompanied by a reporter. I'll address it specifically to that new one who did the piece on homelessness the other week, he did a good job on that.'

'And what's the exercise?'

'We're going to plant an explosive device on the valley's rail line.'

Siôn stopped chewing and stared at his uncle.

'An explosive device? You mean a bomb? A real bomb?'

'A sort of real bomb. Look, there's no point in going up there with a reporter then sticking an old shoe box full of newspaper with 'BANG!' written on the lid under the line.'

'So what is it? Is it dangerous? To us, I mean.'

'No, dead safe. We used to do it when we were kids. You get some bangers, break them open and stuff the powder into some kind of receptacle – we used to use old shotgun cartridges. The important thing is to ram it in hard and make sure its got something tight holding it down. Before that though you've bored a little hole in the side and run a length of that Jetex fuse out from the cartridge. Light the fuse, stand well clear and 'boom!' – a very satisfactory bang.'

'I'm surprised you can get fuses like that in the shops.'

'Well obviously it's not intended for home-made bombs, it's meant for little jet engines that burn solid fuel pellets. You use them on model aircraft, the wooden ones you can fly. They work pretty well. The important thing is to make sure you don't break the fuse wire; if there's a gap, it'll stop burning.'

'What happens if a train comes along after we've set the bomb off? A lot of people go down that line to Cardiff in the morning.'

'It won't do much damage and the first train is just after six. We'll do this around one in the morning, then telephone the police just to make sure someone has noticed.'

'How about getting a photographer along as well?'

The Captain looked at him.

'It'll be dark, Siôn, so if they did take any pictures they'd have to use a flashgun. I can't really get my head round the idea of an undercover military operation in the dead of night with lots of flashbulbs going off. We'll suggest to the reporter that they send a photographer up there first thing.'

The Captain turned back to the typewriter, reached for his packet of cigarettes and lit a fresh one. 'Right then, I'm going to write this communiqué. Make another pot of tea, will you?'

The offices were strangely quiet when Jake got in that Thursday morning. Normally he could hear Wayne and Reg chatting as they sorted out their kit for the day's work, Terry hammering away at a typewriter or just on his way out, sometimes Lotte making the first coffee, but this morning there seemed to be only Mavis at her usual post behind the reception desk.

He wandered into the silent reporters' room. Roland and Dot would, he knew, be on their way to Trefoes but Roland had left him a couple of leads to chase down. He might as well get started.

Lotte drifted in, carrying the day's milk, and headed for the coffee table.

'Morning. Coffee?'

'Please. Quiet around here today.'

'It's Thursday. Since Roland and Dot aren't around we tend to view this as a day of rest and recovery after our Herculean labours of the preceding week – you know, tidy up loose ends, do your expenses, make a few phone calls, nothing too strenuous.'

'Oh, right. I've got a couple of calls to make, not much more than that.'

'Right, well I'm going to pop out for a while when I've had this. If Roland rings, I'm out on a job, you're not sure where. I'll be back mid-morning. If anyone else calls, leave a note on my typewriter and I'll get back to them. If you go out, we usually meet in The Greyhound for lunch.'

Jake made his calls, then wondered briefly if the office had a way of recording the numbers dialled for outgoing calls and then checking to see if they were genuinely work-related. He decided on balance probably not and phoned Amanda. No answer, so he rang his mum and caught up with the news from home.

Lotte came back carrying a bag of shopping and they whiled away the morning drinking coffee and chatting, with the odd phone call to arrange interviews for the following day or next week. At just after 12.30, they walked downstairs and headed for The Greyhound.

On the way they were joined by the Reverend Stanley, wearing a coat and hat and carrying a large leather satchel. Falling into step with them, he complimented Jake on his story, telling them that he'd already sold a good number of bricks and that he was hopeful of getting the current Welsh fly-half, a former Edwardstown player, to come along on the day. Then they were at The Greyhound. The Reverend Stanley politely doffed his hat to Lotte, said goodbye and headed off in the direction of the station. Jake and Lotte turned down the tiled corridor and into the bar.

Wayne and Reg were already there with two men whom Jake had glimpsed passing the door of the reporters' room, on their way in and out of the office. Reg waved the reporters over to their table and introduced them to Jake.

'Meet the Morecambe and Wise of South Wales. Les Trimby and Roger Hinton, our advertising sales reps.'

'And the people who pay your highly inflated wages', said Les, reaching over the table to shake Jake's hand. Roger followed, smiling at Jake and then turning to Lotte.

'Lotts, my love, you must be utterly exhausted by all that talking to yours friends on the phone, typing shopping lists and doing your nails. Allow me to buy you a little stiffener. The usual? And for you, Jake, a pint?' He headed off towards the bar.

Les and Roger were roughly the same age as Reg but more formally dressed than him in dark suits; their customers expected them to look businesslike.

'Any reason you're called Morecambe and Wise of South Wales?' Jake asked Les.

'Well, your trained reporter's eye will already have noted that I wear horn-rimmed glasses and am going very, very slightly bald' – he was, in fact, almost completely bald, with a Bobby Charlton comb-over which only emphasised his lack of hair. 'Roger by way of contrast is short and hairy, although I've never seen his legs; he may shave them for all I know. So it might be said that physically, we bear some resemblance to television's best-loved comic duo.

'Other than that, the only possible reason I can think of is that we don't get a lot of laughs in our line of work, which is keeping the paper solvent, so we do like a bit of a giggle when we can.'

Roger came back with the drinks, a pint for Jake and a brandy and Babycham for Lotte, and settled back down. It turned out that they did enjoy a giggle. Although they had their own line manager in Trefoes and so didn't come directly under Roland's authority, they seem to be infected by the same mitching-off-school mood that gripped the editorial staff. They were good company and quite shortly Wayne went off to get another round. Jake was enjoying himself.

At Edwardstown's railway station, the Reverend Stanley bought a return ticket to Swansea. When he reached Cardiff and while he waited for his connection, he slipped into the gents' toilet, took off his clerical collar, wrapped a silk scarf round his neck and buttoned up his coat.

His train pulled into Swansea just after two. He walked from the station to Wind Street, a busy street near the city centre, and there went into the public bar of a small and unremarkable pub. He bought a pint of bitter and found a seat in a quiet corner, pulled out a book of poems by the Welsh writer Gwenallt and sat quietly reading, occasionally sipping his beer and glancing up at the clock over the mirror behind the bar.

Just after 2.30, he looked up to see a tall, dark man of roughly the same age as himself crossing the bar towards him. He stood and extended his hand.

'Michael, thank you so much for coming. It's good to see you again.'

'And you, Iorweth', said Michael, grasping the extended hand. He spoke with a pronounced Irish accent. 'You don't seem to have changed much.'

'Older but no wiser, I fear. Let me get you a drink and something to eat. What will it be?'

Michael smiled. "I'd hate to ruin any preconceptions so I suppose it'll have to be a Guinness. And a cheese sandwich will be just grand.'

When the Reverend returned from the bar they pulled their chairs closer to the table and began to talk. It was unlikely that anyone could overhear them but if they had it would have become quickly apparent that they'd known each other in Korea. The talk was of former comrades, of shared experiences and lost friends, of what they had done since those days. Then the Reverend moved his chair a little closer.

'Does anyone know you've come over here today?'

'Well I haven't told anyone, and if you mean do the security services keep track of me, then no, I don't think so. I'm sure they've still got a file on me somewhere, but I live a quiet life since the Archbishop removed me from the priesthood.'

'You were defrocked? I thought it was some kind of voluntary resignation.'

'Laicised is the technical term – but whatever, my support for the Republican movement became a little too vociferous, and I think in the end it was for the best all round.'

'But you're still active in that area?'

'I maintain contacts', said Michael carefully, 'and I do what I can for the cause. So now, tell me, what is it I can do for you?'

The Reverend spoke earnestly for some minutes and Michael listened equally intently, not interrupting. When Iorweth finished and leant back, Michael seemed to consider for a few seconds, then he stood.

'Another drink, I think. Bitter, was it?'

'Just a half for me.'

When he'd brought the drinks back and set them on the table, he pulled up his chair and leaned in towards the Reverend. He looked at him in silence, and when he spoke it was in a low and serious tone.

'Iorwerth, I don't do revenge. In particular, I don't do personal revenge. Others have accused me of having done wrong and perhaps they are correct. I will be judged when my time comes, but always I have acted in accordance with my conscience and in the furtherance of what I believe to be a righteous cause.

'Unless you can give me your assurance that what you propose falls within those boundaries, I will have

73

nothing to do with it. What you are asking entails grave risk, for me, for others and for yourself.'

Iorweth held his friend gaze for several seconds without speaking. Then, quietly but firmly, he said 'You have my assurance'.

Michael paused, then nodded slightly and opened his hands in a gesture of acceptance.

'Very well'.

Then he began talking more quickly. The Reverend listened intently, sometimes asking a question, at one point taking a pen from his pocket and jotting down some numbers on the flyleaf of his book of poetry. After twenty minutes or so, Michael stood up and extended his hand across the table.

'I wish you luck, Iorwerth. Please be careful.'

The Reverend took the proffered hand. 'Thank you, Michael. I will consider carefully what you've told me today, and I hope you trust me when I say that the fact this meeting occurred and what we've discussed will never be divulged to anyone else.'

'I do, of course I do.' His smile hardened very slightly. 'And I hope you know that there would, in all probability, be consequences beyond my control were that not to be the case.'

Michael turned and made his way out of the bar. The Reverend remained, a solitary figure in the mid-afternoon lull of the pub, deep in thought.

The by now quite merry men of the Enquirer and their Maid Marian got back to their offices around three o'clock. At some point in the preceding couple of hours Jake had eaten a ham roll and half a packet of crisps; he and Reg had also bought more rounds of drinks. He had wondered if someone ought to go back earlier, just in case Roland rang. No need to worry, said Lotte, they'd be busy putting the paper to bed. If they did ring and got no answer from the reporters or photographers, they'd assume everyone was out on jobs. Or at least, that's what everyone hoped.

Jake made four cups of coffee – for Les and Roger, lunchtime drinking was part of the job and they'd gone back to work - and carried them into the photographers' room. Wayne and Reg were leaning against their workbench, Lotte occupied one of the two chairs in the room. They'd bought back the mood in The Greyhound with them, Reg in particular; his unruly hair seemed even more wild than usual, his glasses were at a slight angle, he waved his hands animatedly as he told stories of strange assignments and valley characters.

Much of his conversation was directed in Lotte's direction. As she laughed at the end of one of his stories, he suddenly stood away from the bench and moved towards the dark room.

'Come in here, Lotts, I want to show you something.'

'No!' she said, still laughing.

'Come on, we can play photographers – you know, turn out the lights and see what develops.'

He took her hand and walked into the darkroom, towing the apparently semi-reluctant girl behind him. A second later, Wayne and Jake heard the lock turn and the red light went on.

Jake was stunned. Like many young people, he was a bit of a Puritan when it came to sex outside his own age group: he knew it went on, it just didn't really bear thinking about. After a few seconds he stopped staring at the closed door and the glowing red light and looked over at Wayne; the young photographer was wearing that increasingly familiar agonised expression. Wayne met his gaze, spread his hands and shrugged his shoulders in a 'What can you do?' gesture then turned back to the bench and began fiddling with a camera.

Jake wandered back into the reporters' room, sat at the desk and stared blankly at a typewriter for a while. What was it he felt – outrage? Jealousy? He picked up the phone and dialled Amanda's number again. Her mum answered. No, Amanda was in town, shopping with a couple of friends. Yes, she was fine, she seemed very happy. Not missing me at all then, thought Jake. Damn. As he said goodbye and put the phone down, Lotte came in.

She sat opposite him, took out a small mirror from her bag and began reapplying her lipstick. Jake watched, silently. When she'd finished, she put mirror and lipstick away and looked across the desk at him.

'I'm sorry, have I disappointed you?'

He shook his head, a little too vehemently. 'No, of course not. Why would you?'

She looked at him for a couple of seconds.

'It's nothing, you know. He's just fun, he's quite attractive in a sort of careworn way and his family life isn't great. He and his wife don't get on too well these days, married at 17 and tired of each other a long time ago. It doesn't go too far and it won't disrupt anything.'

'Absolutely none of my business, Lotts.'

She smiled at him. 'No.'

She stood and gathered her things together, turned and headed for the door. 'See you tomorrow then.'

'Lotts?'

She paused and turned, raising a quizzical eyebrow.

'I think you've buttoned your blouse up wrong.'

Jake left just after, and suddenly hungry, called in at Tolaini's for pie, chips and peas. He walked through the door of Number 17 just as Mrs Probert came out of the kitchen. She stopped when she saw him and sniffed.

'Lunchtime at The Greyhound then?'

"Er, yes. Just a brief one. How did you...?"

'I can smell it from here, boy! Cigarettes, alcohol. It's the slippery slope. Just you be careful.'

She walked down the hallway and began to climb the stairs.

'And if you're sick, don't expect me to clean up after you', she called back over her shoulder.

It seemed a bit early to go to bed. Jake opened the door of the front room. Gareth was in one of the heavy armchairs reading a book and looked up as Jake walked in.

'Aye-aye. Copped by Mrs P, eh? Nice time at the pub?'

'Yeah, good.' Jake slumped in the other armchair.

Gareth put his book down. 'You're looking a bit glum for someone who had a good time.'

Jake sighed.

'The thing is, I sort of miss Amanda.'

He started to tell Gareth about her. She hadn't been his first girlfriend at Aber but when they'd met they'd clicked very quickly. They'd revelled in the freedom of being away from home and parental supervision with the novel experience of grant money in their pockets. They'd discovered sex together, stayed up late putting the world to rights – amazingly easy, it was a wonder that the older generation couldn't see things as clearly as they did – and were part of a big group of friends. It was a cosy world which somewhere at the back of their minds they knew couldn't last, but Jake had cared enough for her to hope that they had a future after graduation.

They'd spoken a couple of times since his first phone call, once when he called her from a phone box again, once when she'd rung him at number 17 at a time they'd prearranged. Neither had been particularly satisfactory; the first time he'd felt uncomfortable in the draughty phone box with its faint aroma of late-night wee and a queue forming outside; when she'd rung him, the unseen presence of the doubtless close-by Mrs Probert had inhibited the conversation. And there always seemed to be people around in the office.

Gareth didn't see a problem. 'Go back home for the weekend or bring her down here.'

'I suppose I'll have to go back. I did mention her coming down but she wasn't exactly crazy about the idea. Anyway, where would she stay if she came? Although it might be nice if she could, she'd get some idea of where I am and what I'm doing.'

Gareth shut his book.

'Look, Mrs P goes over to stay with her sister once a month and I think she'll be off next weekend. I can go back to my mam's – why don't you invite Amanda down then? You can have the house to yourselves.'

Jake thought for a second. 'Bit risky, isn't it? What if Mrs P comes back early?'

'Never has done yet. She goes first thing on Saturday morning by train, comes back on Sunday afternoon, her brother-in-law drops her back in his car. Anyway, a little bit of danger adds to the excitement, doesn't it?'

Jake lay awake for a while that night, arms behind his head, staring into the blackness of the ceiling. A little bit of excitement... He decided: he'd ring Amanda tomorrow. In a slightly happier frame of mind, he turned over and was soon asleep.

Chapter 9

When Mavis came around to distribute the morning's post the next day, Jake was surprised to get an envelope addressed personally to him and apparently delivered by hand. His name was typed on a small sticky label stuck to the front of the envelope and inside he found a sheet of paper with a heading he recognised.

G.L.F.
Glamorgan Liberation Front
Rhyddid!

<u>Communiqué No.2</u>

Further to our earlier communiqué, the GLF will be holding a military exercise on the night of Tuesday 8 October. In order that both true Welshmen and those who would oppose them have knowledge of our seriousness of intent, you are invited to observe this exercise, on the following conditions: that your report is full and fair; that you make no attempt to identify any of the participants in the exercise; that you make no attempt to alert any authority, military or civil, of the existence of these plans; and that you do not co-operate with any subsequent investigation into the exercise by such authorities.

No photography will be allowed during the exercise. No other person is permitted to attend.

You will be contacted nearer the time with details of how you will join the exercise.

Your personal safety is guaranteed by the Commandant of the Welsh Liberation Front.

Stand ready!!
I'r Gad!

Jake studied it with a rising sense of excitement. A real story! He took it in to Roland and stood beside the desk as he read it.

'Tuesday 8 October. That's next week', said the editor.

'Yes. I'm happy to go.'

'I'm sure you are, but it's not quite that simple. As I said when we got the first of these, I'm not inclined to give publicity to a group of nutters who want to play at soldiers. On the other hand, if this really is something serious, then we have a duty to make people aware of it.'

'How about not warning the authorities?'

'I think we could justify that in terms of the greater public interest. I'm sure if anything does happen the police would become involved and you wouldn't have much choice about whether you speak to them or not but as you know, we protect our sources. Some of your colleagues have been dragged before the courts for doing just that.'

'I suppose someone might get hurt.'

'I very much doubt that, unless they trip on a rabbit hole in the dark and break an ankle. I suspect it will come down to a few people running around the woods with toy guns shouting 'bang!' every now and then.'

He put the communiqué to one side. 'Leave it with me. I'll refer it up and see what comes back.'

Jake walked down to Tolaini's at lunchtime for a sandwich and a cup of tea and found Gareth scribbling busily in his notebook at a corner table.

'What are you up to?' asked Jake, pulling up the chair opposite.

'Vox pops on the new factory they're proposing at the top of the valley. They're going to produce gelatine but part of the process means piping waste into the river, so there's a bit of a row going on.'

'Vox pops?'

'Short quotes from members of the public. It's supposed to give a flavour of the cross section of opinion on any given topic. Democracy at work, access to the media, etc, etc.'

'Why are you making them up? Bit unethical, isn't it?'

Gareth sighed. 'Look, I've already done a fair and balanced story on this giving both sides of the argument with quotes from the company, the council and the residents' association. Roland wants a few vox pops to round it off, but if I go out on the streets and ask the great public for their views a lot of them won't speak to me, a lot more don't have any opinions either way, and the opinions of the remaining few are utterly predictable anyway. It's cold, it's going to rain, I'm hungry, and given that I've got to balance out those for and those against anyway, it's just easier to do it this way.'

'What if Roland finds out?'

"How would he? We only give a name and the area they come from, so unless you've claimed to have quizzed Fatima Dashenka Kozonowski of 14 Railway Terrace on her views on the dangers of polluting the river, you're pretty safe. Not quite so easy mind if the boss decides he wants pics to go with quotes, but the boys are busy elsewhere so we're pretty safe. You might as well help. Give me one for the factory.'

Jake thought for a second.

'We need the jobs here and I'm sure the council will be completely on top of monitoring any potentially hazardous discharges.'

'And you are?'

'Mrs Janet Hughes, Cwmphil.'

'And your companion who, judging by the look on his face, doesn't agree with you?'

'No, I certainly don't. We can't risk sacrificing what little we have left of the natural environment round here for profit. I know we need jobs but not at any cost.'

'Well said, Mr...?'

'Ted Rogers, Pontrhyd.'

'Thank you, Mr Rogers, and you too, Mrs Hughes.' Gareth closed his notebook with a flourish and leant back. 'So what's going on in your world, then?'

Jake told him about the invitation to the night exercise of the GLF.

'Sounds intriguing. Probably The Captain but you never know, might be something more. Are you going to go?'

'I'm up for it but I don't know if they'll let me. I think Roland might but he's taken it higher to see what their reaction is.'

'Want me to go with you?'

'No. Thanks, but they stipulate I've got to go on my own.'

'Interesting, but watch your back. I don't suppose they'd invite you along if they intended doing you any damage, I don't reckon blowing up a journalist is going to improve their image, but you never know. Let's see what the powers that be decide then.'

Jake got his answer earlier than he expected. Roland called him in as soon as he arrived the following morning.

'Right, you can go but the editor in chief will want to see your copy before it gets anywhere near the paper. Straight reporting, no glorification of the GLF or whatever they call themselves. To protect yourself, don't make any attempt to find out who's involved. You'll ring me as soon as you can after the exercise, at home and at any time; make sure you've got enough change on you for the public phone box. If I haven't heard from you by 7 o'clock the next morning I'll call the police. All clear?'

'Yes.'

'Are you absolutely sure you want to do this? I want to emphasise that there is no coercion on our part whatsoever and you can decline their offer with no repercussions on your career here.'

'No, honestly Roland, I want to do it. I think it will be OK; a dead or badly dented reporter isn't going get them a lot of public sympathy or a warm reception from the rest of the media. I think I'll be all right with them.'

'Right then. Good luck. And be careful.'

Jake stayed behind that evening, ostentatiously banging away at a typewriter, until the office was empty then rang Amanda. This time she picked up the phone. He told her he was settling in well and hinted at a big story that might be coming up next week, she told him about working in the shop with mum, trips up town clubbing with friends, shopping expeditions. She sounded, as she always seemed to these days, rather detached.

When he asked her if she could come down the following weekend she hesitated. Which was at least better than an outright refusal.

'Where would I stay? I thought you shared a room with another bloke in the house with the dragon landlady.'

'I do but they'll both be away. I could pick you up in Cardiff on Saturday, we could drive down to the Gower, there are nice beaches there and some decent restaurants and pubs. And there's pretty countryside round here too, it's not all slag heaps and pit wheels. I'll put you on the evening train for home on Sunday.'

She didn't sound convinced. 'I don't know. Are you sure it will be OK? It's quite a long way to come.'

But eventually, to his delight, she gave in. She would call him on the Friday evening to confirm all was still well.

Jake spent most of the next three days in a heady mix of moods: excitement at the prospect of seeing Amanda and a big story, apprehension at the thought of what might go wrong with either. At least if the GLF exercise came off he'd have something to tell her about that might impress her just a little bit.

On Saturday he walked into town and bought a black boiler suit and black woolly hat from the local army surplus shop; Roland had confirmed he could put them on expenses, maximum expenditure £5. He hesitated over a tin of camouflage face paint (at his own expense, he had only coppers left from the Enquirer's funds) but decided that might be a bit over the top. And he'd told Mrs Probert that he'd be out overnight on Tuesday or at least be coming home in the early hours on Wednesday covering a story he couldn't talk about at this stage. She'd been sceptical but when Jake offered to ring the Enquirer's editor and put him on the line, she reluctantly agreed.

Tuesday lunchtime came and went, and there was no further information from the GLF. Jake was beginning to give up hope when, late in the afternoon with dusk falling and the street lights coming on, one of the phones on the reporters' desk rang. He picked it up.

'Jake Nash?' said a rather gruff voice which probably wasn't the speaker's normal one.

'Yes.'

'You received the GLF communiqué?'

'Yes.'

'You will be attending the exercise?'

'Yes, but I should just make it clear that– '

'Penallta Colliery, midnight.'

And the phone went dead.

Chapter 10

The Captain, Siôn and the two Jenkins brothers, Iolo and Stefan, sat in darkness in The Captain's old Land Rover, parked on the rough track that led away from colliery. The Captain was behind the steering wheel, Siôn in the front passenger seat, the brothers in the back. The colliery had been shut down a few years before, the shaft filled in and capped, but the pithead wheel was a skeletal silhouette against the sky and the outbuildings, windows shattered and doors hanging from their hinges, still stood. The Jenkins' A35 van was parked nearby. Far from any street lighting and with clouds dense and low, it was very dark indeed.

'Right, let's be clear about the plan of action', said The Captain. 'First, from the moment we pick up the reporter, no names. I'm number one, Siôn is two, Iolo three, Stefan four, OK? So numbers only, and balaclavas on at all times. I don't want to give this guy any clue to who we are. We will go armed, but weapons will be unloaded.'

The weapons consisted of the old shotgun that The Captain used to keep vermin down on the farm and two .177 air rifles that Siôn and Iolo had been given as boys.

'If we're not going to load them, why are we carrying them?' asked Stefan.

'Because at some time in the future we may be properly armed, and I want you to get the feeling of moving through countryside at night while carrying a rifle, OK? And at the same time, I don't want any accidents.

'I will collect the reporter when he arrives, blindfold him and bring him back here to the RV, that's the Rendezvous Point. Wc will then move off in single file, me first, then Iolo, then the reporter, then Stef, Siôn as rearguard. Stay close, no talking – remember, sound carries a long way at night – no lights, no smoking.'

The Captain didn't really think he should have to mention the smoking and lights, it seemed blindingly obvious, but he wasn't going to take a chance with the Jenkins boys. Large, rather overweight lads, Stefan was nineteen, his brother a year older. They lived together in a small house their mother had left them; their father had walked out of their lives when the boys were still young. She had suddenly and surprisingly remarried a year ago, to a travelling salesman from Manchester she'd met in Cardiff on a rugby international night, and moved away as soon as she could. Now the boys lived on benefits and by doing odd jobs on the side for cash.

'Siôn, take the shotgun, the other two the air rifles, I shall be carrying the explosive device.' He gestured towards a tin box lying on the floor of the Land Rover between Siôn's feet.

The Jenkins brothers shifted uneasily in their seats.

'This explosive device – no danger of it going off too soon, is there?' Iolo asked.

'None. It has a fuse which needs to be lit, and I'm not going to be striking any matches until it's in place.'

'That's good. Like you say, we don't want any nasty accidents, do we?'

'Right then, we will proceed up this track for about a mile, then bear right onto the path that takes us through Tafarn-y-Coed Woods. Coming out of that we carry straight on to the railway line, about another half mile dead ahead. We'll stop about 100 yards short of the line; Iolo will move out to the right, Stefan to the left, to act as sentries. Siôn will stay with the reporter, I don't want him getting a close look at the device. I will proceed to the railway line, plant the device and ignite the fuse. After the detonation, we will all return to the RV point.'

'What, the vans?' said Iolo.

'No, sorry, the second RV point, which is where we will have left Siôn and the reporter, close enough to get a flavour of the action but out of harm's way. Not', he added hurriedly, 'that anyone is going to come to any harm.

'Once we have reformed, we will proceed in a swift but orderly manner to the RV – the <u>first</u> RV point. One hundred yards from there we will stop; I will go ahead to make sure no one is around the transport. Assuming that there isn't, we will blindfold the reporter and I shall escort him to his car.'

'What if there is?' said Stefan.

'What if there is what?'

'What if there is someone around the transport?'

The Captain looked at him for a while in silence. 'In that case... I will create a diversion to lead them away while you complete your withdrawal. I shall then make my own way from the area.'

Seeing that Siôn was about to interrupt, he pressed on. '<u>Assuming</u> that there isn't anyone around the vehicles and once the reporter has left we shall move off, the Jenkins boys first, then a one minute gap, then us. Don't drive too fast and draw attention to yourselves. Everyone all right with all of that?'

The three men nodded and they fell into silence. In the Land Rover's rear view mirror, two car headlights appeared in the distance, vanishing and reappearing as the dilapidated road wound towards the colliery.

'He's here', said The Captain. 'Balaclavas on, action stations.'

He swung open the driver's door and stepped out into the darkness.

The Ford Popular didn't like rough roads. Its tired suspension had protested all the way up to the colliery since Jake had left the main road and it was with some relief that he turned into the colliery yard. He swung the car round to face the way it had come and turned off the lights.

It was, he thought, rather spooky – the looming pit wheel, the silent buildings, the darkness. He shivered slightly, then his eye was caught by the flash of a torch in the far corner of the yard. He sat still. A few seconds later, there was another, slightly longer flash. Jake got out of the car, swallowed hard and walked slowly towards the point from which it had come.

'Stop there', said a voice from the darkness about ten feet in front of him. It had something of the tone of the gruff voice on the phone, but not quite. Again Jake thought it seemed a little false. He could make out the shape of someone standing beside one of the shed walls.

'I am the Commandant of the Welsh Liberation Front, and you are Mr Nash, I assume.'

'Yes', said Jake, trying to keep his voice steady.

'Please confirm that you and your superiors have agreed to our conditions, that no authorities have been informed of this exercise and that you have not been accompanied tonight by any other person. If any of these is not the case, please say so now and your presence here can be terminated.'

Jake didn't like the sound of 'terminated' one bit. He drew a deep breath.

'That's all correct.'

There was a short silence.

'Turn around, Mr Nash.'

Jake turned slowly, his boots crunching in the muddy gravel. He'd seen a good many films in which these words were the last a hapless victim heard on this earth. Oh God, he thought, something like real fear growing inside him, is this where it all ends?

'I'm going to blindfold you for our mutual security. Don't be alarmed.'

Jake heard the footsteps approaching him, and then couldn't help cringing slightly as a cloth was placed over his eyes and tied behind his head. A firm hand grasped his upper arm.

'Come with me.'

They walked together, Jake stumbling in potholes and ruts at first, but the hand gently pushed and pulled his arm, apparently steering him around the worst of the obstacles. Then they stopped and the hand disappeared.

Standing blindly in the darkness, Jake heard the sound of other voices speaking quietly and then a vehicle door being opened. There was someone rummaging around inside the vehicle, then the hand was back on his arm.

'Come on.'

They moved off again. Jake was wondering how long this could last when they stopped again, the hand let go of his arm, and the blindfold removed. Jake blinked.

As his eyes got used to the darkness again he saw he was standing in a semi-circle of four men, one short and wiry, another tall and slim, two of medium height and rather tubby. They all wore balaclava helmets that obscured their faces, the slim one with a scarf over his mouth and nose. They were dressed in what looked like a variety of army surplus clothes that doubled, to judge by their well-worn appearance, as work wear. Three of them were carrying what seemed to be weapons, although to Jake's inexperienced eye they didn't seem very sophisticated.

The men regarded him in silence for a while.

'What part of Wales are you from, butt?' said a chunky one finally.

Jake cleared his throat. No point in bluffing.

'Actually, I'm from St Albans, in Hertfordshire. England.'

There was a silence. Three pairs of eyes turned towards a short, wiry man; his eyes refused to meet them.

'Oh bloody wonderful', said the tall slim one eventually. The scarf partially muffled his voice, but the sarcasm was unmistakable. 'Here we are starting a movement to overthrow English hegemony in Wales, a movement to rid ourselves of English tyranny, and we've invited a bloody Englishman along to tell the world about it. Couldn't really have a better start, could we?'

The silence thickened. Jake cleared his throat again.

'Look, I am English, but I have Welsh ancestors and I've lived in Aberystwyth for three years.' He didn't add 'as a student', guessing immediately and probably accurately that this wouldn't add to his credibility.

'I can appreciate your desire for independence and self-determination. And more importantly I'm a professional journalist.'

Again, and for the same reason, he thought it better not to add 'of three weeks standing.' But he was getting into his stride now.

'As such, I'm here to give a true and faithful account of what happens here tonight. And I will do.'

The four continued to look at him in silence. Eventually the tall slim one spoke again.

'Well he's all we've got, and this isn't exactly the kind of thing you want to postpone and readvertise. Let's give him a go.'

He looked at the thin wiry one, who looked in turn at the two chunky men. One shrugged, the other said 'Aye, go on then.'

The wiry one turned back to Jake.

'Right, you're on. But remember, this is a small community. I don't know where you live. But I could bloody soon find out. Right, into file. Let's go.'

He stooped, and picking up a tin box on the ground, led them away. They'd taken only a couple of paces when the figure in front of Jake half turned and leaning round him, whispered loudly 'Oh, Steffo, what's heg–'

'QUIET!!' hissed the smaller figure at the front of the file, fiercely. 'No talking, <u>Number Three.</u>' There was a heavy emphasis on the last two words.

'Sorry, Cap- Number One.'

And for a while, the only sound was their trudging feet.

Chapter 11

The broken road soon became a track, and after a while they turned off to climb over a stile onto an even smaller and muddier path. This wound its way through a thicket of trees which slowed their progress, forcing them to duck below branches and push their way through the undergrowth where it had overgrown the pathway. After five minutes they emerged from the belt of trees into a field and immediately became aware of large moving shapes in the darkness around them. The file behind the leader stumbled to a nervous halt.

'They're only bloody cows', he hissed, 'they won't hurt you.'

Sure enough the animals parted and retreated as they approached, trundling away at a respectable pace. The group moved forward again, treading carefully through the tussocks, Jake occasionally wincing slightly as a squelch underfoot indicated a cowpat. Eventually the leader sank to one knee and held an arm aloft to indicate a halt. They all knelt behind him, Jake stifling a groan as his knee found another cowpat.

'Right' whispered the leader, 'number three to the right, about 100 yards, number four, to the left. Challenge anyone who approaches loudly and clearly, as much to alert us as anything.'

'Sort of, "who goes there?", is it, Cap – number one?' said one of the tubby lads.

'Well you could ask him for his name and address and what he thinks he's doing wandering around fields as this time of night, I suppose, but "who goes there?" is sort of traditional, isn't it? Anyway, if he buggers off, that's fine, we'll be away before he can contact anyone else.

'If he shows any inclination to stick around, we all return to this point and consider our options. Otherwise, if it all goes to plan, wait for the explosion then get back here right away. Mr Nash, stay here. Three and four, move.'

The designated pair moved uncertainly away in opposite directions into the darkness. The leader carefully opened the tin box and took from it a smaller round tin and a tube of cardboard. With a nod to the remaining conspirator, he too headed into the darkness.

The Captain knew these fields and woods well. He had played here as a boy, poached here as a younger man, walked them now at times when he needed to think and be alone. He found the railway line without difficulty and, clambering up the slight embankment, began clearing a hole in the oil-stained stones between the near set of rails. He worked for a few minutes, making some noise but not enough, he hoped, to carry far or be distinguishable from the general sounds of the night.

When he'd made a hollow about six inches deep, he placed the tin inside it, then banked stones all around it, leaving a gap at the top. Inside the tin were the contents of several dozen bangers, held down by another piece of cardboard. A length of the fuse ran from the compacted powder, through a hole in the cardboard and then through a hole in the lid of the tin that was fastened shut with several layers of thick tape.

He carefully unwound a long length of the fuse that had been wrapped around the cardboard tube and laid it on the track in a wide circle, then twisted the nearest end round the length of fuse that protruded from the can. He'd experimented with the second packet of fuse that Siôn had brought back from Cardiff; he calculated he had about a minute's worth laid out. Thank God it wasn't raining. He struck a match, carefully shielding its light in his hand, and held it to the end of the fuse. For a couple of seconds nothing happened, then the fuse spluttered into life and the small, bright flame began travelling along the wire towards the can.

Jake's right knee was getting uncomfortably soggy. As it had sunk into the wet soil it had also found a stone just under the surface; he'd withstood the sharp little pain for a couple of minutes but it was becoming unbearable. He shifted awkwardly onto his left knee. Almost immediately he felt the water begin to soak through his boiler suit. He sighed and glanced across at his minder, who was squatting on his haunches, apparently comfortable. It occurred to Jake that this might be a good time to try for some background information.

'Will you be doing any more of these exercises?' he whispered.

The dark figure ignored him.

He tried again. 'How about recruitment, has that proved fairly easy?'

The minder turned and raised one figure to his lips in a 'keep quiet!' gesture. Jake was trying to decide whether he should have a third attempt at asking a question when the leader arrived back, crouching and moving at a steady trot. He raised a thumb, dropped to one knee, and then all three turned to look in the direction he'd come from. There was a small but bright flickering glow from the track.

Despite his discomfort, Jake found it all very exciting – slightly silly, perhaps, but fun and it would make a cracking story. It was too dark to take notes, of course, but he was trying to remember everything that was happening.

When he thought about it later, he estimated that it was about thirty seconds after the fuse was lit that the air of expectant tension was broken by a quavering voice that came from the darkness on their right.

'Halt. Who goes there?'

The answer came in an angry roar. 'The farmer who owns this land, that's fucking who. And what the FUCK are you bunch of clowns doing on it?'

Jake and his companions froze. Then The Captain stood, turned in the direction of the voice and shouted back.

'This is a Glamorgan Liberation Front exercise. You should know that we are armed!'

'Oh, right', came back the voice from the darkness. 'Fair enough then, that levels things up. So am I.'

Two sharp explosions, close together, two stabs of flame in the dark and two charges of buckshot whistled overhead into the trees.

'Iesu Grist', hissed Siôn.

Then all hell broke loose.

Chapter 12

The most almighty explosion ripped the night apart. Or at least, that's the way it sounded to Jake. A great leap of flame from the railway, a massive bang and then, after a few seconds with their ears still ringing, stones began raining down around them.

There was instant mayhem. Terrified cattle galloped in all directions, the farmer shouted something unintelligible and the GLF contingent took off as one in a panicked run. Jake ran with them, stumbling back over the field, dodging frightened cows and expecting any moment to be trampled by one of them - back through the woods, the branches whipping at his face and the undergrowth tearing at his clothes, pell-mell down the pathway and track.

At some point he was overtaken by the two chunkier men, travelling at impressive speed for people of their size, and before he reached the colliery he heard a vehicle start, the motor rev and then pull away. He ran past a Land Rover; he glanced at it as he staggered by, now nearing the end of his endurance, and somewhere in the back of his mind lodged the distinctive Welsh Language Society's dragon's tongue motif on a sticker in the side window. Then he was into the car park. Heading straight to his car, he wrenched open the unlocked driver's door and flung himself into the driver's seat, gasping for breath.

His inclination was to stay there for as long as it took for his heart to stop racing and he could breathe properly but when the Land Rover drove past, without lights and accelerating hard back down the narrow road, he realised that if he wanted to avoid an imminent encounter with the police, he too had better be making a move.

He started the Popular and hesitated about switching on the lights then decided against it. He swung onto the road and drove down as fast as he dared, and then when he'd swung onto the main road, turned the light switch. The drive back to Number 17 seemed to take forever. Forcing himself to keep to a law-abiding speed, he expected a police car to hurtle into view at any second, cut across the road in front of him and force him to stop. But it was only as he reached the turning into Llanberris Terrace that he saw flashing blue lights on the road coming towards him, and he was out of sight before they reached the junction.

He drove past the house to the phone box and dialled Roland's number. The phone at the other end was picked up almost immediately.

'Roland Griffiths.'

Jake pushed a one-shilling coin into the coin slot.

'Mission accomplished.'

'You're not in the bloody Marines. Are you all right?'

'Fine. A bit muddy and breathless but OK.'

He gave Roland a quick summary of the night's events, ending with his close brush with the police, whom he supposed were on their way to the scene of the explosion.

'Right, go back and wake up Gareth. I'll meet you at the office. You can work with him on knocking out stories for the agencies and the BBC in London; the Welsh papers and the rest will pick it up when their early people come in. I see everything before it goes, and I'll brief the boss.

'I'll give it half an hour or so then tell the local police we had a reporter at the scene, just to make sure those blue lights you saw were the police on their way to the bomb site and not a fire engine heading for a barn fire. I don't want to risk anything going up or down that train line until it's been checked. The police will want to speak to you, obviously, as will a lot of other people. Could you identify anyone?'

Jake hesitated. One had been addressed as Steffo, another as Cap. 'No. They didn't use names and they wore balaclavas.'

'Any other information that might help – physical characteristics like one arm or a heavy limp, vehicle number plates?'

'No.'

'Don't forget I'm going to need a lead story from you for us too. I'll get Wayne and Reg up there at first light. It's going to be a busy day for us all, boy, so I hope you can keep going on coffee and adrenalin.

'OK, get cracking. And well done. Again.'

It was, as Roland had prophesied, a very busy day. With Gareth's help he put together straight news stories to go out to the national media:

BOMB BLAST DAMAGES WELSH RAIL LINE

A bomb planted by a small group claiming to be fighting for 'a free Wales' exploded on a South Wales railway line in the early hours of this morning.
A journalist from the local weekly newspaper, The Edwardstown Enquirer, was with the group. He believes that some damage was caused to the line, but there were no casualties……

Dorothy arrived, tore up the layout for the first three pages of the paper she'd planned for that week and began again. Terry was sent off to find out what he could through his police contacts, Lotte began ringing around to get reactions from local bigwigs and, she hoped, the Free Wales Army (would the GLF be welcomed as allies or resented as upstarts?), Gareth headed up to the Penallta colliery with Reg to report from the scene and Roland sat down to write an editorial:

'Terrorism to some, the armed struggle for freedom to others... The violent face of political confrontation that has disfigured countries across the globe in recent years, from South Africa through Cyprus to Vietnam, came to South Wales this week.'

The other reporters would write the lead story for the front page with whatever updates they could get, while Jake was told to do a straight personal account of the night for page three. Wayne took a suitably dramatic picture of him poring over his typewriter, stubbled chin, hollowed eyes, hair awry, open necked shirt, which would go over two columns beside the headline: **'My Night With The Bombers of the GLF.'**

The police arrived as he was half way though it.

Detective Inspector Wynne Griffiths had been put in charge of the investigation that morning. He'd barely had time to gather his thoughts before he received a call from the Chief Constable which left him in no doubt that he was expected to get results, and quickly.

Fifty-nine years old and dreading retirement, Inspector Richards was a regular drinking partner of Terry Jenkins and had a lifetime's experience of dealing with the criminal underclass of Edwardstown. He prided himself on being able to name the most likely suspects as soon as he was told of the crime, and more often that not he was right. Burglary, assault, car theft, more recently drugs and a few years ago, even a murder: all were all grist to his mill, but politically inspired bombings were well out of his comfort zone. He was a shrewd man and a good observer of character but he had little interest in motives, other than in how they might lead him to the perpetrators; as far as he was concerned, a crime was a crime, and why it had been committed didn't really bother him – someone must be held to account in the courts.

He interviewed Jake in Roland's office, going carefully though the sequence of events from the arrival of the first communiqué to Jake's arrival back at the newspaper office.

Jake repeated what he'd told Roland: he could give some rough descriptions of height and build of the people he'd seen, guess broadly at ages and distinguish what seemed to him to be local accents but he doubted if he could identify them again, given that they'd gone to some lengths to disguise themselves.

Had they used names at all, asked the Inspector?

Jake hesitated very briefly. No, he told the Inspector, they hadn't used names, just numbers.

And once he'd started down that path, it became easier to continue.

No, he hadn't seen any vehicles. He'd heard the door of one vehicle slamming just before they left the colliery area to walk to the rail line, and before he'd reached his car on the way back he'd heard the sound of two vehicles driving away, but he hadn't seen anything.

The hesitation hadn't been missed by Inspector Griffiths. He impressed on Jake the gravity of the situation, the need to nip this in the bud and catch these people before someone got hurt. He emphasised that it was essential that Jake should pass on any scrap of information, no matter how small, that might help the investigation. And finally, he pointed out that should Jake impede a criminal investigation by wilfully withholding information, he would himself be liable to face criminal charges.

Jake said that he completely understood, but that he couldn't help any further. Inspector Griffiths wasn't wholly convinced.

He spoke to Roland behind the closed door of the office, emerging after ten minutes not looking best pleased. He left, casting a sour glance at Jake on the way and taking with him the two GLF communiqués in a manila envelope.

Crews from the BBC and Harlech, the independent television company, arrived at The Castle and interviewed

Jake. He told them what he'd told the police: no, he had no idea of who the bombers were. By the time he'd finished them and his story it was lunchtime and he was very, very tired. Roland sent him home.

As he lay on his bed at Number 17 that night, staring at the ceiling, he wondered why he hadn't told either Roland or the police about the names he'd picked up last night – Steffo, Cap - or about the Land Rover with the Welsh Language Society sticker.

There had been a moment, when the Inspector had warned him that he too would be committing an offence if he didn't reveal all he'd seen and heard, when he'd had a fleeting vision of himself standing in the dock and he'd rather surprised himself with how quickly he'd assured the Inspector that he was being totally honest and open.

Perhaps it was some desire to ensure the story ran on for a while, perhaps he just felt he was entitled to hang on to some information that only he knew.

Too late now, anyway, he didn't think the Inspector was going to be convinced by any explanation that began with 'I've suddenly remembered.'

Despite the fact he was still fully clothed and the curtains were doing a very inadequate job of keeping out the daylight, he soon fell into a deep and dreamless sleep. All round, it had been what he believed journalists liked to call a cracking news day.

For Siôn and The Captain, it had been an absolute nightmare.

Driving away from the town, they'd seen no other traffic on their way home. Their muddy clothing was put into the room just off the kitchen where they kept all the clothing they used for work, and then they scoured the farm for anything that might link them to the explosion. The small tubes of cut-open cardboard that had once been bangers were taken out of a bin and burned in the big range in the kitchen with the bag that had held them; the small pieces of fuse left over from The Captain's experiments followed. The typewriter was put in a sack and buried under several bales of hay at the back of the barn.

The shotgun was cleaned and locked back into its cupboard; The Captain just hoped that the Jenkins boys hadn't lost the air rifles they were carrying. One of them was Siôn's and would have his fingerprints all over it. Neither he nor Siôn had a criminal record and so their prints weren't stored in any police system, but if the gun was found and the police decided to check likely suspects they might be in trouble.

Then they sat at the kitchen table, drinking endless cups of tea and reliving the night. For The Captain, the blind panic of the withdrawal had been humiliating and embarrassing; for Siôn, the whole event had been a mixture of the surreal and the frightening. For both, the breaking dawn signalled a day full of potential disaster.

They briefly considered flinging some clothes into the Land Rover and taking off – but to go where? They concentrated instead on getting their stories straight for the interrogation they felt sure was bound to come.

Siôn was chopping logs and The Captain tinkering with their ancient tractor when the police Ford Anglia pulled into the yard in the mid afternoon. After hours of waiting and growing tension, it was almost a relief.

'Mr ap Siencyn, Mr ap Iorwerth? A few words, if I may?'

After talking to Jake, Inspector Griffiths had gone back to his office. He'd sent a detective sergeant around to talk to the Welsh Language Society boys; while he waited to see if that bore any fruit, he pulled out the file with the letter to the Free Wales Army. He knew The Captain, of course: given to shouting his mouth off, not one to shy away from a confrontation, but he hadn't been in trouble for a while and frankly he didn't seem to be the bomb-planting type. But experience had taught him that life is nothing if not surprising and anyway, he had no other leads.

Now he sat facing The Captain and Siôn across their kitchen table, his notebook open before him.

Were they aware there had been an incident at a railway line nearby?

Yes, they'd heard about it on the radio.

And where were they last night?

Here.

Doing what?

Playing cards, mostly. Had a couple of beers, played till about eleven, went to bed.

What were you playing?

Kings.

And who won?

About even. We only play for matchsticks anyway.

And what did they think about the theory that it might be work of a fringe group linked somehow to the Free Wales Army?

The Captain looked steadily at the inspector. If it was, he said, he could understand why they'd done it.

And did he approve?

The Captain didn't break eye contact with the policeman.

'Like I said, I can see why they done it. All of a sudden, we're in the news and someone's paying a bit of attention to us; they might even start thinking a bit about why we – or rather, they, whoever it was – got pushed this far. And at the end of the day, it's a bent railway line, a bit of a hole and no-one hurt, as I understand it, so no harm done really.'

The policemen held his gaze.

'No-one hurt yet, Mr ap Siencyn, not yet. But a crime committed.'

He snapped his notebook shut. Did they mind if he had a quick look round?

The Captain shrugged. Nothing to see, he said, but help yourself.

The pair went back to what they had been doing while the Inspector wandered around the yard for a while, taking a quick look at the Land Rover and peering into the rubbish bin. Two hearts beat a little faster when he opened the barn door but it was gloomy in there and all that was to be seen was a pile of bales. Then he called across a 'Thank you' to Siôn and The Captain, got into the car and drove away.

They stood watching as it disappeared around a corner, then turned and looked at each other. On the whole, that hadn't gone too badly.

When he got back to the station, Inspector Griffiths found a message on his desk telling him to ring Special Branch in Cardiff. He dialled the number, absently doodling on the large blotting pad in front of him, and when the phone was picked up at the other end told an inspector there what he'd found. Which, he had to admit, wasn't much.

He described the communiqués and said that he'd spoken to two local men who might be suspects; he might ask for a warrant to search their premises but at the moment there was nothing to link them to the explosion. He had a sergeant out questioning other activists in the area and was awaiting his report; he'd know more about the bomb when forensics came back to him.

And yes, he did appreciate the gravity of the situation; and no, he didn't need any help, thank you. Then he paused.

'You could do one thing for me. Lad called Jake Nash, reporter with the local rag but just arrived here from London, was a student at Aber. You could do a quick check

104

on him, see if there's any radical tendencies, anything else known.'

Despite his colleague's assurances that he'd do that, Inspector Griffiths put the phone down rather more firmly than was necessary. Bloody Cardiff, think we're all country boys up here.

He sighed, stood and took his coat from the stand behind him. He'd see if Terry Jenkins was in the pub and if he'd heard anything; he could do with a pint, anyway.

Chapter 13

It was a happy little crowd that gathered in The Greyhound that Thursday. Gareth took the afternoon off and came down to join them, even Terry slipped in early on for a quick one, and the journalists found themselves, to their great surprise, to be minor celebrities among the regulars. Especially Jake, who'd been on the telly.

The bar staff pressed them for the facts they hadn't been able to print: was it true that as well as the four Welshmen there'd been a group of heavily armed men with Irish accents they'd been warned not to talk about? They smiled, shook their heads and said nothing.

Occasionally people in other groups in the pub would look over towards them or nod in their direction; one even raised his glass in a silent toast. The night before, Roland had called Lotte in just as she was leaving and slid two one-pound notes across his desk towards her.

'Buy them a drink on me', he'd said, in response to her raised eyebrows. Which made her think he probably was more aware of their Thursday sessions than he let on.

It was by far the biggest thing that had happened in Edwardstown for a good many years and people basked in seeing their town featured in the national press and in television news bulletins. Everyone was happy, Jake perhaps more than anyone. Being part of a big story, where everyone works together for all hours to get the news out to people avid to hear it, had been an experience he hadn't expected so soon and he loved it. Not even Lotte's disappearance into the dark room with Reg at a later stage in the day for what seemed to him like an even longer period than last week and her even more tousled appearance when she emerged could dent his sense of well being.

As they strolled back to Number 17 that evening, Jake had taken the chance to ask Gareth again, as casually as he could, about The Captain. There wasn't a lot Gareth could add to what he'd already told Jake.

'Not much more to say, really. Bit of a loudmouth who gets himself into odd spots of bother by getting on people's nerves but he's not a criminal and he seems to have been a bit quieter of late, anyway.'

'Do you reckon he could have been involved?

Gareth shook his head. 'Wouldn't have thought so. I think all this armed struggle stuff is just talk, a bit of fantasy to give his life some meaning.'

'How about the lad who lives with him – what's his name?'

'Dunno. They seem quite close, but the younger bloke is much quieter, he stays out of any trouble, in fact The Captain makes sure none starts when he's around.

'Nah, I'd be surprised if it was either of them.'

The Enquirer flew off the shelves that Friday morning and despite an extended print run, you couldn't buy a copy anywhere in the valley by 11 o'clock. It wasn't often that readers saw headlines like **TERROR GANG STRIKE LOCAL RAIL LINK! Bomb wrecks line!** with impressive pictures of police activity and gangs working to repair the damage.

Roland had brought back a congratulatory memo from the editor-in-chief of the group in Trefoes, complimenting them on their efforts and thanking all the staff for their hard work, which he pinned up in the reporters' room.

But as Lotte reminded Jake, today's headlines are tomorrow's chip wrappings. By Saturday, the story had slipped out of the radio and television news bulletins and onto the inside pages of the newspapers. The farmer, who was at first sure that he had come under fire from at least two sources, was now admitting that, what with the darkness and the shock of the bomb going off and all, he might have got that wrong.

No group had claimed responsibility for the action and the police were saying, at least officially, that the 'bomb' had in fact been a small and amateurish device.

It had caused virtually no significant damage and was probably the work of pranksters, they said. Two lengths of rail had been replaced as a precaution, but the line was up and running again in good time for the evening rush hour and by the following morning it was impossible to see where the blast had happened.

Jake's sense of contentment though had lasted through the weekend and into the following week. He joined Lotte in Tolaini's at lunchtime on Monday after he'd spent the morning with Terry in the local magistrates' court. He'd found it found it an interesting, even an entertaining, experience.

The local stipendiary magistrate was a frustrated man much given to extended lecturing of the miscreants who appeared before him, usually dressed in ill-fitting suits that they'd probably borrowed. The rising fury of his denunciations of their crimes, ranging from shoplifting and motoring offences through stealing money from gas meters to brawling outside pubs, always ended in an anticlimax as he mumbled the sentence, usually a not very harsh fine. Requests for time to pay were nonetheless frequent and always met with a baleful stare before being curtly agreed.

Jake particularly liked the deadpan way in which police officers gave evidence, always in that strange formal language which was particularly their own.

'On the night of the twenty-seventh of September at about 11.15 pm, I was proceeding along Cyfartha Road in a northerly direction when I hobserved the defendant' - a pimply 20-year-old who was at that moment staring intently at his feet in the dock - 'urinating against the window of the Sleeptight bedding centre. I happroached him and asked him what he was doing. He replied' (consults notebook) 'I ham laying plans for the invasion of

Poland. What does it look like I ham doing?' I cautioned him, and he then said (notebook again) 'I ham a personal friend of the Chief Constable, so you'd better be careful.' I had reason to doubt this and formed the opinion that he was in drink....'

'You're looking pleased with yourself'. Lotte said, as Jake put his cheese and onion roll and cup of tea on to the table and settled into the seat opposite her.

'Well not so much with myself but life in general isn't too bad, I must admit.'

'Not pining away for the beloved at all then?'

Jake took a bite out of his roll and chewed reflectively for a moment.

'I miss her a bit, I suppose. But she's coming down this weekend.'

'That's nice. Where's she going to stay?'

Jake smiled. 'Mrs P is away at her sister's and Gareth is going over to his mam's.'

'Ah. And while the cat's away... so I expect you'll have a big smile on your face on Monday morning.'

'I hope so.'

'And will she be down again for the Press Ball?'

Jake looked puzzled. 'What Press Ball?'

Lotte raised a surprised eyebrow. The Gwalia Press Ball, she told him, was by some distance the social event of the year, the one time when journalists from all the group's papers got together for an evening of eating, drinking, dancing and whatever might then materialise.

It was also the occasion of the Miss Gwalia Press competition. Each paper would by now have chosen its entrant; the Enquirer's champion was the daughter of a local butcher who had her sights set on a modelling career.

'That sounds like fun', said Jake. 'I'll ask Amanda this weekend if she fancies it.'

The Captain and Siôn were in their usual corner at Y Llew Coch. The gloom of the immediate aftermath of the night exercise had lifted a little over the weekend. Jake's report in The Enquirer had been, as Roland had insisted, straightforward and factual. What The Captain had at first seen as an embarrassing pantomime of an event had emerged in a slightly rosier light.

Jake had started with the receipt of the GLF communiqués at the Enquirer's offices, the first dismissed as a prank, the second taken rather more seriously. He described the meeting with the four masked men, three of whom were armed, although the weaponry seemed very unsophisticated. Although those three seemed to be inexperienced and not very well disciplined, he wrote, the man in charge appeared to have had some kind of military training.

He described the tension of the walk through the darkness of the woods, the increasing nervousness as the leader had disappeared to plant the bomb and as they waited for the explosion; he was frank about the panic that ensued after the shotgun blasts and the detonation of the bomb, and the scramble to get away from the scene.

The story ended with a cross reference to Rolands's editorial, headed 'Local loonies – or a cause for concern?' The editor had abandoned his usual policy of saying nothing that could be considered controversial and had decided this was worth extending himself a little.

'It would be easy to dismiss this small group as either amateurish fantasists or as thrill-seekers latching on to a cause as an excuse for mischief making. Yet the fact that even so small a number are prepared to run the considerable risks of this kind of enterprise and the severe penalties that might ensue must be a cause for concern to those who govern us. Even more so if this group should be neither fantasists nor mischief-makers, but people with a clear vision of an alternative future and a determination to make that vision a reality, whatever the risk to themselves – or to others.'

Siôn and The Captain had read and reread that paragraph with some satisfaction. There had been no further visits from the police, and while The Captain was fairly certain that they would be the subjects of increased scrutiny in the future, they began to hope that they would at least escape arrest.

Taking everything into consideration, they thought, the situation could be much worse.

Jake was, in fact, missing Amanda rather more than he cared to let on to Lotte. As the week went by he began to look forward to the weekend with a keener anticipation; he checked up on some nice places to go to on the Gower and asked Lotte and Gareth about decent pubs down there. He'd pick Amanda up from the station late on Saturday morning, perhaps have a quick coffee and a bite to eat at a Cardiff café then head out on the road west, chatting about what they'd both been up to in the previous weeks, perhaps with her hand resting on his on the gearstick. Or maybe even his knee.

They'd walk on the beaches, find a cosy pub for a meal and a drink, and in the warm, fuzzy afterglow, they'd drive back to Mrs P's, both thinking of what lay in store in that little back bedroom...

Daydreaming in the late Friday afternoon quiet of the reporters' room, Jake had just got to the bedroom part of the fantasy when Roland called him in.

'I hope you haven't got too many plans for tomorrow, because I need you to cover a rugby game.'

Jake's jaw dropped. 'Tomorrow??'

'Yes, tomorrow. Saturday.'

'But my girlfriend's coming down! From London!'

'Well I'm sure she'll enjoy watching too. Rugby is an integral part of the culture here, so she'll be able to get a real glimpse of valleys life.'

'But we were planning on going to the Gower.'

Roland looked at him steadily over the paper littered desk.

'Mr Nash, you appreciate that you've been taken on here as a trainee general reporter. I'll skip the trainee part of that as it's fairly self-evident what that entails; 'general' means that you cover anything that I consider to be newsworthy, be that the second coming of Christ in the market square or the winner of the Funniest Looking Vegetable prize at a local garden fete.

''Reporter' obviously means you report that event by writing about it in the newspaper, but implicit in the job title is the acceptance that you cover those events when and where they happen. If you want to work regular hours, I believe the library is looking for staff.'

Jake couldn't think of anything to say.

'You've played rugby, haven't you? You have a good general grasp of the objectives of the game and its rules?' Roland continued.

Jake nodded miserably.

Roland's tone softened. 'I wouldn't ask and I'm sorry for the short notice, but our usual correspondent has just rung to say he won't be available, although he wasn't very clear about why. Gareth's away for the weekend, Terry and Lotte know next to nothing about the game and anyway, there's a slight issue of seniority here. And it's an important game.'

'Who's playing?'

'Edwardstown and Pantbach. It's a big local derby; Pantbach, as you should know by now, is just up the valley, and close neighbours always make fiercest rivals. Their boys have been fighting with our boys since time immemorial and these games can get a bit heated, so I'm sure you'll enjoy it. Just make sure you get the names right of players sent off as well as the scorers. They were down to twelve men a side by the final whistle a few years ago.'

Jake went back into the reporters' room and stared glumly at the phone for a while. He should really ring her now and tell her plans had changed, but if he did he knew there was a very real chance that she'd cancel her plans. She had come to watch him play when they'd started to go out together at Aberystwyth and they'd been in the first flush of a strong mutual attraction, but the delights of standing on a muddy touchline on a cold Welsh winter's day had soon palled for her. Now the only way she'd watch the game was on television with friends around her and a drink to hand.

Jake gloomily pulled his coat on and headed for The Greyhound.

If he'd had any doubts any doubts about how Amanda would react, they were dismissed within seconds of his announcement of the change of plan.

'Furious' didn't quite cover it. 'Apoplectic' was getting into the general area. As they drove north towards Edwardstown, Jake tried to explain.

'Amanda, I'm really, really sorry. I only found out late last night' - a certain vagueness about the exact time seemed permissible in the circumstances - 'and it just seemed too late to change arrangements.'

The atmosphere in the car would have frozen the heart of a saint. 'Do you know', she said in the very low voice she kept for when she was Really, Really Angry, 'what time I got up this morning to get here? Are you aware that I was invited to a party by a very good friend of mine in Chelsea tonight and gave that up for the promise of some fresh seaside air? Instead of which, I shall be standing on a muddy field watching two groups of thugs pounding the crap out of each other in some sort of ritualistic tribal blood bath while you are hard at work counting the corpses. What are we doing this evening? Do they burn the bodies of the dead on the pitch while we get drunk on mead and leap through the flames?'

'It could be quite a good game, actually.' Even he would have had to admit that sounded very lame.

He swung into the Edwardstown RFC car park, pulled up and turned to her.

'We can still have a good time, honestly, this won't take long'.

And why not float the idea of Plan B?

'And if this weekend doesn't work out quite as we'd hoped, I thought you might like to come down again in a couple of week's time for our Press Ball. Apparently it's an absolute hoot...'

His voice trailed away as she turned a baleful stare on him.

'OK, we can talk about that later', he said hurriedly. 'I'll see if I can get you a cup of tea from the clubhouse while I sort out what's happening. And you won't have to stand in the mud, look, they've got a covered terrace', he added with forced cheerfulness.

From the expression on her face, a covered terrace wasn't going to improve Amanda's mood much in the very near future.

The clubhouse was a long, relatively new building behind the goal posts at the far end of the field. It was split into two sections by the main door: changing rooms with separate exits on one side, while the other was one large room with a bar down one side and windows looking onto the field. In that room, a group of burly men surrounded by kit bags sat around two or three tables in one corner, while at the bar stood older men, some in blazers, talking in low tones to each other. Everyone seemed very subdued, thought Jake, as he made his way in.

One of the men at the bar pointed out the Edwardstown club secretary, a middle-aged man sitting alone at a nearby table on which was small pile of papers. He was wearing a worried frown and a shapeless blazer decorated with a sewn-on Edwardstown RFC badge. Jake went over and introduced himself.

The secretary looked up. 'Oh right, you'll be wanting the team sheet then.' He shuffled through the papers in front of him, extracted one and handed it over. Jake glanced at the list of names, folded it then looked around the room again. There was a very odd atmosphere in the room, quite unlike the usual cheerful bustle of a rugby clubhouse just before a game.

'Bit quiet in here. Prematch nerves?'

The secretary looked up at him. 'Something like that.'

Jake didn't quite know how to respond. He gave a nervous half laugh. 'The thing is, these games are usually covered by one of our correspondents so I've got a bit of catching up to do.'

'Yes, I rather suspect you have.' There was a long pause and the secretary heaved a deep sigh.

'I'd better fill you in a bit. You've probably been told there's always a bit of tension between us and Pantbach. No problem there, really, it's just a local rivalry that goes back a long way, you get a lot of it in valleys rugby.'

'This year, however...' Another long pause; the secretary turned and looked wearily out over the field. 'Well, this year it's a bit more acute, on account of our blind side wing forward leaving his wife and three children this week for another woman. Who happens to be the wife of the Pantbach captain. It's created a bit more than the usual tension.'

'Ah yes', said Jake, 'I can imagine it would.'

'Our boys are convinced she's a Jezebel who's lured him away. I doubt if the Pantbach lot see it like that though.'

'No, probably not. So why isn't your usual correspondent here to cover the game?'

'He's our boy's older brother; I expect he thought it might be wiser to stay away.' He turned again to look out of the window with an expression of hopelessness on his face. 'I just hope they all behave themselves.'

Jake went back to the car and told Amanda the story. Strangely, it seemed to brighten her mood.

'Sex rears its ugly head and looms large over the playing field, eh? Well that should make things more interesting. Was there any tea on offer in the clubhouse?'

'I forgot to ask. Hang on, looks like the opposition's arrived.'

A bus had pulled into the car park. It stopped, the door swung open and a group of men looking very much like those sitting in the bar came down the steps carrying their kit bags. They were followed by a small group of older men who went to the side of the bus, opened the luggage compartment and took out a couple of large bags and two buckets. Then they all filed past the covered terrace, mostly looking down or straight ahead, and disappeared into the clubhouse.

The whole operation was carried out in a silence so profound that the crunch of footsteps across the gravel of the car park was clearly audible. Spectators coming into the ground had stopped to watch, and they too had fallen silent. I bet Tombstone was like this before the OK Corral shootout, thought Jake.

He ducked back inside the car. 'I'll have to go and get a team sheet from them. You OK here?'

Amanda smiled brightly. 'Couldn't be better, thank you. If you could bring me back a large gin and tonic, ice and lemon please, maybe a cucumber sandwich, no crusts, cut into triangles, that would be perfection.' Jake decided she was being sarcastic.

He went back to the clubhouse and following the sign for the changing rooms, found himself in a narrow and rather dark corridor with a door on either side, one marked 'Edwardstown RFC', the other 'Visitors.' Both were closed. He knocked rather gently on the visitors' door and waited for a response that didn't come. He knocked again, then cautiously turned the handle and entered.

The players were sitting on benches around the sides of the room while the older men stood in the middle. All were looking silently at Jake.

'Er, Jake Nash from The Enquirer. Just wondering if I could have a team sheet?'

They continued to look at him as though he suggested they empty their wallets and hand over their cash. Eventually one of the older men in the middle rummaged in his pocket and handed over a crumpled piece of paper.

'Thanks. Um, good luck this afternoon',said Jake. Their expressions didn't change. He backed out of the room with as much dignity as he could muster.

The covered terrace had room for a couple of hundred people, far more than Edwardstown RFC usually drew for their games, but today the tiers were already filling up. Among the spectators was Siôn, on his own because The Captain was more of a soccer fan and usually spent Saturday afternoon at home next to the radio.

Siôn, like everyone else there, knew the backdrop to this game and saw the difference in today's crowd immediately. Fans of different rugby clubs usually intermingled freely when they watched a game and Siôn always thought the banter that went on between them was half the fun. Today though the Pantbach supporters gathered in one end of the terrace; the Edwardstown fans, originally spread out over the width of the concrete steps, were gradually concentrated at the other end. A narrow strip of no man's land divided them; conversation was muted and laughter rare, and there were no exchanges between the rival groups.

Ten minutes before kick off, he saw the reporter from The Enquirer walking up the steps that ran from top to bottom of the terrace and divided the Edwardstown and Pantbach factions. Instinctively, he took a couple of paces backwards and sideways to put himself behind a group of spectators. Peering cautiously round them, he saw that the reporter hadn't glanced in his direction but it was more the girl with him that caught his eye. Striking red hair framed a pert and intelligent, if slightly sulky, face; she had the very pale skin that real redheads sometimes have, and her hair hung down to her shoulders and swayed as she turned her head to look around her. She was wearing a turquoise suede coat that didn't conceal the slim figure underneath and black leather boots. Very nice, thought Siôn.

They pushed through the now crowded terrace and found a space in the row below him and slightly to his left. As they came towards him, Siôn had a moment of panic, thinking that the reporter was bound to recognise him, but he seemed focused on the girl, leaning towards her to speak to her. She turned to the reporter and he heard her reply – 'No really, it's fine. Stop fussing.' She sounded irritated. Posh English, Siôn decided, and stuck up. Pity.

The Pantbach boys ran onto the pitch but instead of going through the usual warm-up routines, gathered in a tight huddle at one end of the field, arms round each other shoulders, heads bowed inwards. The referee stood at the centre spot, nervously playing with his whistle and gazing towards the changing rooms. A minute dragged by, then the Edwardstown team trudged out and formed a similar huddle at the other end of the pitch. A blast from the referee's whistle and the two captains detached themselves and joined him; a toss of a coin, the briefest of handshakes, then the captains went back to their players. The Pantbach fly half placed the ball on the centre spot, the teams arranged themselves to receive or chase the ball, and the ref raised the whistle to his lips again.

Jake felt a little tingle of excitement. Here we go.

Chapter 14

Any hopes the Edwardstown secretary might have had that the game would go off without incident were shattered from the kick-off. One of the Edwardstown forwards caught the ball, the pack formed the usual protective huddle around him; the ball went back to the scrum half, out to the fly half who kicked downfield and was flattened fully two seconds later by one of the Pantbach wing forwards.

The terrace erupted in furious condemnation and both packs immediately came together in an angry jostling mass, pushing, shoving and grabbing jerseys. The referee, a rather stout and pompous history teacher from the next valley, rushed up, furiously blowing his whistle.

Eventually order was restored. Players pulled away, glowering at each other and straightening their jerseys. The referee called the two captains over to him.

'Right boys, this stops now. You're here to play rugby. If you've got other issues, you sort them out off this field, not on it. Any more and someone will be getting a very early bath. Now go and talk to your players and make sure it ends here.'

Fat chance.

A fixture that was always fiercely contested for local bragging rights was this time fuelled by pure venom, and from the restart, it was obvious that the prime aim of both sides was to inflict as much physical damage on the other as was possible. The game was constantly punctuated by more blasts of the whistle; the trainers were starting to sweat as they rushed off and on with their magic sponges and buckets of water, water which became an ever deeper shade of red as the war of attrition progressed.

Every ruck was an opportunity for the vicious boot raking of anyone and anything at ground level, every maul a brawl in which elbows and fists were used with little guile but maximum effort whenever the referee was on the blind side of the struggling mass of bodies. Threequarters attempting to run with the ball were tackled late or taken out early; wings and full backs leaping to catch a high kick were invariably hit viciously while they were in the air; jumpers at the lines-out had their feet taken from under them before they came back to earth, usually ensuring they landed with a sickening thud on their backs.

It was truly the realisation of the maxim beloved of old-school forwards: 'Never mind the ball, get on with the game', but with an added dash of nastiness.

The touch judges, one from each club, saw no wrong-doing on the part of their own players but constantly shouted advice to the referee about the misdemeanours of the opposition, and the opposing factions on the terrace bayed support for their club and condemnation of the other.

Long before half time the referee was sincerely wishing he had decided to spend the afternoon marking the third form's essays on 'Was Henry VIII a good or a bad king? Discuss, with examples', a task he had previously been dreading. When he finally blew his whistle to end the mayhem at half time there was no score, but each side was down to fourteen men after a scrum just before the break had erupted in a flurry of flying fists. He had no idea who had started it but enough was enough; a prop forward from each side was given his marching orders and trudged sourly from the field.

The trainers came on with the orange segments and the players huddled in tight groups on either side of the half way line as the team coaches reorganised their packs to cope with the absence of a man. The touch judges wandered infield to join their respective groups of players, ignoring the referee, who stood alone, pretending to read his notebook.

On the terrace, some spectators had temporarily departed to get a half time cup of tea in the clubhouse but most stayed where they were. There was no fraternisation across the middle strip of no-man's-land, only a few resentful glances and muttered insults.

Jake had written virtually nothing in his notebook. There'd hardly been a decent passage of play to record and no scorers, so it didn't promise to be much of a report. He turned to Amanda.

'I'm going to see if I can get a comment from each side about those sendings-off. Will you be OK here for a while?'

Amanda nodded. She had considered going back to sit in the car, but after a morning sitting in a train and then the drive here, she wanted some fresh air. Jake threaded his way through the crowd, muttering apologies as he squeezed past tight knots of supporters, down the steps and onto the pitch. But none of the blazer brigade seemed interested in talking to him, curtly rebuffing his approaches. Disheartened, he decided to try the clubhouse to see if the secretary might say a few words.

He was still there when the second half kicked off, and almost immediately the game erupted. The ball was caught by the Pantbach number eight, passed back to the scrum half, out to the fly-half, and then unusually, down the line to the wing. He'd had a frustrating and fruitless afternoon, and he felt like a run. Accelerating away down the line, he dummied to go outside the opposing Edwardstown winger then, seeing him committing to the tackle, stepped sharply off his outside foot, cut inside, and was promptly flattened by a high stiff-arm tackle that nearly took his head off.

The following Pantbach threequarters piled into the Edwardstown winger, fists flying, and from all over the field players ran to join the melee around the prostrate bodies of the two wingers. On the touchline the two dismissed props were fighting again; the Pantbach trainer hurled his bucket at the pair, attempting to hit the Edwardstown player but missing both. The Edwardstown trainer rushed forward, swinging his pail at his Pantbach counterpart. He too missed but generated enough momentum to send him staggering into the Pantbach man. The pair, both former players for their respective clubs and well into their seventies, wrestled for a moment then toppled over together into the mud.

The referee stood on the half way line, surveying the chaos. He'd tried blowing his whistle several times, as long and loudly as he could. The sound had been lost in the general hubbub, and he saw now that the touch judges had abandoned their posts, run into the middle of the pitch and were now also attempting to flatten each other with wild haymakers that were all well wide of their target. He shrugged, put his whistle in his pocket, and trudged off.

By the time he'd packed his clothes into his bag in the tiny cubbyhole that was the officials' changing room – he'd thought he wouldn't bother with a bath or changing out of his kit – he'd decided to give up refereeing. Next week he'd buy a pair of walking boots and from then on, he'd spend his Saturday afternoons striding the hilltops enjoying some peace and quiet, far away from vengeful rugby players, truculent teenagers and the troubles of the Tudors.

The partisan bands on the terraces had at first reacted to the battle below them with angry shouts at the combatants on the pitch, but then one red-faced man on the Pantbach side had turned to glare across the divide and yelled furiously, his arm stabbing the air to emphasise his words, 'You Edwardstown boys have always been a dirty bunch of bastards. You want to tell your players how the game should be played. And while you're at it tell that bloody wing forward of yours to keep it in his trousers, if he knows what's good for him!'

A tall bald man in rimless glasses and a bright red muffler took up the challenge for the Edwardstown side. He turned to face the aggressor and shouted back: 'Your bloody lot started it! And if that floozie up there with you didn't put it about so much, there might be three kids with their dad still at home down by here!!'

With an angry roar, the red-faced man advanced into no-man's-land, followed by several others. The Edwardstown man and those around him braced to meet them, and as they came together in a shouting, pushing and punching mass, the crowd around them surged this way and that. Some pressed forward, trying to join in or at least get closer to the action, others pulled back, some tried to get down the steps and onto the relative safety of the field.

Amanda, standing alone in the crowd, was getting really frightened. She'd been in a few sales crowds in West End stores which had been uncomfortable, but none in which people actually seemed intent on hurting each other.

As the crowd swayed around her she tried to move with it, but a sudden surge by the crowd below pushed her backwards and off balance. Her foot was jammed against the step above and she felt herself falling.

An arm around her waist caught her, steadied then lifted her. The arm stayed where it was as a man's voice near her ear shouted above the tumult: 'We're going to get ourselves against the back wall, OK? It'll be better there.' Half turning, she saw that he was a youngish man wearing a green combat jacket, but he was facing upwards into the crowd, trying to spot a way through, and she couldn't see his face.

He started to push through, a pace at a time, pulling her with him. The mass of bodies thinned out as they went up and after a minute or so they'd reached the back corner of the terrace, where a metal support for the roof came down to join a four foot high wall of concrete blocks. He turned and pulled her up beside him, then released his hold on her. Despite her panic, she felt a small stab of regret as he let go.

He stepped down and stood slightly in front and to the side of her, facing the lower terrace and watching the crowd to anticipate any trouble heading their way. Amanda looked at him properly for the first time: he was quite tall, probably around six foot and slim, but she had felt the hardness of his body as he supported her through the melee. He had tight curly hair and the dark, almost Mediterranean looks that some Welsh people have, the looks that gave rise to legends of shipwrecked Spanish seamen from the Armada swimming ashore to the Welsh coast and adding to the local gene pool.

With a high proportion of older people and women in the terrace crowd, the trouble there died down quickly as a chorus of voices called for some sense to be restored. The red-faced man and his bald opponent had been pulled apart and were struggling in the arms of their supporters, apparently eager to be released and continue the fight but careful not to struggle too hard. Generally both seemed content, honour satisfied, to be shepherded apart.

On the field too things were calming down. As the wrestling players disengaged, it began to dawn on them that the referee had disappeared. They stood in small groups, wondering what to do next.

The Edwardstown secretary, however, from where he'd been watching the battle from the safety of the clubhouse – there was no way he was going to risk his dignity by getting involved – had seen the official climbing into his car, still in his ref's kit, and drive out of the ground.

He found his counterpart with a few of his Pantbach committeemen at the other end of the bar. A top-level conference quickly came to the conclusion that the referee, by leaving the pitch and then the ground, had effectively declared the match abandoned. They strode out on the ground together, waving their players towards the changing rooms with shouts of 'That's it, boys, game over, let's get changed.'

As the players began to straggle off the pitch, Amanda's rescuer turned towards her.

'Are you OK?'

'Yes' she said, a little shakily. 'Thanks for pulling me out, it was getting a bit scary. It's funny, you hear about people being hurt in situations like that and you wonder how can it happen, but when you're in it, things just seem to happen really quickly and you can't get away.'

'Aye well, passions were running a bit high today.' He smiled. A nice smile, thought Amanda. 'We're a volatile people, we Welsh, we tend to get a bit more emotional than you cool, level headed English.'

Amanda smiled back. 'You spotted my accent then.'

'I was standing just behind you on the terrace and I heard you chatting to your boyfriend, the reporter.' Chatting wasn't quite the right word; it had been a fairly terse conversation, what there was of it. 'And I know he's English too.'

'You've met him then?'

Siôn seemed briefly confused. 'Well no, not met him exactly... it's a small town, though, and I've met people who've met him.'

He paused and seemed to make a quick decision. 'It's calmed down a bit now. Might be a good idea if you sat down for a while; shall we see if we can get into the clubhouse? I don't suppose anyone from Pantbach is going to be hanging around so it should be fairly quiet.'

It occurred to Amanda that when Jake came back for her he wouldn't know where she was. But he could use his common sense, couldn't he?

'OK.' She put out her hand. 'I'm Amanda, by the way, Amanda Harper.'

He took her hand. 'Siôn, Siôn ap Siencyn.'

They turned and began to make their way down the steps.

Chapter 15

Jake was having a terrible afternoon, both emotionally and professionally. Apart from his rapidly cooling love life, he now had no game of rugby to report either. While he thought Roland couldn't really blame him for that, he didn't anticipate that going back with no story at all was going to be well received.

He'd attempted to get quotes from the respective club officials but had been met with curt 'no comments' from all of them. He'd contemplated going into the changing rooms to see if any of the players wanted to say anything but a brief glance through the doors, and the looks he'd got from the muddied and sometimes bloodied faces inside, had dissuaded him. He was standing disconsolately at the edge of the field when Reg came trotting up, camera bouncing against his chest.

'Duw, what happened here?' he said, looking out over the empty pitch. He'd been booked to cover several games that afternoon, going from one to another to get shots of some of the action. He'd left this one until last, hoping to catch the winning try or kick.

'Massive punch-up, referee fled, game abandoned', said Jake miserably.

Reg grinned. 'Sounds like a better story than a rugby report. You won't get anything from anybody tonight, they'll all be concocting the party line on what happened. Phone them on Monday, they'll have something for you. You want to give the Football Echo in Cardiff a ring though, they'll carry a couple of paragraphs and you'll get paid lineage – you know, so much per line for what they use. We pool it all and share it out every now and then, it's a nice little bonus. I'd do it soon though.' He hitched the Rolleiflex camera round his neck and looked around the ground. 'I'd better go and see what I can get.'

Jake sat on the low wall in front of the terrace and thought for a few seconds, then scribbled some lines in his notebook. He reread them, made some alterations, then headed for the public phone just inside the entrance to the clubhouse. After identifying himself to the operator at the Echo, he was put through to a copy taker and with the phone pressed to his ear and his hand cupped over the mouthpiece, began dictating his story.

'Tag line is 'abandoned', intro is 'A valleys rugby game was abandoned this afternoon after mass fighting broke out between players of both sides, point, new par.'

Jake was feeling quietly pleased with himself by the time he'd put the phone down. Then he remembered Amanda, still standing, he assumed, on the terrace. The terrace, come to think of it, where he'd half-registered what looked like a bit of trouble breaking out. He dashed for the door.

He didn't need to go into the terrace to see that it was by now completely abandoned. Where could she be? Since she didn't know the town at all, the obvious place would be the clubhouse. He turned and began trotting back.

Siôn and Amanda had found a table in a relatively quiet part of the bar, as far as possible from the players coming out of the changing rooms and gathering at the far end. Although the bar itself didn't serve teas and Amanda had turned down his offer of something stronger, he'd managed to scrounge two cups from the ladies who were preparing the players' after-game meal.

'Your first visit here, is it?' he asked Amanda.

'Yes, Jake's just started here – oh, you probably know that already.'

'Where did you meet, then?'

'Aberystwyth University.'

'Did you like it there?'

129

She hesitated, and he smiled. 'Bit too Welsh for you, was it?'

She blushed slightly. 'Not so much that, but it was very different from where I was brought up in London.'

'You might have a bit of the Celt in you though, with that colour hair.'

'Don't think so, although Dad always said he had his suspicions about our Scottish window cleaner.'

Siôn was enjoying himself. A naturally shy and quiet boy, he'd never really had a girlfriend, and living with his uncle on a small farm didn't enhance his attractiveness to the town girls. But talking to Amanda seemed really easy. Perhaps he'd been wrong about her being stuck up.

'Anyway', he went on, 'will we be seeing more of you down here now you've made your first visit?' He certainly hoped so. 'Are you coming down for this Press Ball?' Not that he knew much about it, but he'd seen it advertised in the paper.

'Jake did mention it', said Amanda. She hesitated for a moment. 'Are you going?'

The thought had never once crossed Siôn's mind. 'Oh definitely, wouldn't miss it for the world. Fancy a proper drink now?'

She asked for a gin and tonic. He got up and headed for the bar.

When Jake pushed his way into the crowded room and spotted Amanda sitting by herself at a table, an instant sense of relief surged through him.

'Mandy, I am so sorry', he said, settling into the empty chair opposite her. 'I got really tied up after that fight started on the field. I was trying to get someone from the club, or both clubs, to tell me what was going on – well, it was obvious what was going on, they were kicking the crap out of each other - but I thought I'd better get the official view. Then Reg, he's one of our photographers, turned up. He reckoned I should send a bit of copy down to the evening paper in Cardiff, they don't usually do much on these games but all the players, both trainers, half the committees and a couple of linesmen punching hell out of each other is pretty extraordinary, so then I had to phone it down, then– '

He stopped, suddenly aware that she was gazing up and over his shoulder at someone or something behind him. He turned and saw a tall, dark young man with a drink in each hand hovering there. For a moment, Siôn and Jake looked at each other, Siôn with an expression of acute uncertainty, Jake blankly.

'Jake, this is Siôn' said Amanda. 'He rescued me from the terrace when things started to get out of hand and brought me over here. Which was very nice of him. Siôn – Jake.'

Jake stood and extended a hand to Siôn; Siôn looked at it, rather surprised, then hurriedly put the glasses on the table and grasped Jake's hand.

'Right. Well, thanks a lot for that', said Jake.

'Oh, no worries, I was just sort of there standing a bit behind you and your girlfriend sort of fell into me when the crowd started moving about up there. I thought I should help.'

'Well I'm really grateful. I was a bit busy at the time. I'm a reporter with the Enquirer.'

'Yes, I know.'

There was an awkward pause. Siôn had just decided that the best thing he could do, for more than one reason, would be to make his excuses and leave when Amanda said 'Jake, grab another chair, you've just pinched Siôn's.'

Jake did as he was told, noticing for the first time that there were two empty teacups on the table. 'I'll just go and get a pint', he said and went off towards the bar.

Jake's arrival seemed to have changed the easy atmosphere there'd been between Siôn and Amanda. They sat in awkward silence for a while, then Siôn pushed back his chair. 'Look, it might be better if I took off, you both must have a lot to catch up on.'

'You might as well just finish your pint.' She smiled and shrugged. 'It's my chance to get to know at least one of the locals.'

When Jake came back, Siôn's contributions to the conversation were initially quite brief; Jake, on his part, found himself thinking a couple of times that there was something about Siôn that rang a bell with him, but he couldn't think what and eventually he gave up trying to remember. Gradually all three relaxed and they chatted about the sorts of things that people do talk about when they meet – background, family, education.

Amanda in particular found Siôn's story of his father's death in the pits, his upbringing by his mother then his move to live on his uncle's farm sad and intriguing. Siôn asked her what her plans were for the future and she felt rather foolish saying she had none really, she was just going to see what turned up.

Jake insisted on buying Siôn a drink to say thank you again for looking after Amanda, then they parted.

'See you again, I hope', said Siôn as he pulled his jacket on, looking first at Jake and then for rather longer at Amanda.

'I hope so', she replied, holding his gaze for just a little too long.

Jake didn't notice. 'Seems like a nice bloke', he said, as he watched Siôn thread his way through the crowd.

'Yes, nice enough. Now then, where do you propose to wine and dine me? I'm starving.'

With his plans for a romantic evening in the Gower in ruins, Jake hadn't really given that a great deal of thought. Apart from Tolaini's, Edwardstown didn't offer a great deal in the way of gastronomic delights: two Indian restaurants, a Chinese and a few chippies.

They settled for the Chinese, despite its reputation for spectacularly surly waiters. Not that Jake could blame them, given the kind of behaviour that they frequently had to put up with when the pubs turned out. They had a technique of dropping laden plates from at least three inches above the table when they delivered a meal, and a practise of sweeping the debris of the meal off the table as they cleared the empty dishes, some into a napkin, mostly into the laps of the diners.

Afterwards they found a relatively quiet corner of The Greyhound for a nightcap, where Amanda picked stray grains of boiled rice out of her sweater between sips of her gin and tonic. Jake had another pint, then judged it late enough to move towards what he hoped was going to be the high point of the evening.

'Shall we wander back to the house?'

They wandered slowly. He took her hand, but it seemed to him she let him do that, rather than reciprocated. The house was, as he expected, in darkness when they reached it. He opened the always-unlocked door, switched on the dim single light in the hallway and led her by the hand up the stairs to the back bedroom.

Later, she lay next to him on the cramped single bed and stared at the light of the streetlamp on the ceiling as he slept, his body turned away from her. He had, she knew, been disappointed by their lovemaking. At first the familiar touch of his hands, the feel of his body had been exciting, but somehow she couldn't abandon herself to the experience in the way she used to. She felt sad and a bit puzzled.

She also felt she needed to go for a wee. She got up carefully, opened the bedroom door as quietly as she could and padded down the corridor.

Jake felt her go and rolled over onto his back. Drowsily he thought back over what, with one thing and another, had been a pretty crap day. The sex he'd been so looking forward to had not been what he hoped. She was as beautiful as ever but somehow distant. Something seemed to have gone.

And then suddenly Jake was very wide awake with thoughts of sex instantly banished. The sound of the front door opening then closing was unnaturally loud in the quiet of the night, and unmistakeable. He lay rigid, hoping desperately that it was Gareth coming back early.

Then he heard the heavy, measured tread on the stairs and knew exactly who it was. He closed his eyes and prayed that Amanda had also heard the noise and would stay in the lavatory.

The sound of the toilet flushing stopped Mrs Probert just as she turned the corner onto the landing. She stood stock still under the single 60-watt bulb that illuminated it. There was a brief pause, the sound of water running into a basin, then the door opened and Amanda, wearing only an old rugby shirt of Jake's that barely preserved her decency, emerged from the lavatory.

For a second both women stood immobile then, with as much dignity as she could muster, the younger of the two extended a tentative hand.

'Um, hello. I'm Amanda, Jake's girlfriend.'

There was a long and terrible silence as Jake's landlady slowly looked Amanda up and down. Amanda's hand fell back to her side.

'Well I suppose it's some relief then that he hasn't simply picked you up in some gin palace or at a street corner', said Mrs Probert. Suddenly she was in motion towards Amanda, who instinctively took a pace back. The landlady swept past her towards her own room, threw open her door and then paused. She half-turned her head over her shoulder. 'Please tell Mr Nash that I shall speak to him at breakfast.' The bedroom door slammed behind her.

'Oh my God, oh my God....' Amanda was muttering, her hands covering her face, as she made her way back to Jake's room. He'd turned on the light on the bedside table and was sitting up, ashen faced and speechless. Somewhere at the back of his mind it occurred to him that, just when you thought things couldn't possibly get worse, they had a nasty habit of doing just that.

Amanda sat on the edge of the bed and Jake put a hand lightly on her arm. She stared straight ahead.

'What will she do now?' she asked eventually.

'I've absolutely no idea. At least it looks as though she isn't going to throw me out onto the street in the middle of the night'.

He gave a small and helpless shrug. 'No point in worrying about it now. Come back to bed and we'll sort it out tomorrow.'

She climbed in beside him, he switched out the light and they lay there holding hands beneath the covers. They didn't speak but Jake wondered, among other things, how he would find somewhere else to live. Eventually the dawn light began creeping through the curtains and they fell, somehow, into a troubled sleep.

When Jake made his slow way downstairs later that morning he found Mrs Probert seated at the kitchen table. His mumbled 'good morning' was cut off before he could get both words out.

'Sit down, Mr Nash.'

He sat on the other side of the table, folded his hands together in his lap and awaited the onslaught.

'Despite what Mr Harris may have told you, I am not entirely unaware that times are changing and, difficult though it may be for you to credit it, I was myself young once. Albeit that what was deemed acceptable behaviour in those days was considerably different from attitudes prevalent today.'

Jake nodded and smiled weakly.

'However', Mrs Probert continued, 'my understanding and tolerance does not extend to encountering naked women whom I do not know on my own landing in the middle of the night.'

Jake momentarily considered mentioning the rugby shirt as a mitigating factor but immediately thought better of it.

'I take into consideration that you and the young lady have, I understand, been walking out together for some time and also your attempt at discretion; had my sister not been called away when her daughter was taken suddenly ill, necessitating a visit to the hospital, I should not have returned when I did. Indeed, had I not deemed it inappropriate to stay alone with my brother-in-law overnight I might have remained ignorant of this event. Although you would be surprised, Mr Nash, at how little goes unnoticed by neighbours in this street.'

Jake could quite believe that.

'I shall only say therefore that this incident will not, I repeat, not be repeated. Is that absolutely clear, Mr Nash?'

Jake felt a small surge of relief. Was that all? Not quite.

'I would also add that your rent here does not include my provision of free bed and breakfast for your lady friends. I think another pound on this week's rent should cover it. Is that agreeable to you, Mr Nash?'

'Oh, eminently Mrs Probert; thank you very much.'

She stood up.

'Would the young lady like a cooked breakfast, or is she watching her figure?'

Jake drove Amanda down to Cardiff immediately after breakfast, most of the way in silence. Jake had hoped she'd stay until later in the day but there really didn't seem much point.

He carried her case through the station onto the platform. When the train pulled in, he put her case in through the carriage door, then stood aside to let her climb aboard and slammed the door shut behind her. She stood leaning through the open window, looking down at him on the platform below. He couldn't read her expression.

'So, the Press Ball. Shall I get tickets for us both?' he said, as brightly as he could and more in hope than expectation.

She looked at him for a second. 'Yes, I think I'd like to go to that.' As the guard blew his whistle, she dipped down to let him kiss her cheek, then stepped back and vanished from view as the train pulled away. Jake watched it until it had turned the corner out of the station and disappeared, but she didn't come back to the window to wave.

There was though a lightness in his step as he walked back to Number 17. He'd been surprised when she said yes to the invitation but he felt more cheerful than he had all morning. Maybe things could get better.

Chapter 16

The Gwalia Press Ball was to be held this year at a large hotel just off the Heads of the Valleys road, not far from the group's Trefoes headquarters. This was convenient for the senior management, who tended to live within easy travelling distance of Trefoes, but also roughly in the northern-middle part of the territory covered by the group, so no one had too far to travel. An added attraction was that the hotel offered rooms at discounted rates for those going to the ball, an offer that many who planned to make a night of it gladly took up.

Centrepiece of the evening was the crowning of Miss Gwalia Press, a title that guaranteed the winner a modest cash prize and the right to ride on various carnival floats throughout the valleys for the next year. It didn't rank too highly in the national hierarchy of beauty contests, but it was nonetheless keenly contested by young ladies who had hopes of a career in acting or modelling. Judging was by a panel chaired by the group's editor-in-chief, a thrusting young man by the name of Peter Little, who had his sights set on a move further up the Tomkins Group corporate ladder. He usually co-opted a chief executive from one of the papers' bigger advertisers and a local sportsman to sit with him. The whole event had been compered for the last few years by a well-known local entertainer, Sid Sankey, best known for the annual pantomime he wrote, produced and starred in.

Tickets went on sale first of all to Gwalia Press employees, then to the general public. Most of the latter group who bought them were people who had some kind of link with the papers or wished they did – local councillors, educators and businessmen; for most of the men and women in the valley streets, the closest they got to the ball was reading the result of the beauty contest in their papers.

So Mavis was mildly intrigued when, shortly after she opened the front doors of the Edwardstown Enquirer on Monday morning, a young man in a green combat jacket, worn jeans and working boots appeared in front of her reception desk asking if he could buy a ticket.

'Yes love, there's a few left. Three pounds ten shillings each, that includes a buffet and a free glass of wine. Two, is it?

'No, just the one, thanks.'

Siôn paid his money, pocketed the ticket and left. He hadn't told The Captain about the ball yet. He had to come up with some kind of reason for going; he thought something about 'getting to know the enemy' might be his best bet.

Monday was turning out to be an interesting day for The Captain, too. He'd slipped into Y Llew Coch for a pint and, being on his own, was standing at the bar reading the Western Mail, Wales' daily newspaper, when he became aware of someone standing beside him.

'Anything much in there?' said the stranger – at least, The Captain didn't recognise him as a local.

'No, usual rubbish.'

'I thought they did a tidy piece on that bomb blast you had around here a couple of weeks ago, mind.'

The Captain took a sip of his beer and studied the man. He was in his forties, thick set, with the ruddy complexion of someone who spent much of his life outdoors. He was wearing a duffel jacket and a flat cap, and looked like a thousand other working men in the town; he wouldn't have drawn a second glance from most people.

'That was a good effort by whoever organised that, I thought. And some of my friends thought so too', he went on.

'And who might your friends be?' asked The Captain.

The other man spoke quietly.

'My friends are among those who think it's about time people in Wales stood up for themselves. People who've come to understand that the only way we're ever going to be free of English domination and exploitation is by realising that lickspittle politicians are never going to do that for us, and that the future lies in the hands of those who are prepared to use force in defence of their country.'

The Captain looked thoughtfully down at the half-empty glass in his hand, then back up.

'For all I know, you're Special Branch.'

The man smiled slightly. 'Yes, I could be. But I'm not. Although the Special Branch might have an interest in me.'

He drained his pint and put the glass on the bar.

'I was in the area so I just thought I'd take the chance to call in and let... whoever might have been involved in that exercise... know that they're not on their own. My friends and I are aware of what they're trying to do and we'd urge them not to give up. If things work out, maybe we can work on something together in the future.'

The Captain thought for a moment. 'I think I can promise that the people involved, whoever they were, will carry on the struggle, and that there will be an action in the near future that will prove their worth.'

'I hope so', said the man. He gestured towards The Captain's glass.

'Another?'

The Captain nodded. The man called the barman over and ordered a pint, then when it arrived, paid for it and put the change in the charity box on the counter. He smiled at The Captain and turned to leave, but then turned back.

'One thing though', he said. 'From now on, it might be wiser for them not to send out press releases about their plans. By all means claim the credit if they work out, but at least that way they've got the option of disowning things if they go wrong. And the people who run our country aren't stupid, you know, they've been doing this for a long time. It's best not to tip them off about when or where something might be happening.'

Then he was gone, leaving The Captain with a great deal to think about.

After leaving The Castle, Siôn went to Tolaini's, bought himself a coffee, then sat down to study the details of the ticket. Date, time, place… 'smart/formal dress.' There was nothing in his wardrobe that even remotely fitted that description.

He finished his coffee and walked down to the shopping precinct, and after a brief stop at the Post Office to deplete his savings account, walked into a tailor's shop for the first time in his life.

It was cool and quiet inside and as far as he could see, completely empty. Rows of suits, jackets and trousers, shelves of shirts and ties stretched down both sides of the shop. He was utterly bemused. Where to start?

From somewhere amidst the racks a concealed door opened and closed soundlessly. Siôn didn't see the assistant until a soft voice spoke very nearly in his ear.

'May one help sir?'

Siôn jumped and turned to see a man of middle-age, neatly dressed in a double-breasted dark blue suit, white shirt and grey tie, with thick, grey hair swept back from a high forehead. He had a tape measure draped around his neck.

'Um, yes. I've got to go - well, I haven't got to go, but I'm going to go - er, to a ball.'

'How delightful. And am I to assume that sir's current wardrobe' – the practised eyes took in the boots, the jeans, the combat jacket – 'doesn't quite meet sir's requirements in that respect?'

'No, well, not really.'

With the briefest flick of a hand, the tape measure slid sinuously from around the tailor's neck.

'Very good. Would sir care to remove his jacket and pullover, and I'll just check his measurements.'

Which was another new experience for Siôn, especially when it came to measuring the inside leg. He coped with that by keeping his eyes fixed firmly on an advertisement for a new range of cavalry twill slacks and telling himself that a man of the world would simply take this kind of thing in his stride.

Forty-five minutes later he came out with a light blue shirt, a dark blue tie and a two-piece, three button, single vent black suit. This, he reflected, was turning out to be an expensive exercise. One pair of size nine black leather Oxford shoes from the shop down the road later, he was consoling himself that at least he was now kitted out for weddings or funerals for the next few years. Throwing caution to the winds, he went back to the tailor and splashed out on a pair of cufflinks.

When Siôn got home with his packages, The Captain was sitting at the kitchen table, cradling a mug of tea. His eyebrows went up when he saw the big 'Burton – The Tailor' branding across the bag Siôn had tossed, with unconvincing nonchalance, onto one of the threadbare armchairs by the fire.

'Oh aye, thinking of a career in the Civil Service now, are we? Or a gigolo?'

'Actually, I'm thinking of going to that Press Ball up by Trefoes.'

Siôn didn't say that he'd already bought the ticket, nor had he told his uncle about his encounter with the English reporter and his girlfriend at the rugby game. The Captain had been content with a graphic description of the general mayhem; no need, thought Siôn, to make life any more complicated that it already was.

'The Press Ball? Hobnobbing with the enemy now?' said The Captain.

'They're not really the enemy, are they? That reporter's story wasn't too bad, and if they are, didn't somebody once say something about knowing your enemy? I thought if I could go up there, maybe get the lie of the land, perhaps even get a contact on one of the papers, without telling them exactly why, of course...' He didn't sound convincing, even to himself.

But The Captain didn't seem that interested anyway. He shrugged.

'If you fancy it. Won't do you any harm to get out a bit, anyway, I don't imagine it's a lot of fun sitting around here with an old fart like me every evening. Just be careful what you say. Listen, I had an interesting meeting today...'

The Captain told Siôn about the encounter with the stranger in Y Llew Coch while Siôn poured himself a mug of tea. When his uncle had finished, Siôn sat back in his chair.

'What do you make of it then?'

'Well, I reckon that they want us to have another crack at doing something, make a bit of a stir and see if we can carry that off. And if we do, it looks like they might be taking us under their wing.'

'I'm not sure about any more bombs, Goronwy', said Siôn.

'It doesn't have to be a bomb. We just need to do something that demonstrates we're not intimidated by the power of the State, that we're willing to take action, and it needs to be something that will grab the headlines. Let me have a think.'

Siôn went upstairs to put his new clothes away, The Captain made a fresh pot of tea and went to sit by the fire, balancing the mug of tea on his knee and watching the flames dance in the grate.

Then he had an idea.

Back in Edwardstown the Reverend Stanley sat at his desk, gazing out of the window and tapping the phone with his pen. Then he put the pen down, picked up the receiver and dialled a number. After a couple of rings, it was answered.

'Good afternoon, the Lord Lieutenant's office', said a woman.

'Good afternoon. My name is the Reverend Iorwerth Stanley and I'm calling in connection with the Lord Lieutenant's visit to Edwardstown on the second of November to rededicate the town's war memorial. I shall be conducting the religious aspect of that ceremony.'

'I see, Reverend. I am the Lord Lieutenant's secretary, how may I help?'

'I assume that he will be attending the reception at the Pembroke Pavilion in Edwardstown immediately after the ceremony?'

'I believe so, let me just check.' There was the sound of the phone being put down on a desk, then a rustling of papers. After a few seconds, the phone was picked up again.

'Yes, he will be there.'

'Ah – I'm ringing to enquire whether he might have time after the reception to meet a few of my parishioners at our church hall. They are Korean War veterans and I know he served in that campaign. I thought I would just make preliminary enquiries to see if he had a gap in his timetable.'

'I'm afraid I very much doubt it, Reverend. According to his diary here, he has to go on to an early evening function in Cardiff and I note he has scheduled himself to leave Edwardstown at four-fifteen, which will only allow him about twenty minutes at the reception in any case. He's usually pretty precise about these things.'

'I'm sure he is. The military mind, everything done to a plan.'

'Exactly.'

144

'I suppose that will give him time to relax a little on the drive back to Cardiff. He presumably has a driver.'

'Actually no, Reverend, he always drives himself unless he is accompanying someone, he's a little intolerant of other people's driving abilities. Would you like me to ask him if he can squeeze in a few minutes with your parishioners just in case he can manage that?'

'No, that's quite all right. I understand he is a busy man and I wouldn't like to trouble him further. Thank you for your assistance.'

'My pleasure. Goodbye.'

'Goodbye.'

The secretary went back to the filing she had been doing before the phone call, and after another half hour or so glanced at the clock on the far wall. Ten to six. She tidied the desk and was just wondering if she could slip away a few minutes early when the phone rang again. She wasn't surprised, her boss had a habit of ringing around this time just to check she was still there. But the voice at the other end of the line had nothing like the clipped English accent she was expecting.

'Hello?' said a very Welsh voice.

'Good afternoon, the Lord Lieutenant's office, his secretary speaking.'

'Hello. I'm, um, calling about his visit to Edwardstown in November for the war memorial ceremony.'

'Oh yes. Are you one of the Korean veterans?'

There was a silence at the other end of the phone for a few seconds.

'Sorry?'

'The Edwardstown Korean War veterans. I had a call about them earlier on and I was just wondering if that was the subject of your call too.'

'No, no, my name is Berwyn Thomas and I'm the Boy Scout leader in Edwardstown here. As you probably know, part of the Scout Promise is to do their duty to their monarch, and as the Lord Lieutenant is Her Majesty's representative in the county I was just wondering if he might have time to talk to us after the ceremony. I'm sure he'd have some interesting insights to share with us. The boys are very keen to know if the corgis really are Welsh, for example.'

'I'm afraid not, Mr Thomas, and I'm not sure he knows a great deal about corgis anyway. As I was saying to your vicar only a few minutes ago, the Lord Lieutenant will be briefly attending the civic reception in the Pembroke Pavilion immediately after the memorial ceremony and then driving himself back to Cardiff for an early evening appointment.'

'Driving himself?'

'Yes.'

'To Cardiff?'

'Yes.'

'Right. Oh well, there you go then, worth a try. Not to worry. Thanks for your help, anyway.'

'Quite all right, I hope the boys won't be too disappointed. Goodbye.'

She put the phone down and, as she turned out the lights and locked the office door, she wondered a little at the sudden popularity of her boss in Edwardstown.

In a phone box near Y Llew Coch, The Captain stared at the handset he had just replaced on its cradle. Korean War veterans? The vicar? He had no idea what that had all been about, but no matter, he had the information he wanted.

With the Press Ball just days away, preparation was well under way in Edwardstown and beyond.

In the lounge bar of a quiet hotel some miles down the road towards Cardiff, Sid Sankey was making his own

146

arrangements for what he had every reason to believe would be an enjoyable evening.

As he played with his large whisky and soda, the ice cubes jangling cheerfully in the glass, he gazed over the table into the wide eyes of Sophia Evans, the butcher's daughter who would carry with her the hopes of the Edwardstown Enquirer. To be accurate, he gazed into one of Sophia's eyes; the other was obscured by a gay miniature paper parasol that protruded from the top of a cocktail glass from which she was drinking a luminous green liquid that looked as though it might be radioactive.

'I really think you've got it, Sophia. And I reckon winning the Miss Gwalia title could be your key to a great modelling career and all that brings with it – money, travel, cars, meeting top people...'

Sophia drew deeply on the straw that emerged from the green depths, then sighed.

'Do you really think so, Sid? Some of the other girls are so lovely, and I seem to be a lot curvier than most of them. Models these days are so skinny.' The local beauty contest circuit wasn't a big one and Sophia had already lost a few times to some of the girls she knew would be competing against her.

Sid's eyes wandered down to take in those curves he could see above the table. His gaze lingered on them appreciatively.

'That's why I thought it might be worth our while having this little chat, Sophia. There are different types of modelling and for some of them, believe me, a figure like yours is definitely an asset. Very definitely a major asset.'

His lifted his eyes, and once again they looked with deepest sincerity into hers. 'You just need a few tips on how to go about winning over the jury. And perhaps I shouldn't say this, but I always have a bit of influence on their decision.'

'Really, Sid, do you?'

'Yes, really. Most of the judges know nothing about assessing real beauty and as long as they get their fee and a few free drinks, they don't care too much. So they're always ready to listen to some helpful advice from an old hand, and believe me I've been around this game for a long time.'

His eyes had wandered south again to where Sophia's voluptuous breasts were straining for their freedom from her very tight blouse. He lifted his glass and drained his whisky in one gulp.

'Tell you what, finish your cocktail and we'll go for a drive in my Jag. We can stop somewhere quiet and have a bit of a chat about it'.

In a semi-detached in Edwardstown, Richard was sitting in Lotte's parents' front room, watching her model the dress she'd bought for the ball. It was long and black, low cut at the front and back, and showed off her figure perfectly.

'Cracking, Lotts, absolutely cracking, you look fabulous. I'll be the envy of every man there. Right, gotta go, I said I'd meet your dad down the Institute, they're a man down for the darts team.'

He winked at her. 'Best to keep in with the future father-in-law, eh?'

In her bedroom in Hampstead, Amanda was looking over her shoulder at a reflection of herself in the wardrobe mirror. She coolly appraised the image of the long green velvet dress that perfectly set off her red hair and pale skin and clung to her slim figure in all the right places. That should do it for the boy, she thought to her mirrored image with a quiet satisfaction.

And in a much smaller bedroom in a farmhouse just outside Edwardstown, the boy in question tried on a black suit, a blue shirt and dark blue tie for the third time. But the face that looked back at him was full of uncertainty.

Chapter 17

The following night the Reverend Stanley was in London. After a light lunch, he'd walked down to the station in Edwardstown and bought a ticket to Paddington Station.

Arriving in the late afternoon, he slipped into a public convenience on the concourse and in one of the cubicles, once again swapped his clerical collar and shirt for more inconspicuous clothing, a polo-neck dark blue woollen pullover. He stopped at one of the station's pubs for a pint and a sandwich, then caught the Metropolitan Line tube train to Baker Street, changed to the Bakerloo Line and travelled on to Kilburn.

Coming out of Kilburn station, he'd taken a London A to Z gazetteer out of his satchel and after studying it for a while, strode off. Ten minutes later he was knocking at the door of a rather run-down terraced house in a back street.

After a long pause, it was opened by a thickset man in his thirties, with a shock of wiry grey hair. He said nothing but looked at the Reverend intently.

'My name is Iorwerth Stanley. I believe you are expecting me.'

The man nodded. 'Hello, Father.' He spoke with a heavy Irish accent.

The Reverend smiled slightly. 'Just Reverend. I bat for the other side.'

'Sorry, slip of the tongue. No offence.'

'None taken.'

The Reverend followed the man into a small front room, lit with a single bulb and with the curtains drawn. As the man turned, the Reverend looked at him intently and said, without any further preamble, 'Do you have it?'

'I do, yes. But I have to ask you, are you sure you want it?'

'Quite sure.'

The man looked at him for two or three seconds, then nodded curtly, turned and left the room. The Reverend heard him climb the stairs, then the sound of footfalls and a heavy object, perhaps a piece of furniture, being dragged across the floor overhead. Two minutes later, after more muffled thumps and bangs, the man was back in the room. He carried in each hand a cloth-wrapped bundle.

The Reverend followed him to the dining table set into the bay window and watched intently as the cloths were removed. Two solid pieces of metal lay on the table. Both men looked silently at them for a while, then the Reverend said, quite softly, 'yes.'

They pulled out chairs from the table, sat, and for the next fifteen minutes the Irishman talked, occasionally picking up one or other of the objects he'd brought down to demonstrate something. The Reverend listened intently, sometimes asking a short question. Eventually they seemed to have reached the end of all that was to be said. The Reverend reached into the satchel hanging from the back of the chair and put a thick envelope onto the table.

The Irishman picked up the envelope, lifted the flap and glanced at the contents.

'I'm assuming I don't need to count it?' he said.

The Reverend shook his head.

The envelope went back down onto the table, then the two metal pieces were rewrapped and placed carefully in the Reverend's bag.

The men stood and shook hands. The Reverend made his way back down the dimly lit hallway and stepped out into the night without pause or a backward glance. Behind him the door was shut, quietly but firmly. The sound of bolts being slid into place might have been heard had anyone been close enough, but no one was.

Shortly afterwards the light visible in the small grimy window over the door was switched off, and the house was in darkness.

The Reverend walked for fifteen minutes through the quiet streets until he reached a small, nondescript hotel. The clerk at reception checked his name in a register and gave him a room key.

He had an early breakfast next morning in a workmen's café in Kilburn High Road. Then he walked up and down the road, looking for a particular kind of shop. Eventually he stopped, spoke to a passing postman and was directed to a small store; in its windows were rows of cheap trophies.

Going in, he took one of the objects he'd acquired the previous night carefully from his satchel and showed it to the man behind the counter. He needed an inscription engraved on it, he said, for a presentation, and his sincere apologies for leaving it till the last minute but he needed it for tonight – well, right away really. He was quite happy to pay extra if he could wait for it to be done.

The Reverend took a folded piece of paper from his inside pocket and showed it to the shopkeeper, who studied it carefully, then read back what was written there, letter by letter, space by space. When the Revered nodded his confirmation, the shopkeeper disappeared into the back room. The Reverend took a book from his bag and read while he waited patiently until the man returned and showed his work to the Reverend.

When the Reverend had checked the engraving he paid the shopkeeper, who said there'd be no extra charge. He'd been in the Eighth Army in North Africa himself, he said, always glad to do something for an old soldier, especially one of the Taffs. He'd had a few in his unit, liked them, good blokes. Actually he could knock a little bit off the price.

The Reverend thanked him, wrapped the object in its cloth again and put into the satchel. He headed directly for the Underground station and by mid afternoon he was back in the vicarage in Edwardstown.

Now he sat in his study in one of the armchairs. The room was deep in shadows, lit only by a single lamp on a corner table, and he was still and silent. The two objects stood on the small coffee table in front of him, the lamplight reflecting in their polished surfaces. He was thinking about the Irishman's parting words to him.

'I have to tell you that once you step down the path of action you are contemplating, there is no going back. Things will change, and change irrevocably. Are you ready for that?'

Yes, I am, thought the Reverend. I'm ready.

Chapter 18

The Cascades Hotel was a large modern building, catering in the week mostly for travelling salesmen and senior management staff from various companies on their visits to local factories across the industrial valleys. But it also had a large dance floor, an extensive dining area and a roomy bar, and it had become a popular venue for parties and functions.

On the Saturday night of the Gwalia Press Ball, the car park was packed and the area in front of reception busy with minibuses and taxis dropping off groups of journalists, print workers, management and assorted members of the public. Despite its size, the bar was crowded and the staff serving drinks were hard pressed to keep up with demand.

Jake had driven down to Cardiff in the morning to pick up Amanda after spending the Friday on tenterhooks, convinced that every moment he was about to be told he would have to work the next day; Roland seemed to take a mischievous delight in calling him in every hour or so, only to check some small fact or pass on a thought for next week's coverage. On the last occasion he'd asked Jake if he'd like to take over the regular coverage of Edwardstown's rugby games and seemed surprised when Jake declined the offer. He'd dismissed him with 'you might as well clear off now; see you at the ball tomorrow', and Jake had escaped thankfully to The Greyhound.

Amanda had seemed quite cheerful, even a little excited, and Jake was relieved. Their phone conversations were still stilted and awkward and Jake had found himself running out of things to say. He'd mentioned it to Lotte, who had been quite positive.

'Don't worry about it love, all relationships go through rough patches. You've been living in each other's pockets at University for the last couple of years; now you're doing things she can't share and doesn't really understand, so things are bound to be a bit tense for a while. They'll settle down again.'

Jake wasn't wholly convinced but he was grateful for the attempt at reassurance.

Things did seem to be better between them as they headed north out of Cardiff and into the valleys. Amanda even managed to laugh about the rugby game.

'Are they still at war?' she asked.

'No. Apparently the Scarlet Woman decided to go back to her husband the following Wednesday, the Philandering Wing Forward returned to his wife and kids, the two men met for a drink and ended up shaking hands so officially it's all over and forgotten. Though I suspect they're going to find it difficult to get a ref when Edwardstown go to play at Pantbach next.'

'Dear dear, you boys.'

'Listen Amanda, I really am sorry about leaving you on your own like that. It's just that, you know, being new and wanting to get it right...'

'Sure, don't worry about it.'

'Lucky that guy Siôn was there, I suppose.'

She nodded vigorously, looking straight ahead.

'Mmmmmm.'

Jake had already had to endure what for him had been the excruciating embarrassment of booking in to The Cascades. He and Amanda had never stayed at an hotel together. He'd rung to make the reservation as soon as she had confirmed she'd be coming: a double room, night of Saturday the nineteenth of October, the special rate for the Press Ball, please, and when the receptionist had asked 'For you and your wife?' he'd made a snap decision and said yes.

Amanda had absolutely refused to play along. She had met his tentative suggestion that she wear something that looked like a wedding ring with silent scorn; her tone of voice when she eventually deigned to reply to his half-

154

hearted attempt at persuasion left Jake in no doubt of her opinion of his idea.

'Jake, I do not need anyone's permission to share a hotel room with whomsoever I choose. I am an adult woman living in the sixties. I'm not sure where you are, but I won't be joining you there any time soon.'

In the end she'd agreed not to actively deny her married status, so while Jake had met the receptionist's knowing look and 'Enjoy your stay, Mr and Mrs Nash' with a fixed smile, Amanda had responded with an icy glare but said nothing.

It was a nice room though, with views out over the distant hills and a wide double bed that Jake had taken in with a small thrill of anticipation. He'd changed first and gone down to the bar. Les and Roger, the advertising reps, were already there with their wives; he bought himself the first drink of the evening and joined them.

Their group gradually grew. Wayne and Gareth, with two local girls, had shared a taxi. Roland and Dorothy had driven up because they planned to leave early; they rather obviously viewed attendance as a duty expected of all the editors rather than an occasion to be enjoyed. Lotte and Richard were dropped off by her father, Reg and his wife Rosemary, a pleasant, pretty woman, arrived in their own car too but Jake noticed that Rosemary drank only fruit juices. Lotte and Reg behaved perfectly naturally towards each other, without the undertone of flirtatious banter they had in the office. That must be a bit of a strain, thought Jake. Terry would not be coming. His wife, said Roland, wasn't well enough and he didn't like to leave her alone in the evenings.

Amanda joined them, looking stunning, and was warmly welcomed by the men, slightly more coolly by the women. Les and Roger virtually raced each other to the bar to buy her a drink. Other groups were gathering; members of one drifted across to another to greet old friends or renew acquaintanships. The noise levels rose; the evening was warming up nicely.

Jake noticed four men standing together at one end of the bar, smoking cigars and holding large glasses of short drinks, laughing and talking with the loud self-assurance of men who know they're top dogs. He asked Lotte about them.

'Left to right, Dave Tanner, local boy and outside-right for Cardiff City, although I gather that he's fighting for his place these days; Peter Little, our editor-in-chief; Sid Sankey, star of stage and saloon bar; and Dennis Dugdale, proprietor of the largest second-hand car business in the valleys and originator of Den's Double Diamond, which is like a car-of-the-week promotion but there are two of them. Sid is our compere for the evening, the other three are the judging panel for the beauty competition.'

'Not a very savoury looking bunch.'

'Personally I wouldn't trust any of them with my granny. And she's been dead five years.'

The crowd in the bar thinned as the drinkers carried their glasses into the ballroom, staked their claims for chairs at the tables around the edges of the dance floor and collected their buffet meals from the dining room. The All-Star Vaudeville Dance Band, nine local musicians who made a decent addition to their income from the day jobs by playing at events like this, launched into a selection of popular songs from a dais at the of the room.

During gaps in her conversations, Amanda gazed casually around the room, as she had in the bar, but so far she hadn't spotted the person she was looking for.

Siôn was, in fact, in the furthest and darkest corner of the room. He'd never been to any event like this, and as Saturday evening grew ever closer, he'd become increasingly nervous. At half past four that afternoon he'd told The Captain that he wasn't going to bother going but

The Captain had insisted he should, having already invested quite a lot of money in the enterprise. Besides, said The Captain, he might pick up some useful information. So Siôn, reluctantly, had changed into his black suit, climbed into the Land Rover and driven to the Cascades.

Arriving after most of the guests, he'd parked in a corner of the car park and sat for a while before plucking up the courage to go in. He'd picked up a pint of beer from the bar, then feeling increasingly foolish standing on his own, he'd collected his little pile of cold chicken drumsticks, pork pie, sausages, ham sandwiches and cheese and pineapple chunks on cocktail sticks and found a quiet spot for himself at a table with people he didn't know. His neighbours on either side made tentative attempts to include him in their conversations but gave up after short while. Siôn wasn't really in the mood for small talk.

From where he sat he could see Amanda. She looked beautiful, and she was obviously enjoying herself, chatting and laughing with the others at her table. He poked moodily at a sausage with a cocktail stick.

Waitresses came around to clear the debris of the buffet, and a long table draped with a red velvet cloth was brought out in front of the dais. Sid walked on, resplendent in a white tuxedo, and picked up a microphone that had been left for him.

'Welcome, welcome, ladies and gentlemen, to this glittering event. I hope you enjoyed that delicious buffet – let's all say a big thank you to the catering staff here at The Cascades.' Half hearted applause.

'But now the high point of our evening, the final of the Miss Gwalia Press beauty pageant. Please welcome the judges who'll have the tough but enviable task of selecting the winner from our bevy of beauties!'

David Tanner, Peter Little and Dennis Dugdale came on, smiling and waving, and were introduced by Sid as they took their seats behind the long table.

'And now, let the parade commence!'

The band broke into 'Ain't She Sweet?' and the girls, in one-piece swimsuits, appeared in procession from behind a screen at the back of the dais. They walked slowly around the room, shoulders back, heads high, smiling at the audience and particularly at the judges as they passed their table.

Sophia was fourth in the line, and she seemed to give a particularly wide smile – and was that the hint of a wink? – at Sid as she sashayed by.

Sid read out her short biography from a card, as he had with all the girls.

'Sophia Thomas carries the hopes of the readers of the Edwardstown Enquirer' he said, either not noticing or choosing to ignore the wink. 'Aged 17, she's currently working at the Pat's Pies factory in Edwardstown but has high hopes of a career in caring for the elderly or working with disadvantaged children...'

When all the girls had done their circuit of the room and disappeared back behind the screen, Sid announced a short break while they changed into evening dress. The band started on 'A Pretty Girl is Like a Melody', and conversation at the tables turned to who looked the likely winner.

'Little cracker, that Sophia', said Les.

His wife looked disapprovingly at him. 'I suppose so, if you like the cheap streetwalker look.'

'That's a little harsh, my dear.'

Amanda was distinctly unimpressed. 'It's all a bit degrading, isn't it?'

'Oh come on', said Jake, 'It's just a bit of fun. Although apparently some of the girls take it very seriously.'

'A lot of them do', said Lotte. 'That's her mum and dad over there', nodding towards a very large man and an almost as large woman sitting at a table not far away. 'He's the local butcher. Probably does pretty well for himself, which is just as well because he spends a small fortune on dresses and accessories for her.'

Butcher, thought Jake, very apt. Sophia's dad had taken his jacket off at an early stage of the evening and rolled up his sleeves to the elbow; he had forearms like hams.

Then the girls were back again, one at a time but in reverse order from their first appearances, to be interviewed by Sid. Apparently they all lived at home with mum and dad so they could help out with family chores, most of them had pets that they adored, and their greatest wish was for world peace or just that we should all be more considerate of other people.

As Sid finished his little chat, each girl would be wildly applauded by her own supporters, politely clapped by others, and then would disappear, with a final flash of teeth and a wide smile, back behind the screen.

'There we are then, ladies and gentlemen', announced Sid as the last one made her exit, 'the competitors for the title of Miss Gwalia Press 1968. Who'll be the winner, who'll wear the crown? Let's have one final look at them all as the judges decide!'

Sid smiled broadly out at the audience again. Everything was going smoothly; wrap this up as quickly as possible, a couple of drinks, then he and Sophia could slip away to his room where she could show him again just how grateful she was for this leg-up on the glamour ladder.

With a warm glow of self satisfaction glowing within him, he congratulated himself on a job well done.

Chapter 19

The band broke into 'Isn't This a Lovely Day?', the girls emerged once more to walk in procession around the room and Sid went across to join the judging panel that was already conferring.

The girls completed the two circuits they had been told to do and came to a halt in front and to one side of the judges' table, but it seemed they had yet to reach a decision. Sid turned and with a broad smile and a shrug to the audience, waved them on for another circuit.

By the end of that one, it was becoming apparent that the process of anointing the new Miss Gwalia Press wasn't running smoothly. Dennis and Dave were sitting back, occasionally shaking their heads, while Peter was listening intently to Sid, who looked to be speaking rapidly and earnestly. As the girls began to line up again and the music ended, Sid turned and irritably waved them on, and after some hesitation, they straggled off into yet another circuit.

The band, having played through 'You Make Me Feel So Young', with reprise, was running out of suitable tunes; the music died as they shuffled through their sheet music in search of something vaguely apt. The applause from the crowd had diminished with each successive circuit and had been replaced by a muttering which grew in volume, punctuated by the occasional shout of 'Come on, then!' In one corner of the room, a slow handclap was starting.

Dave had his arms folded over his chest and was staring fixedly away from Sid, while Dennis was obviously making some forceful point to the compere, if the fierceness with which he was jabbing a plump forefinger at the compere's chest was anything to go by. Peter was sitting with his head in his hands.

Finally the girls straggled to a halt in their appointed position, facing the audience. Sid seemed to have slumped a little; he took a piece of paper from Dennis as though it had just been retrieved from a toilet bowl. He turned back to the audience; the power grin was switched back on but its wattage was visibly diminished.

'Well, ladies and gentlemen, what a difficult job for our judges tonight, and no wonder with such a wealth of beauty and talent on display! But they've finally reached their decision so here, in the traditional reverse order, the results!

'In third place, from Pontgarw, Tracey Griffiths!'

Tracey managed a semi-convincing display of surprise and joy as she stepped forward from the line and waved around her. She graciously accepted her third place tiara from Dennis, who had to struggle a little to wedge it into her heavily lacquered hair, but finally she went to stand to one side of the judges

Sid waited for the applause to die, then looked down intently at the paper again.

'Our runner up – and let me say once again what an incredibly close competition it's been this year, <u>incredibly</u> close – our runner up is......' and his grin seemed to become even tighter – 'Sophia Evans from Edwardstown!'

The expectant small smile on Sophia's face froze, then slipped into stunned incredulity. Jake glanced across to the table where her mother and father were sitting, or at least had been sitting; Dad was now half way out of his seat, his face twisted in pure outrage, while his wife desperately hung on to one of his huge arms.

Sid seemed to be in a hurry to bring things to a conclusion. 'And this year's winner, Sharon Morgan from Coedybrenin!'

Lotte leaned across and shouted in Jake's ear above the explosion of noise. 'What an amazing coincidence. That's where Dennis Dugdale has his business.'

Jake didn't hear her. Sharon, a pneumatic but by no means the prettiest girl in the parade, had begun her pantomime of utter amazement and overwhelming happiness but the cheers from her supporters wasn't loud enough to muffle a bull-like roar from Sophia's father.

Towing his wife behind him, he moved with surprising speed towards the judges' table. Seeing him coming they scattered, but he had only one target; grasping Sid by the lapels of his tuxedo, he hoisted him a foot clear of the floor and bellowed something incomprehensible, but which sounded rather like 'You promised!' at him.

'Not the face, don't mark the face!' screamed Sid, through a spray of his aggressors' saliva.

Jake watched the melee for a second then shouted across to Gareth. 'Shouldn't we do something?'

Terry surveyed the mass of bodies and shook his head.

'I don't think so. Way above our pay grade.'

Amanda couldn't quite believe it. Her second visit to Edwardstown, her second brawl. This evening wasn't turning out anything like she'd hoped. At least she was far enough away from the hub of the action to be safe but a tactical withdrawal to the ladies, she decided, might be her best bet.

When she'd allowed what she thought would be enough time for the mayhem to have subsided, she made her way back and stopped in the doorway of the function room. Things seemed to be quietening down; the still-sobbing Sophia was being led away by her mother, her father was being bundled out by friends and relatives, Sid was seated at one side of the dais, cradling a large brandy in a shaky hand and evaluating the damage to his tuxedo. She gazed around the room again and finally saw Siôn. He was sitting at a table with a group but not talking to them. He didn't look very happy. She walked up behind him.

'Does this sort of thing happen wherever you go?'

He jumped at her voice and turned quickly. She looked ravishing.

'Oh – hi. Um, nothing to do with me, again. I'm just an innocent by-stander.'

She smiled and shook her head. 'Perhaps there's a local byelaw that stipulates that every gathering of more than five men must end in a punch-up?'

He thought for a second or so. 'No, I think they repealed that once they got wrestling on the television. I think you've just been unlucky.'

She nodded towards an empty chair beside him.

'Has your partner for the evening taken shelter somewhere?'

'Who?'

'Your partner. The person you brought with you to the ball.'

'Oh, yes. I mean, no, she couldn't make it unfortunately. Tummy trouble. I thought I might as well come anyway.'

'No-one else in your little black book you could persuade to come with you?'

'Too short notice, it only came on last night.' He pulled the empty chair back slightly. 'Do you have time to sit down for a minute? I think there's some of the free wine left if you fancy a glass.'

'You know how to tempt a girl, don't you?' said Amanda and heard herself sounding too clever by half. She looked around as the lights began to dim; a power failure, she thought, just what we need, but as the band struck up again she saw that some couples were moving on to the floor.

'Do you dance?' she asked.

'Dance?'

'Yes, you know, move your feet and body rhythmically in time to music like they're playing now.'

'Well I haven't had a lot of practise.'

Time to move the evening on. She grasped him firmly by one hand.

'That's all right, I have.'

Jake too was sitting by himself, the rest of his table having wandered off either to the bar or onto the dance floor. He was just beginning to wonder where Amanda had got to when he saw Lotte weaving her way back through the tables. She sat down beside him.

'Where did you disappear to?' he asked her.

'Richard's boss and a few of the other managers are back in the bar, he wanted to have a drink with them. To be honest, he wanted to sit at their table tonight, but I told him it was my night out and there was no way I was going to spend it with people I barely know when the people I work with are here. So this was his compromise – first part with me and the Enquirer, second part with the bank crowd.'

'Don't you want to stay with them?'

'No. I've done my duty as the faithful and adoring girlfriend, so he's happy. He can have a drink with his mates now. I don't find I have a great deal in common with them anyway.'

If Jake hadn't had a couple of drinks, he might not have asked the next question.

'How about Richard? How much have you got in common with him?'

She nodded straight away. 'I've told you, a lot. We went to the same school, we've known each other a long time, our families like each other…'

Jake looked at her for a few seconds. 'And is all that enough?'

She smiled brightly. 'Yes.' Then she stood.

'This is getting way too serious. Come on, big boy, ten cents a dance.'

 'Put me down for a dollar's worth.'

The band leader had been playing at this sort of function for a good many years; he was adept at judging the mood and musical tastes of his audiences and after the chaos of the beauty contest, he decided he'd keep the lively stuff fairly brief and move to mellow as soon as he could.

So a good number of the melodies they played were slow. Some of the older dancers could put ballroom steps to them, most of the younger ones, encouraged by the low lights and the alcohol, just took the music as an excuse to get their arms round each other. On the edge of the crowd, in the darkest part of the room, Siôn and Amanda were holding each other and swaying gently to the music.

Siôn could feel the slimness of Amanda's body underneath the dress and smell her perfume. His expression suggested he thought he'd died and gone to heaven. They danced in silence for a while, their cheeks just brushing, then Siôn broke their silence.

'I know you went to Aber but this must seem quite strange down here to you, it's very different.'

'It is. But it has its attractions.'

'Well, if there's ever anything I can do...'

She pulled away suddenly from him and looked at him intently. For the first time in his life, felt his knees go weak.

'Actually, there's probably quite a lot you can do. You can start by ringing me next week.'

Siôn looked at her incredulously, then made a rapid recovery. 'Right, sure. I'll need your number.'

'Ah, we may have a slight problem there. Unfortunately the designer of this dress rather thoughtlessly didn't include a pocket big enough for a pen, and I bet you haven't got one on you either, have you?'

He shook his head.

'So you're going to have to go through the operator. Luckily, my dad's initials are H.P., for Harold Percival, but you can remember them as the sauce – HP. So just think of

165

saucy little Amanda Harper from Hampstead, and the H.P. will spring to mind. He's the only one in the book.'

'Harper, Hampstead, think of the sauce,' said Siôn gravely. 'I think I can cope with that.' Amanda smiled and they started to move back together, but then he stopped.

'Wait', he said, apparently alarmed by a sudden thought. 'I'm only a simple Welsh boy, I'm easily confused. Suppose I think of OK sauce, and look for O.K. Harper? I'll never get through.'

She punched him lightly on the arm, then looked serious.

'Am I too much of a smart alec at times, Siôn?'

'No', he said, as he pulled her back towards him. He'd never met anyone like her before. 'It's quite nice actually.'

Her arms went around his neck, and this time they were very definitely cheek to cheek.

'You will ring, won't you?' she whispered in his ear.

'Oh yes. Yes, I'll ring.'

She moved her head back and looked him into his eyes.

'Actually, there is something else you can do for me right now.'

Siôn was utterly mesmerised. 'Anything.'

'You can kiss me.'

In the diagonally opposite corner of the dance floor, Lotte and Jake were dancing – not quite so closely but with his arms round her waist, her arms on his shoulders. They were also talking a bit more than Siôn and Amanda, inside that bubble of closeness and darkness that lends itself to intimacy.

'How about you?' she was saying, 'where do you see yourself in five years? God, that sounds like a job interview question.'

'I've no idea, really. Except, if I'm honest, not here.'

'Not good enough for you, are we?'

'You're all bloody great for me at the moment, but I'd like to think that five years from now I'll want to try something new. Still news, or writing, or whatever, but a bit more into the big wide world.'

He looked into her pretty, clever face. She felt much softer than Amanda, he thought as they moved slowly in time with the music, somehow warmer.

"If I can say this without sounding patronising, and I probably can't, you're a bright girl, you're good at your job; are you sure running a home and looking after Richard and the kids is going to be enough for you?'

'I can always take up part-time brain surgery in the mornings when the kids start school, I suppose, in between baking cakes for the Women's Institute, carrying the coal in, walking the whippet and scrubbing the front door step, of course.'

They smiled at each other and moved a little closer. For a while there was silence between them.

'I'm glad you came down here, of all places', she said softly. 'And I'll miss you when you go.'

'I'll miss you too. When I said you're all great for me, I had you mostly in mind.'

Their eyes were locked, their lips were moving slowly towards each other and their heads had started that slight incline in opposite directions that makes a kiss so much easier...

'Ladies and gentlemen, please take your partners for The Last Waltz. Last dance of the evening, ladies and gentlemen.'

The bandleader's announcement stopped Lotte dead. She stepped backwards and away from him as the band launched into Englebert Humperdink's big hit from the previous autumn.

'I'd better find Richard' said Lotte softly. 'He's a bit old fashioned about this.'

'Sure, of course', he replied, as brightly as he could manage. 'I'd better find Amanda.'

They turned away from each other, Lotte heading to meet Richard as he emerged from the bar, Jake to scan the dance floor behind him. After a few seconds he saw Amanda making her way in his direction through the slowly circling couples.

'Hi – where did you get to?' he asked her as they came together.

'Went to the loo and bumped into that guy Siôn we met at the rugby on the way back. His girlfriend cried off last night and he was on his own, so I thought I ought to stay and chat for a while.'

They moved together and began to dance, but there was a gap between their bodies which neither tried to close.

'Funny, coming to a do like this on your own, I wouldn't have bothered. Perhaps he just didn't want to waste two tickets', said Jake.

'Perhaps', said Amanda.

After the music was over and the lights had come up, Jake and Amanda stayed for a while to finish their drinks and say goodnight to the others. Then they joined the stragglers making their way into the foyer, some heading up the stairs to the bedrooms, others to collect their coats and begin the journey home.

Just in front of Jake was a group of three, two men and a woman. The woman– a girl really – was in the middle, holding the hand of the man on her left; the man on her right had an arm around her waist. They'd obviously had a good evening, if the erratic way they attempted to get through the ballroom door still three abreast was anything to go by.

In the foyer Jake had expected them to head towards the cloakroom, but they made their rather unsteady way to the stairs to the upper rooms and began to go up them. Then Jake realised who they were: the new Miss Gwalia Press, Sharon Morgan, flanked by the judging duo of Dave Tanner and Dennis Dugdale. A giggling Sharon was attempting to lay her head on Dave's shoulder as they began to climb the stairway to Heaven; Dennis tightened his grip around her waist.

Well, well, thought Jake, there's a turn-up for the books. He turned to draw Amanda's attention to the group but before he could speak he saw, over her shoulder, a rather battered Land Rover drive through the pool of light in front of the hotel on its way out of the car park. On the side window was a transfer: the dragon's tongue, symbol of the Welsh Language Society. And at the wheel, clearly illuminated in the hotel lights, Siôn, the man who'd rescued Amanda at the rugby game.

In that instant, Jake realised why he had seemed familiar.

Chapter 20

Jake lay on his side of the double bed, hands behind his head, staring into the dark. They'd undressed with hardly a word spoken between them. In bed, he'd rested a tentative hand on her shoulder; she'd shrugged, a small, involuntary rejection. She was really sorry, she said, it had been a long day and she was very tired – would he mind if they didn't? Now she lay on her side of the bed, her back towards him, apparently fast asleep.

Strangely, he found he didn't mind very much at all. He wondered what he should do about Siôn. The Land Rover, the sticker in the window, the voice – even though that had been muffled when he'd first heard it he was convinced that Siôn was one of the men who'd been part of the GLF exercise.

He was much less sure about what he should do next.

If he went to the police, he'd have to explain why he hadn't mentioned the Land Rover before; he'd been quite explicit that he hadn't seen any other vehicles. On the other hand, if the GLF became more effective and someone ended up dead or injured, he wasn't sure he could live with his conscience.

But then again, from what little he knew of Siôn, he seemed like a decent bloke and he'd certainly been more than solicitous in helping Amanda when she was in danger.

He drifted off into a troubled sleep, no nearer any decision.

They breakfasted the following morning in almost complete silence in the half-empty dining room and conversation hadn't been any easier during the drive down to Cardiff. After he'd seen her onto her train, she'd leant out of the carriage window and kissed him lightly on the cheek.

'I'll give you a call on Thursday night, 6.30 at your place, OK?' she said, then turned away and went into the carriage. Jake walked along the platform, watching through the train windows as she found a seat, took a book out of her bag and started to read. She didn't turn to look at him.

After a few seconds he began to feel foolish, staring mutely through a train window at a girl who was ignoring him, so he left and drove back up the valley to Edwardstown.

That afternoon, Jake shared a cup of tea with Mrs Probert in her kitchen. He'd perked up a little. Reporters are born gossips and nothing quite delights them as much as having salacious news to share. He'd told his landlady about the beauty competition and Sophia's reaction to coming second, had just revealed the winner – Sharon Morgan from Coedybrenin – and was pausing to savour the moment before telling Mrs P, in the nicest possible way, just how Sharon had shown her gratitude to two of the judges when Mrs Probert broke in.

'Oh I know Sharon won, her mum rang and told me this morning.'

Jake was surprised. 'Really? Why would she do that?'

'She's my sister. Sharon's my niece.'

Apparently not noticing Jake's stunned silence, Mrs Probert went on. Sharon had naturally been delighted with her win, quite a surprise really as she'd never won anything like this before and to be honest, her mum and dad were beginning to wonder if they could find a way to tell her gently that perhaps she wasn't really... equipped for the beauty queen circuit. Although funnily enough she had seemed quite confident about doing well in this particular competition.

Well what with the excitement of it all, she'd got a bit squiffy. She'd been going to ring her dad to come and pick her up – her parents weren't comfortable at that kind of thing and Sharon had said she'd be fine so they hadn't gone – but then she'd called to say not to worry, the girls were ever so friendly with each other and she was going to share a room with one of them, which was very kind of the other girl because she must have been a bit disappointed really.

Then in the morning at breakfast Sharon had got talking to one of the judges, Mr Dugdale, and he'd offered her a lift home. Ever such a nice gentleman, Mr Dugdale, and a very successful businessman. He was very impressed with Sharon, he was even thinking of offering her a job in his office as his personal secretary.

Jake was beginning to appreciate that there was another journalistic skill he needed to master: knowing when it was best to keep things to himself.

The Reverend Stanley and The Captain were both out and about that afternoon. After morning service and lunch, the Reverend climbed into his Morris Minor and drove down to Griffiths Park. He stopped at the side of the road and looked at his watch. When the hands were exactly at two o'clock he set off again, driving at a steady 30 miles an hour.

He headed out of town onto the main Cardiff road and drove until he reached the industrial estate. Keeping his speed constant, he continued along the road as it passed through the factories and assembly workshops on either side until he reached a point roughly in the middle of the estate, where the buildings were set back a little from the road. He pulled into a lay-by just past a pedestrian footbridge and checked his watch again. The minute hand was just short of a quarter past – so, he calculated, a journey of around 14 minutes.

Then Stanley drove on until he came to a roundabout; going all the way round it, he took the exit that led him back onto the road to Edwardstown.

There wasn't a great deal of traffic, but one vehicle which did pass him going towards Cardiff was The Captain's Land Rover. The Captain too was driving carefully and well within the speed limit. He slowed as he approached the pedestrian bridge, then he too pulled into the lay-by.

He got out, walked back to the bridge and climbed the steps. Half way across he leant over the parapet and looked down onto the road below. The side of the bridge was a solid metal sheet that came up to the Captain's chest and mostly obscured anyone on it from the traffic below. Raising his arms, he found he could easily reach over it.

He noted that the footpath below him was set back from the road edge by a wide grass verge, then diverted further away to go around the steps to the bridge. A small service road ran between the pavement and the row of terraced houses set even further back.

On the other side of the main carriageway was another grass verge and another service road that led into a group of industrial buildings; at the weekend, they were all shut and deserted.

The Captain went back into the Land Rover and, following the route the Reverend had taken shortly before, drove home.

By Monday morning, Jake had decided not to tell anyone of his suspicions about Siôn. Other than the Land Rover and the sticker, there didn't seem to be a lot of hard evidence. Admittedly, the voice and the build were similar, but then again there wasn't a shortage of tallish, slimish men with local accents in the area, and he'd never seen the face of the GLF man.

Least said, soonest mended, thought Jake. No point in stirring up trouble, especially for himself. But he'd have a head start in any future dealings with the GLF.

The Captain had spent Sunday evening mulling over his plans, and at breakfast on the Monday morning in the farmhouse he divulged them to Siôn.

'We're going to kidnap the Lord Lieutenant.'

The spoonful of cornflakes that was en route from a bowl on the table to Siôn's mouth stopped in mid-air.

'What??'

'We're going to kidnap the Lord Lieutenant.'

The cornflakes went back into the bowl.

'How? When??'

'When he comes to rededicate the war memorial.'

'Goronwy, I may be wrong but I would guess there'll be a few coppers around then, not to mention maybe some soldiers who may well be armed. I think the chances of us grabbing the Lord Lieutenant while they stand by and watch are pretty slim.'

'Absolutely, Siôn, but we're not going to do it at the ceremony. I've checked and he's going to be driving back to Cardiff immediately after he's been to a reception the council are organising in the Pavilion following the rededication. He'll be on his own. There's a pedestrian bridge over the road roughly half way through the industrial estate. We're going to be on that and when he drives underneath, we're going to stop his car. Then we rush up, bundle him into the Land Rover and drive him off.'

'How are you going to stop his car? Thumb a lift?'

'No', said The Captain, in careful, measured tones. 'I'll have a bucketful of paint. When he drives underneath, I'll tip it over the windscreen.'

'Isn't that a bit dangerous? What if he crashes the car?'

'It'll be no worse than a windscreen shattering. He'll still be able to see out of the side windows, so he should be able to steer it into the side of the road fairly easily. I've checked, there's a grass verge between the road and the pavement so there's enough room even if he gets it a bit wrong.'

'And where are we going to take him?'

'There's an old shepherd's hut on the mountain behind Gwaelod. We can get the Land Rover about half way up the track and leave it in the trees; it's autumn, remember, it'll be dark by then. We get him out and walk the rest of the way. I'll leave some food and water up there the day before.

'You go back down, pick up the Land Rover and get back to Edwardstown. Ring the Western Mail and give them a statement, we can work on that in advance. We'll just say that the GLF have taken the Lord Lieutenant hostage and will be in touch later with their demands. Don't answer any questions. Then come back to the hut.'

To Siôn, it seemed a plan full of holes. Where to start?

'I don't think it will take them long to find us, Goronwy.'

'We'll hold him there until midnight, then leave him. He'll be OK overnight, a bit uncomfortable maybe but he'll survive. If we haven't heard he's been found by the morning, we'll ring again and tell them where he is.'

Siôn thought for a while in silence.

'How long do you think we'll get for it if they do catch us?'

The Captain hadn't even thought about that. He didn't much care, but he suddenly realised what he was asking Siôn to do. His nephew could spend years in jail and come out with a criminal record that would stay with him for the rest of his life. He couldn't ask that of him.

'You don't have to do it. I can manage on my own.'

175

'You can't. You'll need help getting him out of the car and into the Land Rover, then you need two people in the Land Rover, one to drive, one to hang on to the prisoner, otherwise he's just going to try to get free. You need someone to drive the Land Rover back from the mountain otherwise it's going to be spotted sooner rather than later, and you need someone to make the phone call. There's no phone up there and you don't want to leave the Brigadier alone.'

'I'll tie him up or something. Perhaps you could just do the phone call to the Western Mail?'

They argued for a while then arrived at a compromise. Siôn would drive The Captain to the bridge but then rather than wait there together, he'd take the Land Rover back to Edwardstown and go to the rededication ceremony, making sure he was seen. Then he would follow the Lord Lieutenant when he left the reception after making sure the number plates of the Land Rover were obscured with mud, a not uncommon sight in farming country.

Siôn would have an old sweater and his scarf in the vehicle; as soon as the car was stopped, Siôn would jump out with the scarf around his face and help bundle their prisoner into the Land Rover, blindfold him then drive to the hut. He'd leave them there, dump the scarf and his sweater on the way back to Edwardstown, make the phone call and then go home.

What they'd tell the police depended on when the police showed up. The Captain would walk home after leaving his prisoner and reckoned to be back on the farm by early morning. If the police turned up after that, The Captain would say he'd spent the day on the farm, as Siôn had taken the Land Rover to the ceremony; Siôn would confirm he'd left The Captain there in the morning when he'd gone to the rededication and The Captain had still been there when he got home.

If the police turned up before The Captain got back, the story would be that Siôn had dropped The Captain at the railway station on his way to the service. When he eventually showed up, The Captain would say he'd fancied a day out. He'd caught a train to Cardiff and had a few too many to drink; he'd run out of money and ended up thumbing a lift home.

It wasn't foolproof but his uncle was the man who'd taken Siôn in and bought him up, and Siôn felt he owed him this much at least.

But he had a bad feeling about the whole business.

In the vicarage, the Reverend Stanley was sitting at his desk, leaning his chin on his knitted fingers and gazing out into the garden. Now, in late October, it looked ragged and unkempt. One of his parishioners looked after it for him, a labour of love, and by late spring it would be a riot of colour with the lawn carefully mowed and the flower borders neatly weeded. The Reverend Stanley loved to sit there then; it was one of the few places where the anger that seemed to consume him almost all the time subsided, and he could find some peace.

He crossed to the mantelpiece and picked up the framed photograph of the group of soldiers, gazing at it intently for a while, running a thumb along the line of smiling young faces. He carried it over to the desk, set it squarely in front of him then sat back in his chair and gazed again into the garden.

Spring, and peace, seemed very far away.

Amanda had done a lot of thinking on her train journey back to London and in her bedroom that night. When she came down for breakfast the following morning, she'd made her decision.

'I'm going to finish with Jake', she announced to her parents. Her mother was bustling around the kitchen, her father was, as usual, at the far end of the table, invisible behind the Daily Telegraph. The paper rustled slightly and a muted grunt came from behind it.

'Really, darling?' said her mother, dropping two slices of white bread into the toaster. 'That's a shame, I always thought he was rather a nice boy. Have you argued about something?'

'No. We just seem to have run out of steam somehow. I don't really know why exactly, it just doesn't seem to be right any more.'

'Well there'll be plenty more fish in the sea, I'm sure. I met your father when I was eighteen and I thought then he was frightfully dashing, but there were two or three others after me as well', she said coquettishly. The Daily Telegraph didn't react.

'When are you going to tell him?' she continued.

'I suppose I should go down again and do it face to face. We've been together quite a while and it seems a bit cruel just to do it over the phone, especially as he'd either be standing in his landlady's hallway with her listening behind the kitchen door or in a public phone box with people queuing up outside. And a letter just seems really heartless.'

'I suppose that's the kindest thing to do, although it's a bit of a nuisance. When will you go?'

'I might as well do it this Saturday. I'm helping Sarah on her market stall all this week and he'll be working anyway. Mind you, I think he's working on Saturday too, they're rededicating the town's war memorial or something and he's got to go to that, but I could meet him at lunchtime then probably just come straight back.'

The Telegraph moved slightly sideways and her father's face appeared from behind it.

'Is Ormsby-Kirkwood going to be there?'

'Is who going to be where?' said Amanda.

'Ormsby-Kirkwood. He's the Lord Lieutenant of the county. I was friendly with him at Sandhurst and we were in the same unit in the army for a while. We're not in touch any more but I see his name cropping up now and then. Rededicating a war memorial is something he'd be likely to be involved in. If he is there, give him my best wishes, will you?'

And he disappeared behind his newspaper again.

In the Enquirer's office, things seemed much as normal. Lotte smiled warmly at Jake as she came in and greeted him with 'fun night, Saturday, wasn't it?' but hadn't referred to it again. Roland and Rosemary were beavering away in their respective offices and Terry was exacting severe punishment on his typewriter keys.

But when the chief reporter finished his story, he paused on his way out of the office ("Just off down the nick, Lotts") by Jake's chair and leant down towards him.

'Have you heard any more from that Welsh Liberation Front?' he asked in a conspiratorially hushed voice.

'No. Why?'

'A couple of the boys were telling me there was a bloke in The Colliers the other week, west Wales accent, not a local. Someone had seen him drinking in The Llew earlier on and he was moaning in The Colliers that he'd missed his train back. He'd obviously decided to wait for the next one in the pub and it must have been a long time coming because he'd had a few by then.'

Terry leant in even closer to Jake.

'He also started talking about the bomb on the railway line and how we shouldn't think that was the last we'd heard of the GLF. Of course the boys were trying to get more out of him, but he wouldn't say anything else, just a nod and a wink and 'watch out for something.' So you might want to keep your car to the ground.'

179

'OK, Terry, thanks.'

Indiscreet comments in the pub. It was probably just a fantasist trying to get a little bit of notoriety and letting the beer do the talking, thought Jake, but you never knew.

Jake wasn't the only one Terry had shared that information with. He'd mentioned it to Inspector Griffiths in the small backstreet pub where they sometimes shared a lunchtime pint. The Inspector had been intrigued enough to check with one of his contacts who drank in Y Llew Goch, and yes, someone like that had been seen there, buying The Captain a drink.

Interesting, thought Inspector Griffiths. When he went back to the office, he taken the original letter to the Free Wales Army out of the drawer and put it into a file that already contained the GLF communiqués and his notes on his visit to The Captain's farm. It was labelled in large red letters 'BOMB ATTACK'.

Amanda was in the shower when Siôn rang. She'd just rinsed her hair when her mother banged on the door and called 'There's a boy on the phone for you, he sounds very Welsh – Siôn, is it? Shall I tell him you'll call back?'

'No, no, tell him to hang on. I'll take it in your room, if that's OK.'

Two minutes later, still very damp and wrapped in a bath towel, Amanda picked up the phone from the table beside her parents' bed.

'Hello?'

'Oh hi', said Siôn. He'd been screwing up his courage for most of the afternoon to make this call. He had no idea what he was going to talk about but he knew that it was important, that somehow things were moving to a different stage, and he was desperately keen to get it right.

His resolve to be cool, calm and in control melted as soon as he heard her voice.

'Where are you?' said Amanda.

'At home. Goronwy's out in the fields somewhere, so I thought I'd just take the chance to give you a ring.' That made it seem, he thought, as though it was a spur-of-the-moment whim rather than something he'd been thinking about since he last saw her. 'What about you? Have I caught you at a bad time?'

'I was in the shower, actually, so now I'm sitting semi-naked and rather wet on my mum's bed.' She paused to let that image sink in. 'I had a nice evening on Saturday, despite the brawl.'

'Me too.'

The conversation meandered on, surprisingly easily for Siôn. After a couple of minutes, he steeled himself.

'I didn't get a chance to say hello to Jake. Things OK with you two?' he asked, as casually as he could. He very much hoped the answer would be 'no'. True, she'd kissed him, but maybe that was just the wine, the music and the soft lights.

There was another pause before Amanda replied.

'Not really. To be honest, things haven't been right for a while.'

'I'm sorry to hear that', lied Siôn.

'I think things have changed, for both of us. There's no bad feeling, it's just that, well, I think we lived in a bit of a bubble at Aber and when you get out into the big wide world everything's different. And I suppose it's a natural time to make changes.'

'So what changes are you thinking of making?'

'I'm going to tell him it's over between us, that we both need to move on. I'll come down this Saturday, probably.'

Siôn hesitated. He didn't want to push things too fast.

'Will I get a chance to see you?'

'I don't think so. It wouldn't be very nice of me to end a relationship that's meant a lot to us both then go straight on to meet someone else. It's a small place, isn't it, and he'd be very hurt if he got to hear about it.'

'Fair enough, I can see that.'

'But I would like to see you again soon. I'd really like that.'

Siôn took a very deep breath.

'OK then. Well, I'll give you a call again next week, shall I?'

'That would be lovely. Bye. Thanks for calling.'

'Bye.'

Siôn put the phone back into its cradle, jumped up from the stool he was perched on and punched the air, twice.

Amanda sat on the bed and stared unseeing at the pattern on the bedroom carpet for a minute. Then she sighed and picked up the phone again. No point in putting it off.

Chapter 21

As soon as Mrs P called up the stairs, Jake knew this wasn't going to be good news.

'Mr Nash! Your young lady is on the telephone for you.'

Amanda was supposed to call tomorrow. As Jake trudged down to the hallway, a cold hand clasped his heart.

'Hiya – nice surprise!' His forced cheerfulness didn't sound remotely convincing. Amanda didn't waste any time.

'Hello Jake. I know you're working on Saturday, but if I came down then, could we get a little time to ourselves? There's something I need to talk to you about.'

'Well, I'm going to be pretty busy in the day. How about coming down the following weekend? We could have a night out in Cardiff.'

'No, let's do this Saturday. How about if I catch an early train, I'll get the connection up to Edwardstown and we'll just see if we can grab some time somewhere?'

He drew a deep breath. 'I'll come down to Cardiff and pick you up, I'm not going to be busy till around lunchtime. I'll give you a quick call from the office on Friday morning.'

The following morning, Roland called him into his office

'Morning Jake. Got much on today?'

'No, I need to write up the crowded classrooms story but that won't take too long.'

Roland pushed a letter across the desk towards him.

'Give this gentleman a ring and arrange to see him, will you? Gerwyn Price, secretary of the local historical society. They're starting a project on tracing family histories; he might have a few good examples already, could make a nice little human interest piece.'

'Right', said Jake and picking up the letter, turned to leave.

'You're looking a bit haggard this morning', said Roland. 'Night out last night?'

Jake smiled wanly back at his boss. 'No, just didn't sleep too well.'

Mr Price was busy all day, but Jake arranged to call in at his home on the outskirts of the town around half past four that evening.

When Gerwyn Price opened his front door, he turned out to be a small, rotund man with glasses and a permanent slightly startled look on his face.

'Mr Price? Jake Nash from the Enquirer. I arranged to call by about now to talk about the family history project?'

'Oh yes, absolutely. I didn't expect to see you though'.

Jake was puzzled. 'Why would that be?'

'Well I just thought that with that young boy being killed, you'd all be busy with that.'

It took a couple of seconds for Jake to take it in.

'Young boy killed?' he repeated.

'Digging for coal in the river bank. He'd made a tunnel but the roof fell in on top of him and buried him. A couple of the local boys were fishing nearby; they heard his mates shouting and went to get him out but it was too late.'

'Where? When?'

'About half a mile down the road, I think, a couple of hours ago.'

Making hurried apologies, Jake started backing away from the door. 'Don't you worry, boy, history isn't going to go away, you get on with it', Gerwyn called after him as Jake ran back to the Popular and drove as fast as he dared in the direction the history man had indicated. He could occasionally see the river running to the right and below the road, vanishing now and then behind clumps of trees or as the road turned away, but there were no signs of any activity. After a mile he found a small pub. Pulling up outside, he went into the nearly empty public bar and asked a man cleaning glasses behind the pumps if he'd heard anything about the tragedy.

'Oh aye, there's the two who pulled him out', he said, nodding towards two middle-aged men who sat at a table near the window.

Jake steadied himself and, with a fierce effort to quell the butterflies that had suddenly taken flight in his stomach, walked over to them. They were sitting silently, one staring out of the window into the gathering darkness, the other focussing on his hands clasped around his pint glass.

'I'm sorry to bother you, I'm Jake Nash from the Enquirer. I'm told you were the men who pulled the little boy out from the river bank?'

The man studying his hands didn't react, but the other turned his gaze away from the window and towards Jake. He looked very tired.

'Aye, that's right son. Poor little bugger.'

'I know you must be very upset, but could you tell me a bit more about it?'

The man thought for a second.

'Aye, I suppose that would be all right.' He pushed a stool towards Jake with his foot.

As Gerwyn had said, they'd been fishing in the river when they'd heard the boy's friends yelling. At first they'd thought it was just part of their play but then two young lads had come running up, shouting something about their friend being buried. The men had sent them up to the pub, about half a mile away, to tell any grown-up in there to ring for the police and then gone back along the bank in the direction the boys had come from.

A couple of hundred yards away they found three more boys desperately scrambling at a collapsed stretch of the bank. They'd taken over the digging and after ten minutes one of them, the man still holding the glass and who'd yet to speak, had felt a small, still warm hand beneath the earth. They'd cleared the rest of the fall away from the boy as quickly as they could.

But they could tell straight away that it was too late.

The rescuer holding his glass looked up for the first time. 'We were miners, see. We've seen it before', he said wearily.

Jake thanked them, made a note of their names and addresses then, as he got up to leave, the man spoke again.

'No bloody heroics, now. We were only doing what anyone would have done.' He turned back to his glass and resumed his silent contemplation.

Jake often wondered, in the years to come, about the nature of disasters and his reaction to them. Perhaps it was what made reporters able to do their job – the ability to fence off normal human emotions and to focus on getting the story. He had a younger brother, Matt, and some time later he realised how devastated he would be if anything happened to him. But at that moment he couldn't help but feel a sense of excitement as he rang Roland from the pub's payphone.

Excitement, and some satisfaction. A byline on his first story, then the bomb, now being in the right place at the right time and getting those interviews; I do seem to have a talent for this kind of work, he thought.

'Roland? I'm up at Hill View. There's been a young boy killed–'

The editor broke in. "I know, Terry's just phoned it in. What's happening there?'

'Not a lot now actually, but I've got an interview with the two men who pulled him out.' He tried hard not to sound too pleased with himself.

'Right, well done. The boy's name was Derek Chapman, aged 10. His parents live at 45 Deri Terrace. Nip up there and get a photo of the boy.'

Jake was stunned. 'What, now?'

'Yes, now, before everyone else gets them. Bring it in tomorrow.'

Jake drove much more slowly back along the road from the pub, all elation gone and with a sick feeling in his stomach. How you could possibly ask the parents of a boy who'd gone out to play with friends that morning and who would never come home for a photograph of him within hours of them hearing such tragic news?

He found Deri Terrace and parked opposite number 45. The curtains were drawn, but he could see light in the window over the front door. He sat for quite a long time, then he made a decision.

'I just couldn't do it, Gareth.'

The two sat in the front room, facing each other in the two armchairs on either side of the sofa.

'To lose a child, then have someone banging on the front door asking for a picture of him – it just seemed incredibly callous.'

Gareth looked at Jake, not unsympathetically, but Jake could tell this wasn't going to be an acceptable excuse.

'It's not easy', said Gareth, 'but it's part of the job. I always start by offering my sympathies on behalf of the paper, apologise for the intrusion and ask if you could have a few quick words. I've always thought that if I'm told to push off, that's what I'd do, but it's never happened.

'People react in different ways, you'll be surprised. Sometimes there'll be a neighbour or relative there who'll talk to you because the family are too upset to see anyone, sometimes the family actually want to talk to you. Everyone they know is probably equally upset, so someone who's sympathetic but detached, who'll just listen, it helps with the grief.

'And like I say, it comes with the territory.'

At five past nine the following morning, Jake rang the bell at 45 Deri Terrace. He heard the chimes die away somewhere in the back of the house then, through the glass panel in the front door, saw the shape of someone approaching down the hall. Jake took a deep breath.

The door swung open and Jake faced a haggard looking man in his thirties. From behind him, two small boys peered around his legs. The man didn't say anything.

'Mr Chapman? I'm from the Enquirer. I'm very sorry to disturb you at this time, I know it must be very difficult, but I wonder if you could spare me just a few minutes?'

The man nodded and stepped back. 'Go into the front room there.'

Jake stepped past Mr Chapman and the two younger boys, who were staring at him with the unselfconsciousness of the very young. The front room door was shut; Jake turned the handle, and the door began to swing open. The room was in semi-darkness, the heavy curtains drawn, and the first thing that he saw was the end of a coffin. In that instant, he appreciated exactly what the sensation described as 'having your heart in your mouth' actually felt like.

He had never seen a body. The few elderly and distant relatives who'd passed out of his life so far had disappeared first into hospitals or nursing homes, and he'd encountered them next when he stood with his parents as they were carried, safely out of sight, into church. He'd sympathised with others who'd felt the loss more keenly but there'd always been a sense of a timely passing, a life come to an appropriate end, and the whole process had seemed somehow remote from the once living person who was now gone.

But he'd been told about the Welsh tradition of funerals in which the body lay in the family home for a few days before burial. Friends and relatives came there to pay their respects and the funeral cortege went straight from the home to the cemetery. That much he knew, but he wasn't quite sure whether the coffin was left open or not. And he was equally unsure about how he was going to react if it was.

The door swung back with agonising slowness, revealing more of the casket as it went. To Jake's immense relief, it was shut. Derek Chapman and the boys followed Jake in and they arranged themselves on either side of the coffin, which lay on two trestles in the centre of the room.

Jake cleared his throat. 'I wonder if you had a photo of Derek I could borrow, Mr Chapman, for the paper? We'll get it back to you, of course.'

'You're a bit late, boy, the other reporters have taken most of them,' Mr Chapman said in a way that Jake could only think of as brisk. Jake's heart sank. This wasn't going to go down too well back in the office.

'Hang on by there and I'll see what I can find.' He left the room and Jake could hear him climbing the stairs.

The reporter and the two boys, both still staring unabashedly at him from the other side of the coffin, stood in silence for a few moments.

'That's our Derek in there', said one of them finally.

'Yes', said Jake. He couldn't think of anything else to say.

Mr Chapman came back into the room, switching on the light as he did so. He walked to the coffin and spread a handful of snaps on its highly polished wooden lid. 'These are all that's left, I'm afraid.'

They weren't very good. Some were of Derek when he was much younger, but there were a couple of slightly blurred ones that were more recent, one of him behind a sandcastle on a beach, another of him and another boy on bikes. Jake asked if he could take those two and slid them into his notebook. He desperately wanted to be out in the open air again.

'Thank you very much, Mr Chapman. As I said, I'll make sure these are returned to you. And on behalf of the paper, our deepest sympathies.'

Mr Chapman nodded. 'Aye, well. I'll show you out.'

Jake was right. Roland was not impressed.

He put the two photographs side by side, looked at them and sniffed. 'Not nearly as good as the Western Mail's this morning.'

'No. I think they must have got there a bit before me.'

'They must have been pretty fast off the mark then.'

Jake stayed silent.

'Did you get anything from the parents? What he was like as a boy, brothers and sisters, what he like doing best, anything like that.'

'Er, no.'

'Why not?'

'The dad seemed pretty upset and there was no sign of the mum, so I didn't like to push it.'

'Did you try the neighbours?'

Jake shook his head. 'Shall I go back?'

Roland shook his head. 'No, I'll get Lotte to do it. Go and write up what those two told you about digging him out.'

As Jake turned to go, Roland looked up. 'There's a bit more to this job than the ability to turn a nicely crafted sentence, Mr Nash. You might want to have a think about that before you commit yourself to it.' He returned to his moody study of the pictures.

Jake went back into the reporters' room, sat down heavily in front of one of the typewriters and gazed miserably at its empty roller.

Lotte barely had time to say hello when she arrived a few minutes later before Roland called her into his office. Jake, looking through his notes from the day before, could hear the low murmuring of a short conversation, then she came out. As she passed behind his chair, she paused briefly and put a hand on his back, the tips of her fingers resting lightly on his neck.

'Are you OK?'

Jake sighed. 'Not really. I don't think I was quite ready for all that.'

Her thumb gently rubbed the skin on his neck. 'Don't worry about it. We'll talk later.' Then she was gone.

Jake phoned Gerwyn Price and arranged to meet him later that morning, then began writing up his story. He'd nearly finished by the time Lotte came back.

'How did it go?' he asked.

'OK', she said, draping her jacket over the chair opposite his and fishing her notebook out of her bag. 'His mum was there and she wanted to talk; the rest of the family are just in a state of shock. How's your stuff going?'

He nodded to the small pile of paper next to his typewriter. 'Nearly finished.'

'Chuck it over here when you're done, I'll work it into mine.'

For a while, the only sound in the room was the two typewriters clattering, then Jake pulled a final sheet from his machine, put it face down on top of the others, then turned the pile over and began reading them through. He made a couple of corrections, then tapped the sheets together and pushed them across the desk to Lotte.

'There you go. I'm going to nip up and see the bloke I should have seen yesterday before all this started; probably back just after lunch if there are any queries.'

'I'm sure it'll be fine.'

Jake snorted. She looked up at him.

'Look, there's a pub about three miles out of town on the road to Merthyr, on the left, set back a bit, The Black Lion. Why don't I meet you there about eight tonight? I'll buy you a pint to cheer you up, and you can tell me why you think you'll never ever become a reporter.'

Jake was surprised.

'That would be nice, thanks.' He paused. 'What about what's his name, the boyfriend?'

She smiled. 'One of the advantages of this job, we work irregular hours so it's always easy to get out if you want to. Anyway, it's his darts night so he won't be bothered, and he doesn't bloody own me. And it's only a drink, isn't it?'

Jake smiled back. 'Absolutely. Just a drink.'

The Black Lion was a quiet, old-fashioned pub with dark walls, a low ceiling, weak lights and a big fire. Jake and Lotte sat side by side on an upholstered high-backed bench, warmed by the logs burning in the fireplace.

The prospect of meeting Lotte had improved Jake's mood from the moment they'd made the arrangement. Inclined by nature to look on the bright side, he was already in a slightly more optimistic frame of mind by the time they'd got their drinks and settled into the quiet corner seat. At first they'd talked about what he perceived to be his catastrophic failure to do a decent job, but she'd reassured him that it really wasn't that bad. She'd echoed Gareth's words; it was a necessary part of the job that no one particularly enjoyed but it got easier with experience. And when Jake said he thought Roland would never trust him again, she'd laughed.

'He's never Mr Sunshine at the best of times. I think that somewhere there's a course all editors go on in grumpiness. He likes to exercise it every now and then just to keep us on our toes.'

She put a hand on his arm.

'Listen, you had a good start but you were a bit lucky, and a little reality check may be what you need. No one gets it right every time. I don't think your Pulitzer Prize is just over the horizon but that's no reason to chuck your toys out of the pram and give it all up.'

Jake felt a great surge of gratitude towards her. They had another drink, the conversation drifted away from work to more general topics and the gloom that had hung around Jake during the day continued to lift. She was easy to be with; they seemed to share a sense of humour and a view of the world.

And on a more physical level, he was increasingly aware of the warmth of her thigh against his and the swell of her breasts under the shirt she was wearing. Neither of them had spoken about the Press Ball but he hadn't forgotten the softness of her body that night and the kiss they'd nearly, so nearly shared.

'Do you miss Amanda?' asked Lotte.

'Oh sure', he replied automatically. But he wasn't sure any more. He missed something, certainly; sex, of course, but something else they had once shared but seemed to have vanished. He thought about telling Lotte that he was pretty confident that he and Amanda didn't have long to run, but decided against it. He didn't really want to talk about Amanda.

'I guess you'd miss Richard too. Not that you're likely to be apart at any time in the future, I suppose.'

'No, I suppose not. But yes, I would miss him. We've been together a long time, we do get on really well, and as I said, the families like each other and......' Her voice trailed away, and she gave a small shrug.

'And like I said, that's enough, is it?' said Jake.

Lotte held his gaze for a very long second or so, then slapped him playfully on the leg. 'Come on. Don't forget the police have breathalysers now, and we've both got to drive.'

The Black Lion's car park was bordered on three sides by trees. They'd arrived at virtually the same time and their cars were next to each other in the dark and virtually empty car park. Jake walked Lotte to her car door; she unlocked it, then turned to him.

'Thanks, it's been a nice evening.'

'Thank you for the pep talk, and for the company.'

Then he leant forward and kissed her gently, briefly on the lips. When he pulled back, she didn't move. Then she took a breath.

'Do you want to sit in the car for a bit?' she said quietly.

She turned and unlocked her door, then sliding behind the steering wheel, she leant across to open the passenger door as Jake walked round. He was almost unbearably excited. He'd been faithful to Amanda since they'd started seeing each other and the anticipation of what he thought, of what he desperately hoped, might be about to happen was just...intoxicating. As he got in, she started the engine, then turned to him, smiling brightly. 'Might as well keep warm.'

Please, please, he silently prayed, don't let me be wrong about this. Then, very suddenly, they were kissing. For Jake, it was overwhelming – her tongue in his mouth, her hair, her taste, her hand behind his head, pulling him closer. He felt the fierce desire he'd once felt for Amanda surging through him; he slid his hand from her waist to tentatively cup her breast. She didn't seem to mind, and he increased the pressure, feeling its softness. They pulled apart briefly to draw breath; she gazed steadily at him, her eyes bright, then pulled him back to her. His hand slid down to her thigh – suspenders! Oh, God. His hand went

194

further down to the hem of her skirt, then slid underneath it, pushing up. The tops of her stocking, then the magic touch of soft, warm skin. Gently, persistently up...

Then her hand was no longer entwined in his hair but against his chest, pushing against him. She shook her head.

'Jake, stop.'

He pulled his hand away and, reacting to the pressure of hers, sat back, alarmed that he'd messed it all up. 'Sorry, sorry, I was being a bit pushy.'

'No, you weren't', she said, pulling her skirt down but not looking at him. 'It's my fault.'

She stared silently into the darkness of the car park for a few moments, then sighed and turned to him.

'Look, I really like you. But if this starts, where's it going to end? You break up with Amanda – no, don't interrupt - I finish with Richard, ructions all round, then in two years you bugger off somewhere and we either break up or I have to trail around after you, trying to find jobs while you move smoothly upwards. Which you will.'

Jake shook his head fiercely. 'After my recent performance, I don't think I'll ever get beyond covering garden fetes and beautiful baby contests. But anyway, how can any of us know how things are going to work out, Lotte?'

Among the many emotions he was feeling –desire, confusion, a faint hope that this might still turn out as he hoped – exasperation pushed its way to the front of the queue.

'It just seems to me that settling for what you know deep down is second best, because you're frightened that if you don't things might possibly get worse, isn't much of an option.'

'Besides', and exasperation turned to irritation, 'playing photographers with Reg doesn't seem to bother you too much.' Oh shit, he thought. I shouldn't have said that.

He was right.

'Ah, that's it, is it?' Her tone was a couple of degrees colder. 'Not that it's any of your business but for what it's worth, that's never going to disrupt anything. He's not going anywhere, things aren't going to change because of... it's not even a relationship, we're just friends.'

She looked out of the window again. 'But you're right. I'm not doing myself any favours there, am I?'

Lotte turned back to him and put a hand out to take his. 'Not the greatest of ends to a nice evening. I'm sorry, Jake, but it's only going to ever end in tears. Can we be friends, please? Good friends?'

Jake looked at her for a few seconds, then shrugged and smiled. God, she was gorgeous. 'I think you're wrong about where it might go but yes, of course we can be friends. Why wouldn't we be?'

He leant across, kissed her on the cheek then got out and walked back to his car. As he started the engine, he glanced across. She'd turned on the interior light and was redoing her makeup in the driver's mirror. When she finished, she put her bag on the passenger seat, turned and with a small smile, waved briefly to him. He watched her as she drove off.

Professional failure, love life in tatters... I should have stayed in St Albans and worked for the council, thought Jake. He put the Popular into gear and slowly bounced across the car park to the main road.

Lotte pulled up outside her parents' home, switched off the engine and sat for a while in the car, her hands resting on the steering wheel. The curtains of the front room were drawn but there was a small gap through which she could see the blue and white flickering of the television screen. It was what her mum and dad did most nights, stay home and watch the telly.

She got out of the car, locked it and walked up the garden path. As she opened the front door, her shoulders went back, she smiled brightly and called out into the darkness of the hall 'Hiya, I'm home.'

How can we know how things are going to turn out, Jake had asked her. You can't, she thought, of course you can't. But sometimes you can make a pretty good guess.

Chapter 22

The rededication ceremony was going to be a difficult one to get right. Coming just over a week before Remembrance Sunday, it hadn't felt appropriate to plan a full-blown military affair, but there were still veterans of the First World War alive and active in the town, and more who remembered relatives lost in that and subsequent wars.

Many of the councillors were acutely aware of the resentment that had been caused when the memorial had been dismantled and moved from its original site, and they were anxious that the rededication be an occasion of dignity and reverence. The memorial had been rebuilt in a green and wooded area of the park exactly as it had been but with the addition of a new inscription recording the move, and the council had been delighted when Ormsby-Kirkwood had agreed to attend; to have an eminent military man bestow his favour upon the project was, they felt, some form of official vindication of their decision.

For Councillor Jones, chair of the committee that had overseen this delicate task, it had been a busy, not to say anxious, week. He'd checked and rechecked the arrangements, but as he awoke that Saturday morning he lay in bed looking at the slight crack in the ceiling immediately over his head, running through the plans for the day again in his mind. He'd just come to the part where he was standing to accept, in a modest and humble way, the grateful thanks of the dignitaries assembled in the Pavilion, when his wife brought in his morning cup of tea. Everything seemed to be in order.

Jake had other things on his mind as he drove down the valley. The weather matched his mood; it was a gloomy day, dry but with the threat of rain constantly in the air, and the dark clouds hung low in the sky.

When he and Lotte had met in the office the morning after their night out at the Black Lion she'd been as friendly as ever, but Jake had the feeling that a door had been closed which would not be reopened.

He'd rung Amanda as early as he could. She'd already left and it was her mother, Celia, who'd told Jake what train she'd be on. Jake and Celia had always got on well and enjoyed a little chat when they saw or spoke to each other, but this time, she'd been brief and to the point. Apart from a polite 'How are you getting on?' she'd simply answered his few questions, and her 'Goodbye Jake' at the end of the call had sounded ominously final.

He'd been standing by the ticket barrier for about ten minutes when he saw her coming towards him. She was wearing the suede coat again, her red hair moved and shone as she walked and he felt that familiar tug at his heart. She gave him a small smile and a quick hug, then they walked to his car. On the way back to Edwardstown the conversation didn't exactly bubble, but they maintained some kind of dialogue about this and that: friends, family, what they'd both been doing.

Jake drove to the Pavilion car park and they walked back through the park to Tolaini's. She found the quietest table she could and when he came back carrying the coffee cups, they sat and looked at each other. She held his gaze in silence for a few seconds, her head tipped quizzically to one side.

'It's not really working any more, is it?' she said finally, gently.

He thought afterwards that it was much like someone close to you dying: you may have known it was going to happen for a while, you may even know, deep down, that it's for the best, but that doesn't soften the impact. He felt slightly sick and he could feel his eyes prickling. Don't cry, he told himself, don't you bloody dare cry.

He put both hands across the table and covered hers with them.

'I know it hasn't been going that well, but I thought maybe it's just a bad patch. We could make it work again, couldn't we?'

She turned her hands to grasp his and squeezed them. 'I don't think so.'

'I remember the night I first met you at that disco', said Jake. 'I'd seen you around a few times, but we'd never spoken and I thought you were right out of my league. I was with Rhodri, and you were with your mate, the one with the blond hair and irritating laugh – '

'Nicky'.

'Yes, Nicky. Rhodri said let's go and ask them to dance. I didn't think I stood a chance, but he was dead set on Nicky and I thought, well, one dance and what the hell, can't let a mate down.'

''We'd been watching you for a bit. You looked absolutely terrified when you finally did come over, but it was sort of sweet. And I'd fancied you for ages.'

'I didn't have a clue.'

'Men never do.'

They both smiled at that.

Jake asked the question he didn't really want an answer to.

'So, do you fancy someone else now?'

She hesitated momentarily. 'No, no one else. It's just that... I think what we had was wonderful, I had so much fun with you and you're a lovely person. But somehow it was of its time, and now we're out in the big wide world, we seem to have left it behind.'

For a few seconds they sat in their own small world of sadness, oblivious to the hustle and bustle, the everyday life around them. Then he sighed and gently slid his hands away from hers.

'OK. What do you want to do now?'

'I'll go back home.'

'I've got to cover this rededication thing but if you can kill time for a couple of hours, I'll drive you down afterwards.'

'That's fine, I'll come with you. Dad asked me to say hello to a friend of his he thought might be there anyway – Ormsby-Kirkwood?'

'Yes, he'll be there. He's kind of the star of the show, actually.'

They stood, and as they turned to leave, she reached out and grasped his hand.

'Thank you. Thanks for it all.'

He managed a small smile. 'Yeah, you too.'

As he pulled his coat on, he had a thought. 'I rather lost touch with Rhodri after that disco. What happened with him and Nicky?'

'They're getting married next year. I'm a bridesmaid.'

Obviously, thought Jake, he didn't find her laugh quite as irritating as I did. Fingers crossed for them it stays that way.

There were no marching bands or mass of waving banners at the memorial. Each branch of the armed forces was represented by a single figure, and three members of the local British Legion carried their flag, the Union Jack and the Welsh Red Dragon. Youth organisations from the town, army and air cadets, scouts and guides, had been distributing a short order of service as people arrived; now they formed a single group.

The memorial itself was a rectangle of three steps, on which was a central block of granite inscribed on four sides with the names of the men and women of Edwardstown who had given their lives in war. Mounted on the granite block was the statue of a soldier, his head bowed and his rifle reversed, muzzle down, in the traditional attitude of mourning.

There was a new inscription carved into the stone of the top step: '*This memorial was erected by the people of Edwardstown in 1922, in grateful memory of their relatives, friends and neighbours who made the ultimate sacrifice for their country. It was moved from its original site in Cyfartha Road to this location in 1968. In peace and tranquillity, we will remember them.*'

The dignitaries had gathered on the top step on either side of the inscription, facing a crowd of around a hundred people. Many of them wore medals, some the faded berets of different regiments and branches of the services. Jake and Amanda stood with Reg, slightly to one side of the crowd.

The chairman of the council spoke first, recalling the disquiet that the decision to move the memorial had caused in the town. He hoped that all could now agree that this new location was a more than fitting alternative, and he thanked Councillor Arthur Jones and his committee for their hard work in ensuring that the transfer had been carried out smoothly and in good time for the Remembrance Sunday ceremonies. Councillor Jones nodded gravely in response, then the chairman introduced the Lord Lieutenant.

Brigadier Nigel Ormsby-Kirkwood cut a splendid figure in his smartly cut dark blue uniform with its silver braid and the Prince of Wales feathers against the red band around his hat. He wasn't tall but he held himself erect and his voice carried out clearly over the crowd.

When he had heard of the plan to move the memorial, he said, he too had been disturbed. But he had gone on to reflect that while we carried the past with us, we live in today, and the needs of today often mean that we must accept that some things must change.

'But standing with you now in the quiet of this park, I am content that the sacrifice of those who are named on this monument is not, and will not be, forgotten. Their names live forever more, and the presence of you all here at the rededication of this monument to these brave men and women, which has been so carefully and lovingly reconstructed, is evidence of that.'

He paused for a few seconds.

'I shall now ask the padre to lead us in prayer.'

The Reverend Stanley stepped forward, flanked by two non-conformist ministers. They read a prayer, each taking a paragraph in turn. After the amen, all bowed their heads as a bugler from the South Wales Borderers regiment played The Last Post.

The last strains of that sad call died away across the park, and after a few seconds silence, the Reverend asked them all to join together in singing 'Abide With Me'. Then the chairman thanked everyone for attending and hoped to see them on the following Sunday for the Remembrance Day ceremony.

Reg, from a discreet distance, had got the shots that would appear in next week's paper; he said goodbye to Jake and Amanda and left. The crowd began to drift away towards the park gates, and a small group turned in the opposite direction, heading for the Pembroke Pavilion and the civic reception.

When the Reverend Stanley reached the Pavilion, he found one of the council commissionaires on duty there.

'Is there somewhere safe I could slip out of this surplice and cassock and leave my bag, please?' He indicated the heavy leather satchel he was carrying over one shoulder.

'Certainly, Reverend. There's a door just the left as you come in, beside the gents. It's a small storage room, they'll be quite safe in there. I'll keep an eye out.'

'Thank you very much.'

The Reverend found the room, took off his clerical wear and folded it neatly into the satchel. Then he put the bag on the floor behind a chair in the corner and went out to mingle with the other guests.

Amanda was standing on her own in one corner, twirling a glass of warm white wine, watching Jake as he circulated among the guests, notebook in hand. He'd changed, she thought. He seemed at home here, more confident than she'd seen him before, walking up to people much older than him, engaging with them, smiling, nodding, making notes. She wasn't quite sure how she felt; certain that she'd done the right thing, sure, but a little shakier than she thought she would be.

Perhaps coming to the reception had been a mistake, and the drive down to Cardiff was going to be uncomfortable for them both. It might have been better to go straight away; she could have caught a train to Cardiff, there were bound to be trains heading into the city on a Saturday evening. She made up her mind. She'd go and say a quick hello to Ormsby-Whatsisface then walk down to the station.

The Lord Lieutenant's first large whisky and soda had barely touched the sides on its way down, and he was now well into his second; it wasn't a drink that was available to most of the gathering but his secretary had made his alcoholic preference clear when she'd accepted the invitation to the reception. He couldn't abide the cheap plonk they usually dished out at this sort of do, although she hadn't put it quite like that, and they'd made sure that he would have access to a decent Scotch. Not quite as good as the one in the hip flask he'd left in his car, he always found that a little nip before these events set him up nicely, but good enough.

Just at that moment he was particularly thankful for their cumulative effect. It was partially anaesthetising him to the very boring conversation he was locked into with a pompous local councillor, who was telling him at great length of the enormous amount of tact and negotiating skills it had taken to affect the transfer of the memorial. Ormsby-Kirkwood was beginning to wonder if he could decently make a graceful exit before his scheduled departure time and was more than ready to be distracted by the very attractive young lady who tentatively approached them.

'Brigadier Ormsby-Kirkwood? I'm sorry to interrupt–'

He eyed her appreciatively. 'Not at all, my dear.'

'-but I promised my father I'd say hello to you. Harold Harper? I believe you were in the army together for a while.'

'Harry Harper? Good lord, yes. How the devil is he these days?'

'Very well, thank you. Still in insurance but looking forward to retiring.'

'And you're his daughter?'

'Yes – Amanda.' They shook hands. Councillor Jones waited to be introduced; when he realised he wasn't going to be, he mumbled an excuse and drifted disconsolately away.

'And how is your mother – Cynthia?'

'Celia.'

'Of course, Celia, I was at the wedding. Charming woman. Harry and I have rather lost touch over the years, I'm afraid. And what brings you down here?'

'My boyfriend – my ex-boyfriend – is a reporter on the local newspaper. It's just a flying visit, really, I'm going to catch the train back from Cardiff later.'

Ormsby-Kirkwood glanced at his watch. Definitely time to go.

'Look, I'm going back to Cardiff myself. Can I give you a lift? You can tell me what Horrible Harry – sorry,

Army nickname, no offence – has been up to all these years.'

Amanda hesitated, but only briefly. 'Well, that's very kind of you, are you sure it's not an inconvenience?'

'Not at all, the station in Cardiff is barely out of my way and I'd be glad of the company, especially such charming company. I'll just make my farewells. My Bentley's outside, it's the only one in the car park; shall I meet you there in five minutes?'

Across the room, the Reverend Stanley was with the two non-conformist ministers and a small group of parishioners, but he was taking little part in the conversation. Ever since his arrival he'd made sure that the Brigadier was always just within his line of vision. Now he watched as Ormsby-Kirkwood and the young lady he'd been talking to moved apart, and the Brigadier began to say his goodbyes. He murmured his excuses to the group and backed gently away. Then he turned and, more purposefully, headed for the door.

In the far corner of the car park, tucked in between the bushes that lined its boundaries and a caterer's van, Siôn sat in the Land Rover. He'd watched the ceremony from the back of the crowd and he'd seen Amanda with Jake. There was no way of knowing from their body language if she'd told him yet; they didn't seem to talk much but perhaps the occasion had something to do with that. Anyway, much as he might want to, he couldn't risk trying to speak to her, for several reasons.

After the ceremony he'd walked with the group heading out of the park, gradually falling behind them, then he circled back to the car park and the Land Rover. He'd pulled on an old sweater he used for work around the farm and a woolly hat, then wrapped a scarf around his neck and the lower part of his face. It was quite a big car park and this corner was quiet; he was pretty confident he hadn't been noticed there, but he couldn't quell the queasy tension that was knotting his stomach. From where he sat, he could see both the front door of the Pavilion and a large blue Bentley, and his eyes rarely strayed from them.

He leant back into his seat and his hands drummed a nervous rhythm on the steering wheel.

'Come on,' he muttered to himself. 'Come on, come on...'

Amanda found Jake sitting at a table, scribbling in his notebook. She put a hand on his shoulder and he looked up.

'Jake, I'm going now.'

He was taken aback. 'Oh, right. I just need to get a couple of quotes from the British Legion, then I'll be ready.'

'No, don't worry, the Kirkwood guy is going to give me a lift back to Cardiff, he's going there anyway and he wants me to tell him about my dad. They knew each other in the Army, apparently.'

Jake suddenly looked very forlorn. Her face softened and she put her hand back on his shoulder.

'I know it's going to be strange for a while, Jake, but it's for the best, and we'll always be friends if you want us to be. It's just going to take a bit of time to sort ourselves out. I really hope you'll be happy. I think you will.'

She leant down and kissed him gently on the cheek, then turned and went to get her coat. Jake stayed at the table, a horrible empty feeling inside him. Why was it that all the women in his life wanted to be just friends now?

Leaving Ormsby-Kirkwood to make his farewells, the Reverend had gone back to the small room in which he'd left his satchel and carried it into the adjoining toilet. He carefully locked the door behind him, lowered the toilet lid and sat down. Undoing the straps on his satchel, he lifted lifting out the clerical clothes on top then carefully removed the two heavy bundles, still swathed in their cloths. He unwrapped the bigger of the two and carefully stood its contents on the floor. It was the base of a Bofors anti-aircraft shell.

Old soldiers and collectors of militaria had long prized old ammunition of all sizes as souvenirs of war. Complete, they were in two parts: the business end, the part that left the muzzle and exploded, and the base that contained the propellant charge and remained in the weapon, to be discarded once it had been used.

Easily available in curio shops and jumble sales, the empty bases of larger calibre shells could be seen in the homes of many ex-servicemen, at the front door as umbrella holders or by firesides, holding poker and tongs. This one, about eighteen inches long, was highly polished. It had an inscription on the side, and unusually, had a lid that sealed its top. The lid had a small protruding handle that Stanley gripped and turned; it lifted away.

Tilting the shell towards the overhead light, he reached in and made some adjustments to a mechanism inside. He set the base carefully upright again, and unwrapped the second, smaller bundle. When he'd finished, he held the explosive end of the shell in his hands. This was unusual. Empty bases were common, complete shells, emptied of all explosives, less so but still not difficult to get hold of. But the shell in two separate parts – that was rare. And what made this shell rarer yet was that, from the explosive part trailed two wires, their ends stripped of the protective plastic sheath.

Carefully lowering the wires into the top of the base, the Reverend attached them to two small crocodile clips just below the lip, then reached rather awkwardly further inside. There was an almost inaudible click. He settled the top part of the shell into the bottom, taking care not to snag the trailing wires, and turned it firmly clockwise. Another faint click, and the two halves were locked together.

Wrapping the discarded lid in the smaller of the cloths, he put it back into the satchel and put his clerical garments on top of it. The now complete shell he wrapped in the larger cloth, then took the satchel back into the cloakroom, left it there and carried his heavier burden outside the front door of the building. He walked a few yards from the door, glanced at his watch and waited for the Brigadier to emerge.

Ormsby-Kirkwood came out about two minutes later, striding purposefully. The Reverend stepped forward to intercept him. He smiled and his voice was light, but his eyes were cold.

'Brigadier, I wonder if I may just have a minute of your time?'

Ormsby-Kirkwood glanced across to his car and saw Amanda waiting there.

'What is it, padre?' He sounded irritated. 'I'm on a rather tight schedule.'

'Of course, this won't take a second. I rang your office during the week about a group of my parishioners, all veterans of the Korean campaign, as I know you are. They were hoping to meet you.'

'My secretary didn't mention it...'

'No, quite, when she explained that you had another appointment to go on to I asked her not to bother you with it. The men were rather disappointed, but they had prepared a small memento of today for you, and I thought you might like to have it anyway.'

He unwrapped the shell and passed it over to the Brigadier.

Ormsby-Kirkwood took it and, turning the gleaming shell over in his hands, examined it with appreciation. When he spoke, his tone was softer and he sounded rather embarrassed.

'This is absolutely splendid, padre. I do have a couple of others, of different calibres but not complete, as this one is; it will go very well with them. I see there's something engraved on it in Welsh. I don't speak the language, can you tell me what it means?'

'I can, Brigadier. 'Taro ergyd dros ryddid i Gymru'; 'They fought for the freedom of Wales and the world.'

'Very apt, padre, very apt.' He glanced towards Amanda again and hesitated. 'Look, I'm terribly sorry I haven't got time to meet your chaps this afternoon, I really do have to go on to another engagement, but next time I'm in the area I'll leave enough room in my schedule to do so. Could you ring my secretary next week and make sure she has your telephone number and address?'

'Of course, Brigadier, thank you.'

'And thank your group for this magnificent gift, I really am very grateful.'

The men shook hands and the Brigadier turned back towards his car, the shell cradled in his left arm. The Reverend watched him for a second, then turned and walked briskly back to the Pavilion.

Amanda, standing by the gleaming Bentley, had watched the meeting between the Reverend and the Lord Lieutenant.

'So sorry, m'dear' he said, as he walked round to the passenger side of the car to unlock the door for her. 'Padre wanted to present me with a memento of the day. Rather splendid, isn't it?'

'What is it?'

'Bofors shell – light anti-aircraft. Damned effective.'

'Is it safe?'

He laughed. 'Oh yes, no need to worry about that. They don't let these things out to the general public till they've been made absolutely safe. Wouldn't do to have people blowing themselves up in their own homes, would it?'

Amanda settled herself in the front passenger seat. He closed the door and began to walk round the front of the car, then stopped briefly with an expression of irritation on his face. Then he continued to the driver's door, opened it and put the shell on the seat.

'Forgotten my damned gloves. Won't be a second.'

He strode off back towards the Pavilion and she settled back to wait for him. Lost in her thoughts, she jumped slightly when there was a knock on the driver's side window. It was Jake. She gestured to him to open the door.

He leant in. 'I wanted to say thanks for coming down here today; it must have been a temptation just to call. I do appreciate it. It all seems to have been a bit of a rush today, what with me working. I was wondering - I'm going to be going back home for a weekend some time; perhaps we could meet up for a coffee and a chat, if you're free? And if you think it would be OK.'

'I'm sure it would be.' She hesitated, then leant towards him. 'Jake, there is something...' Then she stopped. 'No, don't worry about it, we'll talk again when you come up next.'

He looked slightly perplexed. 'Well, if you're sure. Right, then.'

He leant in and kissed her on the cheek, then noticed for the first time the shell on the seat in front of him.

'Bloody hell, what's that?'

'The vicar gave it to the Brigadier, it's a memento of the ceremony today.'

'Looks a bit lethal.'

'I don't think so, you see quite a lot them in antique shops around Hampstead. He reckons it's quite safe and I guess he should know what he's talking about. I suppose you wouldn't be able to get them if they were still dangerous.'

Jake leant in further to examine the shell and read the inscription. 'Taro ergyd dros ryddid i Gymru.' Way beyond his very limited Welsh, but somewhere in the back of his mind, a small bell rang. An alarm bell.

He heard footsteps approaching on the gravel behind him and, stepping back, found Ormsby-Kirkwood looking at him quizzically.

'Just saying goodbye to my gir – my friend, Brigadier', he said. He raised a hand to Amanda, then stepped back further to let Ormsby-Kirkwood get into the car.

'Don't worry, young man', said the Brigadier, 'I'll make sure she gets to the station safely.'

He picked up the shell and, leaning through the gap between the front seats, dropped it onto the back seat. He eased himself behind the steering wheel, the car door shut with a smooth click, the engine purred into life and Jake watched the Bentley as it made its stately way across the car park and onto the road.

Jake was on his way back towards the Pavilion by the time another vehicle, an old Land Rover, followed it out. He was walking slowly and thinking hard, trying to bring something to mind, something half remembered. Then it came, and he realised why that little alarm bell had rung.

'Ryddid.' He'd last seen that, or something like that, on the GLF communiqués. As for the rest of the inscription, 'Ryddid' was freedom, 'Gymru' was Wales, that much he knew; the rest was beyond him. But the Rev was at the reception, he'd know. With a sense of urgency he couldn't quite understand, he quickened his pace.

The Reverend Stanley was coming out of the front door, walking quickly with his satchel slung over his shoulder, just as Jake reached it. The Reverend nodded curtly and made to walk round Jake but Jake stepped in front of him. There was a question he needed to ask.

'Sorry to bother you, Reverend, but I've just seen an inscription on that shell you gave the Brigadier, and I was wondering what it meant. It was something like, er, 'Tar', something, 'ryddid' –'

'Taro ergyd dros ryddid i Gymru'.

'Right. And what does that mean, Reverend?'

The Reverend was looking coolly, levelly at Jake, and he spoke softly.

'It means 'striking a blow for the freedom of Wales.'

And suddenly Jake saw it all – the shell, the inscription, the GLF communiqués, Terry's warning about something big in the offing. His eyes widened, his body tensed.

'Jesus, you're one of them, aren't you?'

The Reverend's gaze did not waver.

'One of them? One of whom? I have no idea what you mean', he said quietly.

Jake was shouting now. 'That bloody shell is going to go off, isn't it?'

And the Reverend's voice was now very quiet.

'Yes. Yes, it is going to go off.'

Jake stared back in horror. 'You bloody madman. My girlfriend is in that car!'

For a second, the Reverend's face changed to an expression of distressed bewilderment. He looked down, then he braced his shoulders and when he looked up again, his features were once again impassive.

'I am truly sorry about that, Mr Nash. Truly sorry.'

Jake stared at him in anguish. 'You're sorry? You're fucking sorry?' He had an almost irresistible impulse to punch the face in front of him, but then he turned and ran towards his own car.

'You won't get away with it!' he screamed over his shoulder at the Reverend.

'No', said Stanley quietly to himself, as he watched the small blue car accelerate as hard as it was capable of out of the car park and away up the road, 'I won't get away with it.'

The Captain, dressed in white overalls, was painting the bridge over the road to Cardiff. A keen observer might have been puzzled that he seemed to be doing the same patch repeatedly, the part of the parapet just over the lane that carried traffic from the valley towards the city, but there weren't many people using the bridge in that industrial area on a Saturday afternoon, and the few that were didn't seem to notice.

He and Siôn had been waiting at the Pavilion car park when the Lord Lieutenant arrived, much earlier than was strictly necessary. They'd noted his car, not a difficult one to spot, then Siôn had driven The Captain to the lay-by and dropped him there. The Captain had changed into his overalls and tipped several tins of paint into a bucket. Then he'd climbed the steps of the bridge, settled himself in place and started work.

He glanced at his wristwatch. 4.30. Any time now, and the sooner the better; daylight was going and already there were lights to be seen in some of the houses set back from the road. Traffic was thankfully light in both directions; those who'd be heading into Cardiff for the evening had yet to make a start, and those travelling home from the city shopping trips had mostly not started back.

One man had addressed him as he passed by. 'Bit late to be doing that, butt.' 'Aye well, I'll finish soon and what I do now I don't have to do on Monday', The Captain had replied and the man had walked on without further comment.

His eyes didn't leave the road except to check the time on his watch or to dip the brush into the bucket of paint. Although he had a clear view of the road for a couple of hundred yards, he knew he would only get one chance at this.

Then he saw it, the big blue Bentley. A low evening sun was reflecting from the windscreen so he couldn't see the driver, but there was only one car like that in the area today. He heaved the bucket onto the parapet and waited. The car was closing on him at an even speed, and it would

215

pass right below him. Steady...steady... NOW! The bucket tipped and the paint flowed.

Ormsby-Kirkwood had been enjoying the drive. The whisky had induced a warm glow inside him and he always liked talking about the old days in the regiment, especially when the listener was an attractive and attentive woman. He'd been careful to observe the speed limits driving through Edwardstown, but then they were travelling through an industrial estate. The road here was quieter and straighter, so he could turn and look at Amanda more often and for longer than he'd cared to risk on the town roads. The needle on the speedo crept a little higher.

He was telling Amanda about the time he and Horrible Harry had fallen in with two American officers on a week's leave in Berlin; probably not quite the right quality to be effective officers, in his opinion, but up for a good time and with loads of cash. He'd just got to the bit where they'd challenged each other to drink a bottle of champagne inside a minute, and he turned to gauge her response. She was watching the road ahead, and in the space of seconds, he saw her face change from polite interest to perplexity and then to alarm. A little too late, the Brigadier turned his attention back to the road and found he was about to drive into what seemed to be a thick green waterfall.

Before he'd properly taken it in, his view through the windscreen vanished. In sheer panic, his right foot stamped on the brake and in the same instant he wrenched the wheel to the right in an attempt to get away from the green stream; with a shriek of tearing rubber from the tyres, the heavy car skidded as it went under the bridge, mounted the kerb and slammed sideways and hard into a concrete street light stanchion twenty yards down the road.

The impact shattered the passenger window, showering Amanda with fragments of glass; her head hit the upright between front and back doors, stunning her. At the same time Ormsby-Kirkwood was flung against her, his forehead bouncing hard off the steering wheel, knocking him out and opening a deep cut. The stanchion snapped under the impact, the top part of the post toppling down and crashed across the car. Then everything went quiet. Inside the car, the sun, filtering through the green paint that covered most of the windscreen, lit the two still faces with a deathly hue.

In the split second between The Captain upending the bucket over the edge of the parapet and the paint hitting the car, he registered that there was someone in the passenger seat beside the driver. By then it was too late. As the car passed out of sight below him, he dropped the paint bucket and ran across to the other side of the bridge, hearing the tyres squealing below him. By the time he reached the opposite parapet, the car was back in sight, moving sideways; he watched, frozen, as it hit the street light and the post smashed down on the roof of the car. For a couple of seconds, he couldn't move.

'Oh Jesus', he hissed under his breath. Then he turned, ran to the steps to the road, hurtled down them and sprinted towards the car.

Jake had driven as hard as the car and traffic had let him. The only thought running through his mind was that if anything happened to Amanda, he would be responsible. Had he told the police the truth about the night of the exercise, about hearing The Captain named, about seeing the Land Rover with the sticker, then none of this might have happened.

He hit his fist, hard and repeatedly, on the steering wheel. Stupid, stupid, stupid, he screamed silently at himself, and crouched forward, urging the little car on.

As he left Edwardstown behind he saw the Land Rover ahead; by the time they reached the bridge he was almost on its bumper. When its brake lights suddenly came on and it skidded to a halt he had to stand on his own brakes to stop himself running into it. As he flung his door open, he saw its driver leap out and start running down the road ahead of him. Jake sprinted after him and saw for the first time the reason for the sudden stop.

Ahead of him, the Bentley was slewed across the side of the road, a concrete post across its roof; a man in white overalls was tugging frantically at the driver's door. The Land Rover driver ran up to help him.

Jake rushed to the passenger side. The broken base of the stanchion was wedging the front door shut. Through the shattered window, he could see the back of Amanda's head slumped against the door pillar. Blood was seeping through her hair.

'Amanda! Are you all right? Can you hear me?' he shouted but she didn't move. Oh God, what if she was dead? What if the car caught fire? And what if the bomb exploded now?

He tugged desperately at the rear passenger door, but that too was jammed shut by the impact. Suddenly another hand closed over his on the door handle and joined in his frantic tugging. He spun, and instantly recognised Siôn's face above the scarf. Jake let go of the car door handle and swung a wild punch, which bounced off Siôn's shoulder.

'YOU FUCKING MANIACS!!' he screamed.

'This wasn't supposed to happen!' yelled Siôn, pushing him away. 'Just help me get them out.'

Siôn ran back round to the driver's side, managed to get the rear passenger door open and climbed into the car. Amanda was dazed but her eyes were open; Ormsby-Kirkwood had been thrown across her and was pinning her in her seat. He was unconscious and blood was pouring from the cut on his head, running down his face and soaking into his tunic.

The Captain, leaning through the driver's door, had got hold of the cross strap of Ormsby-Kirkwood's belt and was trying to pull him away from Amanda. Siôn crawled across the back seat and, cupping the side of her face in his hand, began talking to her quietly.

'It's OK, you're OK, we'll have you out in a minute, just hang on...'

She lifted her head slightly and tried to focus on him. Jake ran around to the driver's side of the car.

'Get the bomb, just get the fucking bomb!' he screamed in an agony of frustration. How long had they got?

Siôn and The Captain both turned to him, bewildered. 'Bomb? What bloody bomb??' said The Captain.

'Don't give me that crap - the bloody shell. The one your mate the Reverend gave the Brigadier.'

They stared at him with blank faces. Jake gave up trying to explain and flung himself through the back door of the car, squeezing in beside Siôn. The back seat; he'd seen the Brigadier drop it there...

The Captain watched Jake for a second, then dropped his grip on the General. 'Siôn, get out of the car!'

Siôn stayed where he was. He turned and looked at his uncle for a second, then back to Amanda. 'Don't worry, it'll be fine, nearly there', he said softly to her. Her hand moved up to cover his, still on her face. 'Siôn?' she whispered.

Jake was beginning to get really frightened now. There was no sign of the shell on the part of the seat he could see. He reached behind Siôn to feel along the back of the seat then tried to reach around him. Nothing.

Siôn was not going to move, but somewhere in the part of Jake's brain that was still functioning rationally he realised that if Siôn had been sitting on the shell, he'd know about it. Jake stopped for a second and tried to think. He was sure the shell had been on the back seat but wherever it was when the car hit the lamp post, it wouldn't be there now - the force of the impact must have moved it.

He couldn't see anything on the floor between the front and back seats; he reached down and began feeling blindly under the front seats, his face pressed hard against their leather backing. Nothing, nothing at all, not even any rubbish. He pushed his shoulder hard against Siôn's leg to give himself more room, reached further into the darkness... and there it was, a smooth, cylindrical coldness, directly underneath Amanda. With his fingertips, he rolled it back towards him as slowly as his panic would allow. Then he could see the base. Grasping it as gently as possible, he pulled it towards him and when he could get his other hand on it and he was sure his grip was firm, he lifted it and backed slowly out of the Bentley.

Other cars had pulled up and now there was a small circle of on-lookers around the wreck. Jake, the shell cradled in his arms, stared uncertainly round about him at the gathering crowd. There was a low murmur when they saw what Jake was carrying and a few took an involuntary step backwards. Jake's mind refused to work; he had absolutely no idea what to do next.

Then the shell was wrenched from his arms.

Chapter 24

The Captain too was trying to make sense of a situation that seemed to make no sense. After the reporter had shouted at him about a bomb then dived back into the car, he stood for a few seconds trying to untangle it all. Why was there a girl in the car? Who was she? How did the reporter come to be here? And what was all this about a bomb? Who would put a bomb in a car – this car?

But watching Jake's frantic search, hearing the panic in his voice and with Siôn refusing to get out, he needed to make sure. He could see some of the floor on the driver's side and that seemed to be clear; he pushed his hands under the seat and tried to reach round Ormsby-Kirkwood's legs, feeling in the darkness. Nothing. He was going to have to somehow get across to the passenger side, and with the broken lamp stanchion blocking that door, it was going to be difficult. Perhaps he should try to pull the Brigadier out again. Then he realised that the reporter was now standing beside the car.

He was facing a small crowd that had gathered, God knows from where, and in his arms he cradled a shell as though it were a sleeping baby. He was staring at the crowd and they were staring back, but nobody was doing anything at all.

The Captain looked at the shell. It was highly polished but it looked the genuine article; there was no way of knowing whether it was live or not. He waited for someone to do something. Nobody did. The Captain had never seen active service but he knew well enough what would happen if that shell did go off; for many of the people in the crowd, for those in the battered, paint-bespattered car and for the young man holding it, it would be goodnight, Vienna. And for Siôn too, of course.

The Captain reached across and pulled the shell away from the reporter.

221

'Stay here, all of you. Nobody bloody move!' he shouted.

He knew he had to get the shell away, but to where, and to do what with it, he had no idea.

Lowering one shoulder, he barged his way through the crowd. It parted readily enough to let him pass, people stumbling backwards away from him. Then he began to run.

On one side there was a row of houses; he turned instinctively away from them and saw on the other side of the road a group of small industrial buildings. It was getting dark now, but no lights showed there.

He headed towards them and when he reached the empty parking area in front of the biggest building, he stopped, uncertain of where to go. There was a narrow lane down the side of the building to the right, separating it from what looked like a warehouse next door. Contain the blast, he thought, contain the blast and it will do less damage. He turned into the lane and ran down it for twenty yards or so, then saw an even narrower footpath running at right angles between the warehouse and the building behind it. Swinging sharply onto the path, he trotted until he was halfway along it, then slowed and stopped.

Panting, he looked up and around. The brick walls of the buildings on either side of him were high, he could see only a narrow strip of sky, and at either end of the path, more buildings. This was the best he could do. If he left it here he could try to find something to cover it with, sandbags, rubbish, anything that would deaden the blast even more.

He put the shell down in the middle of the path. There was something engraved on the side, and he bent down to see what it was. Words, Welsh words. He couldn't understand them, but Siôn would. Not that he was going to let Sion anywhere near. He straightened up slowly and looked down at it.

Obviously it had been worked on to get it that shiny. In which case, it was very unlikely to be dangerous. He couldn't imagine anyone vigorously polishing, much less engraving, a live shell. And what on earth would someone like the Lord Lieutenant be doing, driving around with one? He began to wonder if he'd made a bit of an idiot of himself, snatching it away from the reporter and dashing off like that.

Now he had time to think a bit, it began to dawn on him that he was in a very difficult position. Lots of people had seen him run in this direction and he could hardly just stroll back to see how things were going. Perhaps he could work his way round behind these buildings and get back to the Land Rover from further down the road. But he couldn't just leave Siôn. Shit.

Right. The only thing to do was to dump the overalls, get back to the road either further up or down from the bridge, then come back as discreetly as possible. He might be able to catch Siôn's eye without being noticed. With more people gathering by the minute, there was still a chance they could both get to the Land Rover without drawing attention to themselves and get away. There was nothing they could do now for Ormsby-Kirkwood or the girl, and the emergency services were bound to be on their way.

If that bloody reporter hadn't turned up screaming about a bloody bomb... He looked down at gleaming cylinder at his feet. Shit, he thought angrily, I'm making a complete idiot of myself here, it's probably completely harml-

A flash of light, orange and red, then the violence of the explosion sent a tremor through the ground that many of those who had gathered around the wrecked car would remember all their lives. Windows shattered, debris was flung high into the air, a pall of dark smoke rose from the factories and warehouses and hung over them. But the buildings, as The Captain had known they would, absorbed most of the blast.

As the reverberations died away, people in the crowd clutched at each other, some started to hurry away and a hubbub of voices arose. An acrid stench drifted across to them. Jake was the first to move. He dived back into the car, where Siôn was still holding Amanda but gazing blankly in the direction of the explosion.

'Siôn, you've got to go.'

Siôn turned to him, looking almost as dazed as Amanda.

'What happened? Where's Goronwy?'

So that was who it was. Jake should have guessed. 'He took the bomb, Siôn, and ran off with it. He took it to where it wouldn't hurt anyone.'

Siôn looked uncomprehendingly at him.

'Is he all right then?'

Jake looked at him for a long moment.

'I don't know. Probably. I expect he put it down somewhere relatively safe then got away. He won't come back here though, too dangerous. He'll make his own way home somehow.'

'Yeah, probably, he's a clever little bugger.' He nodded vigorously, then looked beseechingly at Jake. 'We didn't know anything about a bomb, honestly. It was just going to be a kidnap, a sort of symbolic kidnap, it wouldn't have lasted very long.'

Watching him hold Amanda, Jake believed him. 'OK, but you've got to go too. The police can't be far away and you'll go down for a long time if they tie you into this. Go home and wait for Goronwy. I'll look after Amanda, I promise. Go on, now.'

Siôn studied his face for a few moments, then turned back to Amanda and kissed her gently on the forehead.

'See you later, cariad', he whispered.

He climbed out of the car and as he passed Jake, paused briefly.

'Thanks.'

Jake nodded. 'Might be a good idea if you drive down towards Cardiff and then circle back to Edwardstown. I would guess that's where the police will be coming from first.'

'Right'. Head down, shoulders hunched, Siôn pushed through the confused, milling crowd. No one seemed to notice.

Turning onto the quiet roads as soon as he could, he drove the Land Rover carefully home. His hands were still shaking as he made himself a cup of tea and some toast, which he couldn't eat. He sat for a long while in the darkness and silence of the kitchen.

Eventually, he dragged himself upstairs to his bed and lay on it, fully clothed. After a while, he got up and undressed, then tugged on his pyjamas. If the police came in the early hours, it wouldn't do for them to find him still in his day clothes.

It was a long and sleepless night. He was waiting for the sound of a single set of footsteps in the yard, the unlocked door opening. When dawn began to lighten the gloom of his bedroom, the police still hadn't arrived. But by then he knew he wouldn't see his uncle again. He turned over and buried his face in his pillow.

Chapter 25

It was a busy night for Detective Inspector Griffiths. By the time he arrived at the scene and examined the paint-spattered car and the site of the explosion, the Brigadier and Amanda had already been taken to hospital and Jake had followed them.

There were still plenty of witnesses eager to give the Inspector their version of events, although no one had actually seen the crash or could explain the paint on the car. There'd been two, perhaps three men trying to get the occupants out of it, they said. One of them had got out of the car holding what looked like a big bullet or a shell, one of the others in white overalls had snatched it from him and run off. Then there'd been a massive bang.

A short walk over the bridge, past the patch of fresh paint over the Cardiff-bound carriageway and the discarded bucket, helped connect some of the items in the sequence of events for the Inspector. Where the shell had exploded was now a cordoned-off heap of rubble, surrounded by shattered walls that tottered dangerously. Near the middle was a canvas tarpaulin, laid neatly over a small, smoother-shaped mound.

Back at the car, the first policemen on the scene filled in a few more blanks. He'd found the reporter from the Enquirer, Jake Nash, there when he arrived.

The Inspector's eyebrows were raised ever so slightly, but he didn't interrupt.

Mr Nash, said the constable, had told him he'd been on his way down to Cardiff when he arrived at the site of the accident although, no, he hadn't actually seen it happen. Two casualties had eventually been removed from the crashed car, with the help of the fire brigade, and Mr Nash had been able to confirm their identities as Brigadier Ormsby-Kirkwood and a Miss Amanda Harper, as he'd been with them at a function at Pembroke Villa in Edwardstown earlier that afternoon.

He also confirmed that a man in white overalls had apparently been trying assist the casualties of the crash. Mr Nash had discovered what seemed to him to be a suspicious object in the car while attempting to aid the casualties and had retrieved it, then the man in white overalls had seized it from him and run off with it. He had no idea who that man was.

The officer confirmed that one of his colleagues had gone to the site of the explosion and had found what appeared to be the remains of a person dressed in what looked to have been white overalls. He was quite definitely dead. The officer in question had been a bit upset; he'd been sent back to the station to write his report.

Mr Nash had confirmed that as well as himself and the man in overalls, there had been a third man involved in the rescue attempt. The reporter didn't recognise him and could give only a brief description: thirty to forty years old, he thought, a bit stout. The man had said only a couple of words, possibly an English accent, and he'd just seemed to disappear after the explosion.

Mr Nash had then accompanied the occupants of the car to hospital, following the ambulance in his car. He was, apparently, close to the young lady and wanted to be able to give her family news of her condition.

When Inspector Griffiths arrived at the hospital in the early hours of the morning, the senior doctor in Casualty told him that both Amanda and the Brigadier were under sedation and in no immediate condition to talk. They'd both suffered head injuries, the Brigadier's the more severe of the two, but neither was in danger and barring unforeseen complications, Amanda would probably be released the following day. The Brigadier would remain a while longer for observation.

The Inspector found Jake sitting in the corridor outside the side ward where Amanda lay sleeping. He settled heavily into the chair beside him and looked at him intently for a few seconds before he spoke.

'Well, Mr Nash, you seem to have a gift for being in very close proximity to this sudden rash of explosions we're getting down here. Why would that be, do you think, just bad luck? Or I suppose from a reporter's point of view, good luck?'

Sitting in that dark corridor, Jake had had time to think about what he was going to tell the police; he'd decided that honesty, as far as that was possible, was going to be the best policy.

He told the Inspector something the detective already knew, about the drinker in the pub talking, in the aftermath of the first explosion, about something more to come. There'd been no more communiqués from the GLF, but when he'd seen the shell in the back of the Brigadier's car and read the inscription on it, he'd recognised one of the words as something he'd seen in the earlier communiqués.

He'd asked the vicar what it meant simply because he knew he spoke Welsh; the Reverend had admitted the shell was going to explode.

'What exactly did he say, Mr Nash?'

'I said, you're one of them, aren't you, and the shell is going to go off, and he said, I don't know what you mean by one of them, but yes, it is.'

'And by 'one of them', you meant...?'

'The GLF.'

'Who are...?'

'I don't know. I told you earlier, I didn't recognise any of them on that night time thing and I haven't met any of them since.'

The Inspector looked down at his hands, clasped in his lap, then back up at Jake.

'Do you know Goronwy ap Siencyn, also known as The Captain?'

'No, I've never met him, although I have heard of him.'

'So you wouldn't know if he was the man in the white overalls?'

'No.'

'And his nephew, Siôn?'

Jake hesitated slightly. 'Yes, I met him at a rugby game. We chatted a bit. He'd helped my girlfriend – my ex-girlfriend - out of a spot of bother, but that was all.'

The Inspector stared levelly into Jake's eyes.

'And could he have been the other man who helped get your ex-girlfriend out of the car?'

There was no hesitation this time.

'No, Inspector.' Jake shook his head. 'It was all a bit confused and I couldn't see much of him, he was pretty muffled up, but it wasn't Siôn.'

Two cars set out later that morning from Edwardstown police station. When the first of them arrived at the dark Victorian house beside Holy Trinity church, two officers got out. Getting no answer when they knocked on its door, they went over to the church. They found the Reverend sitting in the semi-darkness in one of the back pews, a small bag of clothes and personal necessities beside him.

The verger, arriving to get ready for the first service of the day, was treated to the unusual site of his vicar in handcuffs being escorted down the church path and into a police car. Unlike the verger, the Reverend seemed totally unperturbed.

The second car, with four officers inside it, arrived at the farm at about the same time. Siôn was already up.

Two constables stayed at the farm to search it again, the other two took Sion back to the station. There he told the Inspector that he hadn't seen much of The Captain the day before. They'd driven into town together, but then The Captain had gone off somewhere, saying he was going to be busy for the rest of the day, perhaps go down to Cardiff. Siôn had gone to the rededication of the War Memorial, then driven home and spent the rest of his day doing odd jobs around the farm.

No, he hadn't noticed anything at all unusual about his uncle's behaviour in the last few days.

Yes, he had been a bit worried about this uncle not coming home, but he was a grown man and he could look after himself.

Yes, of course he'd heard about the explosion on the news.

And for the first time, his voice broke.

He'd heard about the crash on the early morning radio news and that someone had run off with the bomb before it exploded. He had no reason to suppose that it might have been his uncle. Goronwy knew about bombs and shells though and would have known what would happen if this one had gone off. Carrying it away like that would have taken a lot of courage. But it was something that his uncle would probably do.

The Reverend admitted it all straight away. He refused to say where or how he had obtained the bomb, but everything had been his idea and his alone, conceived and executed without the assistance of anyone else.

He sincerely regretted the involvement of the young lady in the incident, that had never been intended.

Other than what he'd read in the press, he had no idea who or what the GLF was, and he was not a member of any organisation other than the Church in Wales.

Inspector Griffiths was genuinely bemused.

'I can accept that you didn't intend to harm the young lady and that her presence in the car was unforeseen, but what if there'd been another car passing in the other direction when that bomb went off? What if he'd stopped to let someone cross the road in front of him?

'Why, Reverend? Why this, and why you, of all people?'

The Reverend thought for a few seconds, then shrugged slightly.

'Perhaps I'd reached a point where just being angry wasn't enough.'

The second police search of the farm was much more thorough than the first, but the typewriter had long gone from beneath the mound of hay and they found nothing incriminating.

They organised an identity parade. Siôn stood in a line of other men roughly the same height and build as himself. A man and a woman who'd witnessed the rescue attempt from the car and thought they might be able to recognise the mysterious third man walked slowly past, carefully studying each of the men. Neither had picked him out.

Jake was the final witness the police asked to attempt an identification. Inspector Griffiths watched intently as Jake passed Siôn; as far as he could see, neither had behaved unusually. Jake had seemed to scrutinise each man in the line equally carefully, Siôn had kept his eyes focussed on the far wall, as he had with the previous two witnesses.

Inspector Griffiths wasn't the least bit surprised when Jake turned and told him, no, there was no one there he could identify as the third man.

He wasn't going to lose any sleep over it. Much as the policeman in him suspected there was more to this than he could prove, he'd been in the service too long to let it worry him. He'd got a culprit and a confession, the case was closed, and if retirement was just over the hill, this was a good enough way to end his career.

They buried The Captain on a day when heavy clouds hung low over the hilltops around the valley and the rain fell in a remorseless drizzle. He had no family left other than Siôn and there were few mourners at the graveside. Three cameramen stood at a respectable distance from the grave; two were from the press, the third seemed more preoccupied with taking shots of the small group that had gathered to witness the burial.

Jake was there, standing on his own, slightly apart from the other mourners. He'd thought of asking Amanda to go with him, but he remembered the way Siôn had spoken to her in the car and how she'd held his hand to her face, and in the end he didn't.

From where he stood he could see her with Siôn, huddled together under one umbrella, her hand covering his on the handle, their shoulders touching. When the coffin was lowered into the wet earth he bowed his head, and she leant hers gently onto his shoulder.

When the brief committal was over, he shook hands with Siôn and kissed Amanda briefly on the cheek then walked alone down the hill to collect his car. He drove out of town and parked in the lay-by under the bridge. The Captain's handiwork had been painted over and the bridge returned to its uniform dark grey.

Jake climbed the stairs and crossed over to the row of buildings where The Captain had taken the bomb. The area of the explosion was still cordoned off and a sign warned of danger from unstable buildings but there was no one around to prevent him slipping under the tape.

The most dangerous walls had already been knocked down, and the rubble was piled into several heaps in the small clearing created by the explosion and subsequent demolition. Jake stood for two or three minutes in silence, his hands thrust into his coat pockets.

So much had changed in such a short time. Welcome to being grown up, he thought.

The rain had stopped and a weak late afternoon sun was breaking through the clouds. He turned to go and as he did so saw a glint of metal in the rubble. Stooping, he pulled it clear.

It was brass, dull and discoloured except for the bright, sharp edge of torn metal that had caught the sun's rays. He recognised the base of the shell from the arc of the rim; a piece of the upper casing was still attached to it, twisted away by force of the explosion. He examined it for a few seconds then pulled a handkerchief from a trouser pocket and, wrapping the shell fragment carefully in the cloth, slid it into his coat.

He took one last look around the site then turned and started to walk back to his car.

Time, he thought, for a pint.

Acknowledgements

I owe a great debt of thanks to friends and former colleagues for their invaluable help in reading the many drafts of this book and for making invariably helpful and constructive suggestions for their improvement, principally Wynford Emanuel, Grahame Lloyd and Adrianne Leijerstam. Thanks too to Trent van der Werf and Anne Simmonds for helping clarify my over-complicated thoughts on the cover design.

My wife, Mary, was a source of unwavering support as well as sound advice, for which I shall be eternally grateful, during the long process that has resulted in this book.

And finally my thanks to you, gentle reader, for persevering long enough to get to this point. I hope the task has not been too onerous, and you have enjoyed at least the odd bit here and there.

27626904R00139

Printed in Great Britain
by Amazon